A cop. Why hadn't Tasha told him? Was she undercover in some way? Was that why she wasn't in uniform?

But if she was undercover, why had she responded to a simple neighborhood argument?

Rick had hated the look in her eyes when she saw him—the pure shock that soon became deep disappointment. Apparently she hadn't expected to be arresting him on Monday morning. It was probably lucky for both of them that he had turned down her offer to see him again. This wasn't what either of them had in mind.

He leaned his head back against the cracked leather seat. He was being arrested—arrested!—and all he could think about was the way it would change Tasha's opinion of him. His priorities were screwed up. Not to mention the fact that this was yet another way for the Creep to mess up his life.

An arrest. What would his family think of that?

Well, Rick already knew what they would think. They wouldn't be surprised. Although he was.

And the amount of anger he'd experienced when he was facing down the Creep—or the guy he'd thought was the Creep—worried him too.

The car moved forward and Rick closed his eyes.

He had no idea how he would get out of this one.

# THE PERFECT MAN

## KRISTINE KATHRYN RUSCH

PUBLISHING

**The Perfect Man**
Copyright © 2018 by Kristine Kathryn Rusch
First published in 2008 by Five Star
Published by WMG Publishing
Cover and Layout copyright © 2018 by WMG Publishing
Cover design by Allyson Longueira/WMG Publishing
Cover art copyright © Curaphotography/Dreamstime, Pixattitude/Dreamstime
ISBN-13: 978-1-56146-047-2
ISBN-10: 1-56146-047-8

ALSO BY KRISTINE KATHRYN RUSCH

NOVELS

*Bleed Through*

*Simply Irresistible* (written as Kristine Grayson)

*The Death of Davy Moss*

SHORT STORIES

*"Spinning"*

*"Cowboy Grace"*

*"Drinking Games"*

# THE PERFECT MAN

# CHAPTER 1

*R*ICK CHANCE SAT on the front steps of his new house, and watched as the neighborhood came alive. He had moved to an upscale development in Portland's West Hills. The homes were large and only ten years old, and they all looked the same.

Most of the people on this block worked nine to five. As the chill of evening approached, cars showed up, people returned, and leisure time began.

A cup of coffee cooled in his left hand. He felt comfortable for the first time in years.

He liked the rhythm of this place. It calmed him and almost made him believe he could belong.

The alarm on his watch beeped, and he sighed. He set his coffee down, then turned his wrist, shutting off the alarm.

The only bad thing about his move to Oregon was that he now lived near his family. And tonight would be the first big family gathering since his return. He wasn't ready for all the questions, the comments, the sideways looks.

He would have turned Gerald down if it weren't for Jane. Rick's big sister had been his only support and comfort during his years away. She had begged him to take part in family events, which he would do until it got too uncomfortable for her. And it would. He wasn't about to defend himself to these people. He wouldn't explain himself either.

Rick picked up the mug, downed the last of the coffee, and went inside the house. Time to find something to wear. Since he was the family's black sheep, he figured it was only right to dress the part.

~

Natasha Morgan stood knee-deep in garbage. Her khaki pants were ruined and so were her shoes. Good thing she didn't spend much money on her work clothes.

The stench—a mixture of rotting meat and sour milk—was incredible.

Tasha resisted the urge to wipe her nose. She'd done that once already and it had been a mistake.

The sun reflected off windows of parked police cars. Tasha had to be careful which way she faced so that the light wouldn't blind her. She glared at the precinct itself—a white brick building that had faded to gray—wishing some other detective would come out here and help, even though she knew *she* wouldn't dig through garbage to assist another team.

Her partner, Lou Rassouli, used his gloved hands to take another bag of garbage off the pickup truck. Lou was a barrel-shaped man with biceps the size of her thighs and strong hands, scarred from years on the street. His face was lined—compassion lines, she called them, because they could ease into the most sympathetic features she'd ever seen.

The bag was a self-tie white plastic, and he was having trouble opening it. Finally, he ripped out the bottom of the bag and dumped the contents onto the precinct parking lot.

"How much more do we have?" she asked.

"Half the truck." Lou sounded discouraged. They had found the garbage at Damon Pfeiffer's building, but had been unable to determine which bags were his. So they'd had to take the entire Dumpster load.

Even so, Tasha had a horrible feeling this would be a dead-end. It seemed that nothing they did could tie Pfeiffer to his brother's murder.

"What do you think we're going to find?" she asked.

"If we're lucky, a note Pfeiffer wrote to his brother, threatening to kill him. It would be really nice if he signed and dated it."

"Seriously, Lou."

Lou grabbed another bag, then grinned at her. "That's the nice thing about garbage. You never know what you're going to get."

Tasha shook her head as Lou dumped the next bag. When she had gotten promoted to detective she somehow hadn't imagined herself sifting through someone's garbage. Some silly part of her had expected to solve crimes in less than sixty minutes with the help of her trusty partner and a sudden flash of insight.

Actually, the insight came often. She had a knack for this job. But the problem with insight was that it didn't stand up in court. She needed evidence too. And in this case, especially, evidence was particularly hard to find.

The sun went beneath a cloud, sending a chill across the lot. It was getting late. Tasha sighed as Lou threw more bags onto the pile. Not only would they have to search, but they'd have to clean up this mess as well. The lieutenant wouldn't appreciate losing a corner of the precinct parking lot to a mountain of garbage.

Lou tossed the last bag in the mix, then put his hands on his back and stretched. "Most of this stuff is going to be pretty easy to sort through. Food scraps, coffee grounds, things like that. It's the other stuff we gotta keep an eye on."

She sifted through a stack of magazines, all of which were addressed to an apartment below Pfeiffer's. She picked them up by the corners and shook them. Little subscription cards fell out, but nothing else.

"People don't believe in recycling any more," she said.

"Any more?" Lou asked. "Like they ever did."

He kicked aside some beer cans and started on the outer edge of the pile. Then he looked up at her. "Say, Tash, don't you have a thing?"

She had just tossed aside an unidentifiable ball of slimy material. "A thing?"

"Tonight. Don't you have a family thing?"

She froze. "What time is it?"

He had to push aside his glove to read his watch. "Almost five."

Tasha swore. "It's not just a family thing, Lou. It's Brooke's rehearsal dinner, and I'm covered in garbage. Oh. My. God."

Lou gave her a sympathetic look. He knew how much trouble Tasha had with her family. They had never understood her—particularly her desire to take such a challenging job. They would hate it if she canceled. She'd be in trouble if she were late, and they'd never let her forget it if she showed up covered with filth.

But she had no choice. She had to stay here.

"I'll cover for you," Lou said.

She shook her head. "This mess—"

"Won't be that hard to go through, especially if you send one of those desk jockeys out here on your way out."

"Lou, no."

He grinned. There was a yellow dab of something stuck to his chin. "You'll owe me."

"I'd rather stay here."

"I know, Tash. But you don't dare miss this one."

She knew it. She had even told him to push her if she balked. In a fit of weakness, she'd agreed to be Brooke's maid of honor. It had been a big mistake. She'd been forced to attend showers and girl parties. She'd even had to host one herself, which would have been a nightmare if it weren't for Lou's wife who volunteered to help her.

Tasha simply wasn't good at girl things. She had never placed a priority on them, and for the most part, she didn't enjoy them. She hadn't been kidding when she said she would rather be sorting through garbage than going to the dinner.

"Tash," Lou said. "You made me promise to get you there. I'll drive you if I have to."

She nodded. "I'm going. I'm sorry, Lou."

"It's all right," he said. "I'll think of suitable payback."

She had no doubt about that. She had a hunch she'd be paying for this one for a long, long time.

～

It had taken Herbert Beebe two days to find the house. The streets in Portland ran on a grid pattern, but the house was in a neighborhood filled with oddly named housing developments. The streets in those places shared names: Paradise Drive, Paradise Avenue, Paradise Court. The house numbers didn't run in order either.

The place was a deliveryman's nightmare.

Beebe finally located it on a quiet block. The house was large and beautiful. From the outside, no one would be able to see the horrors that happened inside.

He took a deep breath. His hands were shaking.

"I'm here, Jessamyn," he whispered, hoping she could feel his presence through the locked doors, the thick walls. "I'm here, and I'm finally able to help."

# CHAPTER 2

TASHA PAUSED OUTSIDE the Harborside Yacht Club, trying to compose herself. She had raced home, taken a hot shower, and dried her hair. Nothing had completely taken the stench of garbage out of her nose. She applied perfume, something she usually avoided, more for herself than for anyone else.

Her blond hair was already flying out of its neat bun, and her feet ached. She wasn't used to high heels at all. She felt ridiculous in the pale green gauze dress she bought a few days before. She was more comfortable in her work clothes. This dress made her feel like someone she wasn't. Someone her family wanted her to be.

There was nothing more she could do about her appearance. Considering how filthy she'd been at five o'clock, just the fact that she made it here looking slightly presentable was a victory.

She sighed and opened the large glass doors. Immediately the restaurant's view caught and held her, just like it was supposed to. The walls facing the Columbia River were made of nothing but glass. The setting sun glinted off the water, and shone whitely on the mountains beyond. For a moment, she didn't even see the yachts docked at the edge of the pier or the patrons sitting under umbrellas outside. For a moment, all she saw was her beautiful city, stretched out like a jewel on the river's edge.

"Nice, huh?" The voice in her ear was rich and masculine, so deep and resonant that it made her shiver. She looked over her shoulder at the man standing just behind her. In fact, she had to look up to see his face—and she rarely looked up at anyone.

He had rugged features, square jaw, prominent cheekbones, and dazzling blue eyes. His dark hair was a little too long, and his dark mustache was too shaggy for modern style. But on him, it worked. He looked like a poster boy for a Western—a man who would be as home in chaps and spurs as he seemed to be in his faded blue jeans, tailored white shirt, and expensive corduroy blazer.

"The view," he said as if she hadn't understood him. "It's nice."

"Um, beautiful," she said, wondering if pretty dresses made her act like the imbecilic debutante her mother had always wanted her to be.

"I think the view's the best part about this restaurant." He sounded regretful.

She wouldn't know. She'd never eaten here before. She'd managed to avoid the place.

He smiled. It was a self-deprecating look that changed his rugged-ness into something close to movie-star handsome. "Not used to talking to strangers?"

Sure she was. She talked to them all the time. Interrogated them was more like it. She wondered what this man—this yacht club member—would do if she told him she was a cop.

His smile would probably chill, then he'd say something polite and disappear into the restaurant. Men did that to her when they found out what her job was. They seemed to think it made her some kind of leper. Or they asked to have their parking tickets fixed, which annoyed her even more.

His smile faded. "I'm sorry. I'm embarrassing you."

"No," Tasha said. "I'm the one who should apologize. It's been a long day, and I was just trying to get my bearings before going into the fray."

"The fray?" he asked.

She waved toward the private room her family had rented. "Rehearsal dinner. I'm not good at these things."

"I prefer the bachelor parties myself," he said.

At that moment, so would she, but she bit that comment back. Her cousin had asked her to be on her best behavior for the wedding. Tasha suspected "best behavior" also applied to the showers, rehearsal dinner, and other events before the wedding itself.

"But at least rehearsal dinners have food." He held out the crook of his arm, as if he expected her to take it. "Shall we?"

She frowned. "Are you going to a rehearsal dinner?"

"I'm afraid so."

"The same one I am?"

"Probably, given that this place only has one private room large enough for friends and family."

"You're going to the Halliwell dinner?"

"Actually," he said in a conspiratorial tone, "I'm going to the Flesner dinner, but I suspect they're one and the same."

She felt a blush warm her cheeks. How long had it been since she blushed? Her first day in the precinct, years ago, when she'd been a rookie. She'd learned then that blushing only resulted in more teasing and a general lack of respect. Somehow she'd learned to control the blush, so it was a surprise that it had returned.

"You're a friend of Gerald's?" she asked, ignoring the man's arm.

"No," he said. "He's my nephew."

Tasha frowned. "But you look like you're the same age."

The man raised his eyebrows, seemingly startled. "I'm four months younger," he said in mock indignation.

"And he's your *nephew?*"

He shrugged, apparently used to this. "My sister—his mother—is twenty years older than I am. I was, as my parents put it, a surprise."

"I'll bet." Tasha glanced across the crowded restaurant. Silverware clanged and something fried smelled sinfully delicious. No one had seen them yet, not even the maitre d'. She wondered if she could hide in the entry all day.

Then she realized what the good-looking man beside her had said to start the last interchange.

"What's wrong with Gerald?" she asked.

"Excuse me?"

"Gerald. I asked you if you were his friend, and you said, 'No' in a tone that implied if you weren't related, you wouldn't speak. What's wrong with Gerald?"

He dropped the crook of his arm. Apparently she had gone into interrogation mode. No one expected it from a tall willowy blond in a suit, let alone one wearing gauze.

"Before I put my foot in it farther," he said, "who's he marrying? Your sister?"

"My cousin."

"A close cousin?"

Tasha glanced toward the door leading to the private party. She couldn't see inside, but she knew Brooke was in there, waiting. They had been close once, as little girls playing Barbies. But as Tasha got more athletic and interested in the law, Brooke had watched her as if she were a subspecies of bug.

To Brooke's credit, she had tried to understand. And she had always included Tasha, even though the inclusions were torture. Like the time she had chosen Tasha to be a member of her homecoming court.

Like this wedding.

"A close cousin?" Tasha repeated. "I guess so."

His magnificent eyebrows met in the middle. He had obviously noticed her pause. "Bridesmaid close?"

The blush hadn't completely faded. Or if it had, it was making a return appearance.

"Maid-of-honor close," Tasha mumbled.

"Wonderful." He let out a sigh and looked away. The sun was glinting off one of the yachts, sending a stab of white light into the restaurant.

"You were going to tell me about Gerald." She didn't want this conversation to end. She was enjoying it. If Lou were here, he'd say she was flirting.

Which was nonsense of course. She never flirted. She left flirting to Brooke.

"Gerald." Her companion sounded like he wished he'd never heard his uncle's name. "He's not a bad sort. He's probably the marrying kind. He's stable, reliable—"

"Dull," Tasha said.

He looked back at her. In just a few moments, she had forgotten the power of those blue eyes. "You know him?"

"No," Tasha said. "But you're implying that there's something wrong with stable and reliable."

He sighed again, clearly a man who was trapped. "Listen, I got stuck with Gerald my entire childhood. I'm sure he's a great guy. He's just not..."

His voice trailed off.

"What you consider a great guy?"

He ran his hand through his dark hair. It caught the light, then fell slightly out of place. Carelessly attractive. So few men could actually pull that off, but he could.

"He was, you know, the kind of kid who got hit with the ball instead of catching it." Her new friend sounded exasperated. "I know that guys like Gerald are taking over the world right now, and I suppose it's their revenge for being picked last at baseball, but every time the family got together—and that was once a week whether we needed it or not—I had to spend time with Gerald. I tried to teach him how to shoot baskets. I tried to teach him how to play catch. I tried to teach him how to run, for godsake. He couldn't even do that."

Tasha laughed. "Then he and Brooke are suited. Because I tried to teach her all that stuff too, and she didn't want to sweat. 'It's icky,' she used to say."

He smiled.

"You're not the best man, are you?" Tasha asked.

"Best man for whom?" he asked, his eyes twinkling.

"The guy Gerald chose as his best friend," she said deliberately misunderstanding his misunderstanding.

"You mean the guy who gets to walk you down the aisle?"

"Yes."

"The guy who gets to dance the first dance with you?"

"Yes."

"The guy who is supposed to be at your side all day tomorrow?"

"Yes."

"Nope."

"What?"

He grinned. "I'm just an usher."

Tasha felt a spark of disappointment. To hide it, she looked at her watch. Now she was officially late. "We'd better get in there before someone notices we're missing."

"We can't be missing," he said, "if we haven't arrived yet."

"You like to play with words," she said.

To her surprise, his smile faded. "I never play with words."

"But—"

"I work very hard at them."

She smiled again. But she felt that some of the lightheartedness had left the conversation. She wasn't quite sure why.

"Since we know everything else about each other," he said, "maybe we should add names. I'm Rick. Rick Chance."

"Tasha Morgan," she said.

"Well, Tasha," he said, holding out his arm. "Shall we march into the fray?"

She took the offered arm. His skin was warm and smooth, but she could feel the muscles beneath. "I guess we'd better."

And together they walked to the back room as if they'd known each other all their lives.

# CHAPTER 3

$\mathcal{O}$NLY TWO SEATS remained when Tasha and Rick arrived, and those seats were side by side. The table filled the private dining room, which had once been a small patio overlooking the pier. Someone had encased it in glass, and placed large ferns against the only wooden wall. The table was polished oak, and the chairs were so heavy that Tasha felt she could get a workout just by lifting one.

There was a large bare spot of floor between the kitchen and the table, and Tasha looked at it with alarm. A piano, a drum set, and instruments stood in a corner.

No one had told her there would be dancing later. Usually Brooke warned her about these things.

Of course, when Brooke warned her about dancing, Tasha always found a reason not to show up. She wasn't a dancer. Her feet got in the way of each other and usually landed on her partner's, much to his chagrin. Or she ended up slow dancing with someone she didn't like, who pawed at her and sweated on her and whispered clichéd nothings in her ear.

Tasha looked away from the dance floor and finally faced the group. Relatives she knew all too well, friends of Brooke's, and strangers who bore a faint resemblance to Rick shouted greetings. Tasha smiled and let Rick lead her to the open chairs in the center of the table.

Her cousin Brooke sat at the head, looking radiant. But then Brooke always was radiant, with her short cap of red hair, her dainty features, and her peaches-and-cream complexion. She wore a sea-green dress that made Tasha's green gauze look as if she had accidentally put on a robe for the evening.

Gerald sat next to Brooke. He had a square sort of Clark Kentish build, but without the muscles. When his metabolism slowed down, he would have the soft, squishy belly and flabby arms of a man who never exercised or even went outside. Still the jacket he wore suited him, and the pale peach shirt he wore brought out what little color his skin had. Obviously Brooke had been dressing him, and doing a good job of it.

Brooke and Gerald didn't notice that Tasha was late—they were too wrapped up in each other—but Tasha's father shook his head slightly as she entered. Her mother glared at her, and Tasha's brother collected a five-dollar bill from Brooke's brother Elliot.

Rick saw the interchange too, and he put his free hand over hers, giving it a squeeze before they separated to take their seats.

The rehearsal dinner proceeded through toasts—hers was inane, Rick's elegant—salads, wine, and food as bad as Rick had predicted it would be. Midway through the dessert (chocolate cheesecake, the only edible part of the meal), the band members filed in and began tuning up.

"Can we leave now?" Tasha whispered to Rick.

"You're the maid of honor," he said. "You're supposed to stay to the bitter end."

She groaned. Why had she agreed to this? It had already forced her to buy two dresses—the one she was wearing tonight, and a pink hooped thing that made her look like a petit four. Not to mention the matching shoes, purse, hat, and earrings. Or the hair appointment at the preferred salon, which was going to be another sixty dollars out of her very meager pocket.

She would be damned if she asked for any of the family money to pay for her part in this ridiculously expensive wedding. She'd declared her independence too long ago to crawl back now. Besides, her parents didn't need to know how badly a thousand dollars broke her budget.

The band was poised and in position. Fortunately, someone had decided to make another toast with the after-dinner drinks.

"No one'll notice if we just fade away," Tasha whispered.

"If I fade away, maybe," Rick said. "But you have to dance."

He seemed to be relishing her discomfort.

"Why do I have to dance?"

"Bride and groom first, followed by the maid of honor and best man, then the attendants."

"I thought that was after the wedding."

"And this is rehearsal," he said. "You don't think they'll follow the same traditions here?"

"How come you know so much about this stuff?"

He leaned back in his chair and took a sip from his long neck bottle of beer. He held the bottle between two fingers, and tilted with practiced ease.

"You go to enough of these things," he said after his sip, "you figure them out. This is one of the traditional ones. They're the easiest to predict."

"How many have you been to?" she asked.

"Enough." He still wasn't looking at her. Apparently something in the marina had caught his eye.

Brooke stood up. She had a bit of color in those delicate cheeks, and her eyes were a little glassy. "We need to dance!" she said, and swept her arm toward the band.

The band glared at her. Tasha had a hunch this was not the introduction they'd wanted. A piano player, a drummer, a guitarist, and, of all things, a trombone player. All of whom were male and all of whom looked like they had seen better days.

But, obligingly, they launched into their first song, and it was a pop-swing thing that had "dance to me" in every beat. Tasha was surprised. They were very good.

Brooke and Gerald slipped onto the dance floor. The other attendants were standing. Rick nudged Tasha.

"You'd better get up," he said.

"Not until I know who the best man is," she said.

"Weren't you at the rehearsal?"

"They had it in the afternoon. I had to work."

"Oh, well. Your weekend's date is over there." Rick nodded to the only blond man at the table. He was pudgy, and too short to make the pudginess look good. He wore glasses that didn't fit his face. When he caught her looking at him, his eyes lit up and he smiled.

He seemed harmless enough, but she was terrible at small talk and she didn't like dancing with strangers.

Although she wouldn't have minded dancing with Rick.

"Side by side," Rick said, "for the entire wedding."

"You're enjoying this too much for a man whose just met me," Tasha said.

"Believe me it's nothing personal. Usually I'm the only person who is uncomfortable at a wedding. It's nice to meet someone else who shares the feeling."

The best man had worked his way around the table, and bowed before her. The tips of his wispy hair fell forward as he did so. He looked as nervous as Tasha felt.

"May I have this dance?" he asked.

Tasha had promised Brooke. So she gave the best man her best smile. "Sure."

She didn't look at Rick as she took the best man's hand and let him lead her onto the dance floor.

His hand was damp, but his grip around her waist was surprisingly sure.

Right away, she apologized for her lack of dancing skill.

"It's not a problem," he said as he expertly guided her across the floor.

"I'm sorry," she said as she caught her breath. "I don't remember your name."

"Howie. Howie Klatch." He adjusted his glasses, as if he were trying to see her better. When he put his hand back on her waist, the glasses slid down his nose.

"I'm Tasha."

"I know." He smiled at her. His smile made seem rounder, but pleasant somehow. "It's okay. We were never properly introduced and you couldn't come to rehearsal."

The floor was filling up with the rest of the attendants. And after they straggled on, so did the parents and the other couples. She couldn't see Rick.

"What do you do?" she asked Howie.

"I run an Internet startup. We went public a few years ago. Maybe you've heard of us—"

"The same company that Gerald owns?" she asked.

Howie nodded, then his smile turned into a grin. Now he looked impish and almost cute. He apparently liked it when people figured out he was rich. "We started it together. We never expected it to go so well, but we're not complaining."

"I guess not."

He was leading her pretty well. Her feet hadn't gotten tangled yet, and she'd managed to avoid stepping on him. He was still looking at her, and so was Brooke—casually, over her shoulder. Tasha got a scary feeling that she and Howie had been matched in this wedding for more than one reason.

This song seemed like it was going on forever. She glanced at the clock and realized that the song *had* been going on forever. Five minutes at least with no end in sight. Damn Brooke for hiring a jazz and swing band.

Howie was still smiling at her. Actually, he was smiling *up* at her. He was short enough to make her uncomfortable.

"So," he said, "Brooke tells me you're pretty good with computers."

"Computer crimes," Tasha said.

"Oh?" His eyebrows went up. "You're a hacker?"

She laughed and was about to correct him, when she saw Rick loom up behind him. Rick tapped Howie's shoulder, and said, "Mind if I cut in?"

Before Howie had a chance to answer, Rick swept him aside and took Tasha in his arms. His grip was firm, his hands were dry, and he was the perfect height for her.

"Thank you," she said.

"My pleasure." His voice was deep and low, and in her ear. "I've never danced with a hacker before."

"You're not dancing with one now."

"You told him that to impress him?"

"He misunderstood me."

"Oh."

Over his shoulder, she saw Brooke frown at her.

"I think Brooke and Gerald are trying to fix me up," Tasha said.

"With him?" Rick sounded surprised. "Don't date much, huh?"

"Don't like dating," Tasha said, not wanting to get into it. If she wasn't careful, she would confess to him what her job was, and she didn't want to do that. Not tonight. It would only ruin a lovely evening.

"Enjoying yourself yet?" Rick asked.

"I've got to admit, you've made this a lot nicer evening than it would have been."

He pulled her even closer. She had never danced with a man who made her feel small. Maybe that was why she always tromped on them.

"You've made it nice for me too," he said. "I was afraid that I'd spend the entire evening fending off polite queries about my work. You know, the old 'have you figured out yet what you're going to do with your life?' question."

He smelled faintly of wood smoke. His shirt was soft against her cheek. She had no idea how her head found its way to his shoulder, and she looked up at him abruptly.

"That's a familiar question," she said. "It comes when you're not working or when you're working at a job that the people in your life don't approve of."

"Sounds like you've heard it a few times."

"Too many." She winced again. The next question would be "so what do you do?" and she didn't want to answer that. So she said rather quickly, "Want some punch?"

"Not really." He eased a hand up her back. She could feel the warmth of his palm through that silly gauze. "I'm enjoying the dance."

She was too. She couldn't remember the last time she'd been held like this. The music had slowed down and she hadn't even realized it. She put her head back on his shoulder, and he wrapped his other arm around her.

How could she feel so close to someone she didn't even know? Maybe one of her fantasies was finally coming true. A handsome man, a wonderful flirtation, a great dance. Nothing had to go beyond this night. Maybe nothing should. After all, reality was always worse than the fantasy. If her job had taught her anything, it was that.

The music stopped, rather abruptly.

She and Rick kept dancing, but he turned so that he could see the band. Then she noticed that everyone else stopped too. She felt self-conscious, and she pulled away.

For a moment, he continued to hold her close, then he let her slip out of his grasp. She looked at the band. Gerald was there, talking to them. And Brooke was heading her way.

Tasha cursed. She knew what was going to happen next.

"Think we goofed up somehow?" Rick asked.

"I think we ruined best-laid plans," Tasha said just as Brooke got close.

"Tash!" Brooke gave her a quick airy hug. Her cousin smelled faintly of lilies, and she seemed perfectly put together despite the stress of the day, lateness of the hour, and her alcohol consumption. "We haven't had a chance to talk. Excuse us?"

She didn't even look at Rick as she said that last, just led Tasha to the bar. Friends still gathered there, but the family moved out of the way. Apparently this had been a Plan to make sure that Tasha Learned the Errors of Her Ways.

Or maybe it had been a Plan to Invite Tasha Back into the Fold. Or maybe the Plan had been to Find Tasha A Man So That She Would Stop This Nonsense.

Whatever it was, Tasha, as usual, had screwed it up.

"What are you doing?" Brooke asked in a tone which said How-Can-You-Do-This-To-Me-On-The-Night-Before-My- Wedding?

"I was dancing," Tasha said.

"And flirting."

Tasha shrugged. "Rick seems nice."

"Nice? Nice? Do you know anything about him?"

"Only that he's Gerald's nephew and he'll be an usher at the wedding."

Brooke sighed theatrically. "How do you always pick the wrong men?"

It was Tasha's turn to sigh. She was never going to live down Bobby Bailey, from high school. Bobby had been a dope-smoking musician who had seemed romantic at the time. Eventually he got arrested on a DUII and disappeared into the court system.

"I didn't realize I'd picked anyone," Tasha said.

"You were supposed to spend the evening with Howie."

"I hadn't been informed there were rules." Tasha had to struggle to keep her voice down. She could see Rick at his spot near the table. He hadn't sat down. He was watching them. His gaze was intense.

He saw her looking at him. *Need help?* he mouthed.

She shook her head slightly, then wished she hadn't. Maybe she did need help.

"Tash, at a wedding, the maid of honor always spends her time with the best man."

"But this is the rehearsal dinner."

"E-yay-aaah," Brooke said, making the word into three syllables. Whenever she did that, it meant "how dumb can you be?" Tasha was amazed at how much of her conversations with her cousin were always in this kind of code.

"I just thought we'd eat and leave. I didn't even know there'd be dancing. Howie asked, I danced with him, and then Rick cut in."

"You let him."

"It's polite to dance with the cuttee," Tasha said through clenched teeth. "Did you want a scene?"

"It would be just like Rick to provide one." Brooke tapped a manicured finger against her perfect white teeth.

Tasha saw the wheels move, saw Brooke's opinion shift from blaming Tasha to blaming Rick. Brooke slipped her arm through Tasha's and pulled her close, just like she used to do in high school when she wanted to gossip. "Listen, Tash, Rick's not your kind of guy."

"I thought you just said he was."

Brooke let out a little whistle of air, her extreme exasperation sound. "He's trouble, Tash."

"I'm a cop, Brookie. I can handle trouble."

"I don't want you to blame me for it," Brooke said. "He's not the kind of guy you should be with."

"Even for one night?"

"Tash!"

"Sorry," Tasha said, but now she was intrigued. "What's wrong with him?"

"Everything," Brooke said, and looked at him. Tasha couldn't help herself. She looked too.

He smiled and waved two fingers, just as if he knew what they were discussing. It was a roguish smile. It suited him as much as the twinkles in his eyes did.

"He's good looking," Tasha said.

"They all are."

"His family?" Tasha asked.

"No, silly," Brooke said. "Womanizers."

"He's a womanizer?"

"He's got a woman for every day of the week, and twice on Sundays."

Tasha turned toward her cousin in surprise. Brooke rarely spoke in clichés. In fact, that particular cliché was the province of Tasha's mother, who usually said that of any handsome man.

"Oh, so he likes women," Tasha said.

"He doesn't like them. He uses them," Brooke said.

"He seemed nice to me."

"Tash! That's how they get their victims."

"Victims?" Tasha frowned.

"You know what I mean," Brooke said.

"No, I don't."

"Look, Tash, he's a user. He can't hold a job, so his women support him. And he's macho. He does all those guy things."

"What guy things? He watches too much TV? Scratches himself in public? What?"

"You sound testy," Brooke said.

"I don't know what I've done to deserve this kind of talking-to. Did you want me to spend more time with Howie?"

"Tash, Howie's stable. He's rich, and he's really nice. He'll take care of you."

"I don't want to be taken care of, Brooke." Tasha slipped her arm out of her cousin's grasp. "How come no one in this family understands that? I take care of myself."

"Tash, you know what I mean."

"You've been saying that for the entire conversation, and I've been saying, 'No, I don't.' What does that tell you, Brooke? I'm dense. I can't figure this stuff out sometimes."

"Clearly," Brooke said softly.

"Brooke, I know you mean well, but—"

"Tash, you're going to have to get married some day. You're right at that age, and you're too naïve by half... ."

Naïve? Tasha thought. She was a police officer, for heavens' sake. If anyone was naïve, it was Brooke.

". . . you'll get hurt, and I don't want to be responsible for it."

Tasha had missed some of that diatribe. "How would you be responsible for it?"

Brooke bowed her beautiful head. "Gerald didn't want to invite Rick. He's the family black sheep, you know. But I wanted everyone in both families in my wedding. You know how important family is. I really pushed for it. It would be awful if it backfired in my face."

"Seems to me," Tasha said, "that if I got involved with him and he was half as bad as you say, it would backfire in my face."

"You know what I mean!" Brooke said.

Tasha sighed. Ironically, this time she did. Brooke really cared about Tasha. Brooke didn't understand her, but she cared.

"Brookie," Tasha said, using her cousin's childhood nickname. "I'll spend as much of tomorrow with Howie as I can. And I'll be good. It's your special day. But I can take care of myself. They train us how to do that at my job."

"Not emotionally," Brooke said.

"Even emotionally," Tasha said. "You don't have to worry about me this weekend. You have enough to worry about. Like the fact that the guests are getting confused and the band's antsy. Don't you want some of that lovely music you're probably paying for?"

"Oh, damn," Brooke said and hurried off toward the band. Gerald was still standing there, looking concerned.

Tasha turned to the bar and ordered a beer. The bartender gave her a tall glass with foam that spilled over her hand.

"I'll get that," a voice said behind her.

Rick. She already recognized his voice, and the feel of him against her back.

He ordered a beer for himself, then took out his wallet, only to have the bartender tell him it was part of the dinner. Still, he put a five in the bartender's nearly empty tip jar.

To impress her? Tasha wondered. Or because he was just that kind of man?

The band started up. Tasha could feel Brooke's gaze on her.

"How bad was it?" Rick asked, moving her to the side of the bar.

"Bad enough that Brooke would be mad if we went back out on the dance floor."

"Because she wants you with Howie?"

"Because she says you're not right for me."

He sipped his beer, seemingly unperturbed. "Let me guess. She called me a deadbeat."

"Yes."

"The black sheep of the family."

"Yes."

"A womanizer."

"Yes."

"And?" he asked. "What else?"

"Macho."

He nearly snorted his next sip of beer. "Since when did that become a crime?"

"It's a new century," Tasha said. "Apparently the old ways are no longer our ways."

He grinned. "How much of this stuff do you believe?"

"What I believe doesn't matter," Tasha said. "My cousin believes that if I spend time with you tonight and tomorrow it'll ruin her wedding. So I have to respect her wishes."

His grin faded. He glanced at Gerald and Brooke, who were dancing, but were watching them.

"Fair enough," he said. "This is their weekend. They get to call the shots."

He set his beer down, then took her beer and set it beside his. For a moment, she thought he was going to lead her to the dance floor—the true black sheep, thumbing his nose at everyone. Instead he took both of her hands in his.

He ran his thumbs over her knuckles. The movement sent little shivers through her. His gaze caught and held hers.

"For what it's worth, Tasha," he said. "You were the highlight of my evening, maybe even the highlight of my week."

"There go those words again," she said, teasing gently. "You bend them to your own purposes."

"No purpose involved," he said, "except to thank you for making what would have been an ordeal a lot of fun."

He squeezed her hands, and then let them go.

"I should thank you, too," she said, but he was already walking toward the door. He didn't even say goodbye to Brooke and Gerald.

She wondered if she would have been as understanding if someone had said all those things about her.

# CHAPTER 4

$\mathcal{R}$ICK PULLED HIS beat-up truck into the garage and punched the remote. The door eased down behind him. He shut off the ignition and listened to the engine tick.

If Gerald hadn't wanted Rick at his wedding, why had he invited him? And what was wrong with flirting with the most beautiful woman there?

Tasha had been a dream—a vision. Rick had often imagined the perfect woman, but he'd never seen her in the flesh before. She was even wearing a fantasy outfit—a form-fitting green dress that flowed around her legs, a dress so thin that he could feel the texture of her skin beneath it.

He let out a small sigh. Better not to think of it. The edict had come down from on high: Spend time with Tasha and spoil the wedding. And, no matter what his family thought, he was not the kind of man who would do that.

He opened the car door and stepped into the dimly lit garage. It smelled faintly of gas, old oil, and dust. The previous owners hadn't used the garage much, and he hadn't been here long enough to make it his own. The shop sat in the back, workbench ready with all of his tools, but he hadn't touched them since he moved.

He hadn't touched much of anything. All he had done was work and unpack. Doing both of those had taken more time than he actually had. Tonight was the first night he had done anything social since he had come to Portland, and he'd been lucky enough to meet a beautiful woman.

Even if he was forbidden from spending time with her tomorrow.

He'd get her phone number, and see if their flirtation could last beyond the stress of a family gathering.

Feeling resolved, he crossed the still-too-clean garage floor, headed for the stoop—and froze.

In front of the door leading into the house was a basket wrapped in a dusty rose cellophane. He felt his blood pressure go up. He hadn't expected anything like this. Not here. He thought he'd left all of that in Chicago, left all of it in the past.

He took the last few strides to the door, and crouched, staring into the basket. Perfumed bath soaps, oils, lotions, and a variety of towels and washcloths, all thick and a tasteful light pink. This had cost a lot of money. Seventy-five to a hundred dollars at least.

His old friend was announcing himself in style.

Rick scanned for the card. He knew there had to be one. It took him a minute to find it in all the ribbon that tied the cellophane closed. He plucked the card off, breaking the ribbon.

The envelope read *Jessamyn* in flowing script.

Familiar script.

Dammit, the Creep was back. Or more accurately, the Creep had moved here too.

Rick slid a finger under the edge of the envelope, ripping it open. He pulled out the card. The cover was a picture of a rose, newly opened, and photographed slightly out of focus.

He opened the card.

*My Jess:*

*He believes he can take you away from me. But he can't. I love you more than he does. I always will.*

*I am waiting for you—*

And, as usual, the card was unsigned.

Rick cursed, and flung the card into the metal garbage can beside the door. Then he picked up the basket and threw it inside too. It landed with a loud clang, but that wasn't satisfying enough. He picked up the can, opened the garage's side door, and carried the can to the curb.

If that harassing twerp was spying on the house, he'd know that his little gift wasn't appreciated.

Rick resisted the urge to kick the garbage can. He turned around and went back into the garage, this time locking the side door behind him. Then he grabbed the emergency flashlight he'd hung near the door, and checked all of his possessions.

None of the boxes had been moved. All of his tools were in place. There was a smudge mark near the woodpile left by the previous owners, the pile that Rick had been planning to move to outside so that it wouldn't draw termites.

He crouched near the smudge, saw the ridges of a shoe print, but didn't know what kind. Not enough for him to even judge size. Damn the man. He was elusive.

Rick scanned the rest of the garage, but saw no other signs of his visitor. Then he hung the flashlight back in its place, and went inside the house to call the alarm company. He knew better than to call the police, at least for something this small. He'd gone through hell in Chicago, and ended up with a terrible reputation. He wasn't going to go through that here.

He wanted a life.

And dammit, he was going to have one, no matter what.

Beebe put down his binoculars, hands shaking with rage.

He saw the hideous truck with its Illinois plates return, saw Jessamyn's husband stalk out of the garage with the garbage can, heard it thunk even though he was watching from three blocks away, and knew that she hadn't gotten his gift yet again.

He hadn't seen her yet. This house was bigger, though, and Chance spent a lot of time in the basement, where he blocked all the windows with dark black-out curtains, even where the plants had grown up around the house.

Such torture she suffered.

Beebe had gone to the only window he could get close to, shouted for Jess when he knew her husband was gone, but she hadn't answered. He'd tried to peer inside, but he could see nothing around the curtain. She might not have even been in that room.

She might have been in another part of the house, another part of her prison, waiting for him to set her free.

He nearly freed her in Chicago. He'd free her here.

He had to.

Her life depended on it.

# CHAPTER 5

*H*OWIE INSISTED ON walking her to her car. Tasha didn't mind. If he wanted to be polite, she would let him.

She was, after all, on her best behavior.

She had parked in the outdoor lot near the yacht club. The club's lights reflected on the water, revealing all those expensive boats. The cars in the lot were expensive too.

Even hers.

"Big day tomorrow," Howie said when they reached her red Mustang. It had been her high school graduation gift from her parents, and the only luxury she owned. It cost her. She could barely afford parts on her salary, and it used more gas than she liked.

But it was the one thing that her family had ever given her that suited her, and she treasured it for that reason.

"Big day," Tasha repeated, fishing for her keys.

"Should be fun," Howie said. He was smiling at her again. She had spent the rest of the evening talking to him. He'd wanted to dance, but she didn't like dancing with men who were shorter than she was.

Especially not after dancing with someone as perfect for her height as Rick Chance had been.

"It should be fun," Tasha agreed in a chipper voice that she barely recognized. She unlocked the car door.

"I'm glad we're going to spend time together," he said, and he sounded so hopeful that she sighed.

"Howie," she said, "I know that Brooke and Gerald think we're perfect for each other, but I'm not interested in dating right now."

"Not at all?" He raised his eyebrows, and she knew he was thinking of Rick. So was she. She hadn't stopped thinking about Rick since she met him.

"Not at all," Tasha said. "Did they tell you what I do?"

"Brooke said you had gotten a job to prove to your family that you could be independent."

"I'll bet she said that I proved my point and was ready to be taken away from all that."

Howie bobbed his head like an eager three-year-old.

"Brooke thinks I should be taken away from all that," Tasha said. "But I'm not ready to be."

"I don't mind women who work." Then he shook his head. "That came out wrong."

"It's all right. I know what you mean." Tasha had a hunch Gerald wanted his wife to work too, and she knew that Brooke was all too ready to stay at home. "But they didn't tell you what I do, did they?"

"No," Howie said. Confusion was making its way into his voice.

She leaned against the car. The metal was cool against her skin. "I'm a cop, Howie."

"A what?" He sounded stunned.

"A police officer. A detective, actually." Her voice was gentle. "And it's more than a job to me. It's a way of life."

"You don't look like a cop," Howie said.

How many men had said that to her over the years? Usually she demanded they tell her what a cop looked like, and all too often they stammered something about a big, solid woman, a woman who cared more about muscles than men, or said that a woman shouldn't be a cop at all. Then they'd get embarrassed as they realized that they'd insulted her, and they'd try to apologize, usually making it worse.

But Howie didn't deserve that. He was a nice man who'd been mislead by her cousin. Brooke had given him expectations, and it was Tasha's job to let him down as easily as possible.

"Howie," she said, "it takes a special person to be friends with a cop, let alone date one. We have to put our jobs first, and a lot of times our jobs put us in danger. They also let us see a part of humanity that no one can look at without being affected. We bring our work home with us, spend too much time brooding, and then clam up when a well-meaning friend asks us how we are."

"I know."

"No. You don't. I didn't know how it would be until I went to the academy, and even then, I didn't completely understand it. I said I wasn't ready to date anyone, and that's because it's just as hard from my side as it would be from yours."

"Gotcha," he said, then patted her hand. He gave her a rueful smile. "I'm glad Brooke put us together tomorrow. I think we'll make it a day to remember."

"I'm sure we will," Tasha said. She wanted to get into her car.

"I'll wait," he said, "make sure you get out of here okay."

She smiled at him, and this time, she was sure he blushed.

"I mean, you know how to defend yourself and all, but it's a habit—"

"It's a good habit, Howie," she said, opening her door, and climbing into the driver's seat. "I'll see you at the church tomorrow. Sleep well."

She closed the door before she heard his answer. She turned the key, heard the great engine roar, and backed out of her parking spot at a speed that wasn't prudent. As she drove away, she looked into the rearview mirror.

Howie stood below a street lamp, making sure she got out of the parking lot okay. The light caught his wispy blond hair, making it seem almost white. He looked lonely and a little sad.

She wished she could be attracted to a man like him. A nice man who wanted nothing more than some attention and respect. Who wanted to build a good home for his family, who probably had decency down to a science.

Maybe Brooke was right. Maybe Tasha did pick the wrong men.

Because she had a hunch Rick didn't think about good homes, nice women, and creating a family.

She wondered what he was doing right now. He was probably in some trendy bar, nursing a beer. He was probably having a good time just to spite them all.

She knew if she weren't so tired, she would be doing the same.

# CHAPTER 6

*R*ICK PACED IN his remodeled kitchen, the cordless phone pressed against his ear. He walked across the polished hardwood floor to the security keypad, stared at the digitized map of his house and grounds, and frowned at the blinking red area.

"I have it now, Mr. Chance," the woman on the other end said. She had identified herself only as Leanne, and he had written that down, anticipating problems early. "There was a perimeter alert at 9:15 on the southeast basement window and—"

"Alert?" he snapped. "Someone was trying to get into my window and you people call it an alert?"

"Sir, we—"

"Did you call the police?"

"No, sir. If you remember when we set up your system, we explained that perimeter alerts happen all the time. A cat could have brushed against the window. A branch could have fallen. It probably wasn't an intruder. Intruders don't brush against buildings. They try to enter them."

She verged on patronizing, but he probably deserved it. They had explained that to him.

"What if I go outside tomorrow and find footprints there?" he asked.

"Then we misjudged."

"Well, you misjudged," he said. "Someone got into my garage."

"Are you all right?" She was all business now.

"Fine," he said. "And nothing was stolen. But someone was here tonight."

"We can secure the garage, Mr. Chance," she said, still using that businesslike tone. "I'm sure your salesperson explained that as well—"

"And the routine I'd have to use just to go in and out of it." It had seemed like a lot of bother at the time, but now that the Creep had found him, maybe it wasn't. "I'll think about it."

"Do that, Mr. Chance. Was anything damaged?"

"No," he said.

"Then how do you know—"

"He left something."

"He?"

"In English," Rick said, "'he' is the generic pronoun."

"Excuse me?"

"Nothing," he said.

"Is everything else all right?"

"No windows are broken," he said.

"We know that." She sounded so businesslike. It exasperated him, as if they were discussing something other than his new house, the place that was supposed to be his sanctuary. "We'd get that reading."

"Then you'd call the police?"

"Of course. But if you want a higher level of attention, we can set up your system to call the police for every perimeter alert. However, I must warn you that the police get easily irritated. If your perimeter alerts are frequent and the police find nothing, they won't be easy to contact when you do have a problem."

"I know that," Rick said through clenched teeth. That was the reason he'd not taken that part of the service in the first place.

"Would you like to upgrade at this time?"

"No." He'd take care of it himself.

"I do think you should report this incident to the police, Mr. Chance. It sounds as if you do have a problem."

*Of course it does*, he thought. *Because I do. Why do you think I hired you people?*

"Mr. Chance?"

"I appreciate the advice," he said, and hung up. For a long moment he stared at the maple countertops, the new tile he'd had the contractor put in, the flat-topped stove, and the refrigerator with a state-of-the-art computer system that allowed it to talk to him if he left the door open too long or if the temperature was wrong and started spoiling food.

What did he really have here worth protecting? His stuff. But stuff could be replaced. His privacy. But the Creep had already invaded that.

Rick sighed. He had three options: he could barricade this place up like a fortress; he could whine to the police; or he could go after the Creep himself.

He glanced at the closed windows, the shades down, protecting him. Was the Creep watching even now? Did he see Rick's shadow playing against the shades? Rick's skin crawled. How could one person make his life such a living hell?

He opened the magic refrigerator and stared at the beer, longing for one. But he'd had enough for one night. Instead he grabbed the milk and drank it straight from the carton, then wiped his mouth. Maybe a small meal would calm him. The food at the Yacht Club hadn't been that good.

The Yacht Club, and Tasha. He should be thinking about her, thinking about tomorrow. Instead he was obsessing about a bastard he didn't even know.

Rick closed the refrigerator door before the thing could yell at him, went into the bedroom, and flicked on the light. His tuxedo was hanging from the closet door, pressed and ready to go.

His entry back into his family's good graces hadn't gone that well either. They hadn't liked the fact that he had moved back to Portland, and they clearly hadn't forgiven him for all the things he'd supposedly done.

He wondered why he was even a part of this wedding. He and Gerald really hadn't spoken for years. No one had even been in his house, with its remodeled interior, its solid wood furniture, and comfortable coverings. Maybe he hadn't invited his family because he wanted them to think little of him. Maybe he liked cultivating the image.

Or maybe he really, really valued his privacy.

Which brought him back to the Creep outside.

That bath oil basket was the first volley in the Portland side of a war. Rick was going to volley back. As soon as this wedding was over, he'd buy some cameras and place them around the garage doors, and the window.

He'd catch the guy on film, track him, and then put an end to this nonsense once and for all.

# CHAPTER 7

$\mathcal{M}$AYBE IF TASHA had been sitting in the congregation, she would have thought the wedding beautiful. But as she stood in the front, listening to her cousin recite her vows in a shaking voice, Tasha had the horrible feeling that she was one of several frosting flowers on a particularly ugly sheet cake. The dress itched and rubbed in all the wrong places, she kept banging the hoop on anything within a fifty-mile radius, and the shoes were higher than she was used to.

By the time the wedding party had recessed, stood in the greeting line, and straggled to their cars, Tasha's calves ached. She wished she would stop moving, but she couldn't.

She had agreed to ride with Howie to the reception because she didn't want her Mustang decorated for the bridal procession. When she saw what happened to the procession cars, she was glad she'd made that decision. Someone had covered Howie's black BMW with streamers, a big sign reading *Honk at Newlyweds in Limo* with a giant arrow pointing behind them, and several bright pink bows that matched her hideous dress.

The hooped skirt didn't fit into the car, and she had to wrestle the thing into submission every time she wanted to sit down. She and

Howie had beaten the dress back just so he could steer, and then he'd had to help her out of the car when they got to the rented hall near the Rose Garden.

Apparently a lot of people who weren't invited to the wedding had been invited to the reception. People poured out of the building, and applauded the bridal party as it arrived. All the guests watched as Tasha struggled to find her feet so that she could shove them to the pavement when she got out of the car.

Howie, bless him, kept pushing down the top of her skirt so that it wouldn't flare up and reveal the lace panties she had so inadvisably decided to wear underneath. The only consolation she had was that she knew all the other bridesmaids were suffering the same indignity.

Brooke's skirt was hooped as well, and had a train that looked like it belonged to another dress. But somehow Brooke carried it off. She swept out of the car like a princess, and let Gerald guide her to the door, to the continued applause of all of their guests.

The bridesmaids trickled behind, swatting at their skirts, adjusting their large brimmed hats, and tripping on the damned skimpy shoes. The groomsmen's biggest duty seemed to be preventing their partners from falling on their hooped butts.

The reception was on the fifth floor and there was no elevator, so by the time Tasha arrived, sweat prickled her back. Maybe she became a cop because it was easier than going the debutante route. The dress and the shoes were a torture worse than any criminal could dish out.

But she did stop as she entered the large room and not just because she needed to catch her breath. Glass surrounded her on three sides, presenting a view of Portland that was nothing short of spectacular. Mount Hood stood majestically in the distance, the Columbia glittered below, and the city itself stretched across the hillsides like a painting.

The room—which was closer to a ballroom than anything else—had statues, potted plants, and expensive wicker furniture scattered throughout. The caterers had set up toward the back, and two bars stood in the corners, with most of the guests milling around those.

Gifts stood on a table near the door, and on the floor near the door, and against the wall near the door. Such a scattering of white wrapping paper and silver bows Tasha had never seen before.

A chamber orchestra played softly in the corner, but a band was setting up on the other side of the room. Soon there would be dancing.

Again.

Tasha groaned, and let Howie lead her to a seat. The wicker creaked beneath her weight and her skirt flew up like an umbrella accidentally popping open. She tamed the skirt, then held her hands on it firmly, trying to make it stay in place.

Howie took one look at her, and smiled gently. "I'd better get your food. Anything you can't eat?"

"Nope," she said, wondering if it showed.

He disappeared and she scanned the room for Rick. She'd been doing that all day. She'd seen him briefly before the ceremony, ushering some old lady toward the groom's side of the sanctuary. Rick in a tuxedo was delicious. The tux, which was a tasteful black, accented his broad shoulders and narrow hips. The cummerbund drew attention to his muscular torso. Finally she understood the purpose of the cummerbund. On most men, it simply looked like a sagging piece of fabric masquerading as a girdle. On Rick, it was an accessory. A handsome one.

He hadn't seen her looking at him, and as she walked down the aisle after the ceremony, his gaze was on the bride and groom. He looked sad. Tasha hadn't seen him since.

There had to be three hundred people in this large room, and still it seemed empty. The chamber orchestra was playing "Jesu, Joy of Man's Desiring," which Brooke had used as her recessional. Everything was about as perfect as a family wedding could be.

Howie came back and set two plates before her. One heaped with food-food, and the other with desserts. The food-food was, for the most part, unrecognizable: puffs-this, and pastries-that, and sauce-covered whatchamacallits strewn with nuts. The desserts, on the other hand, were recognizable and they made her mouth water.

She thanked him, and he smiled, then went back to fill his own plate.

A hand brushed her shoulder. She looked up and saw Rick behind her. He smiled, and there was nothing gentle in that look. It sent a tingle all the way through her.

"Somehow you manage to pull that dress off," he said.

She grinned. "I would like to pull this dress off."

"Then you would be the talk of the wedding."

His words reminded her of her promise to Brooke. "We said we wouldn't flirt today."

He nodded. That sad look was there, just a hint of it, near his eyes. "I just wanted to take a moment to tell you that you look beautiful."

"Despite the dress?"

"And the hat." His fingers brushed it too. "A dance later? After the bride and groom are gone?"

"I don't know," she said. "I'm not sure I can make it that long."

His grin seemed automatic. Something was bothering him. "You'll have to. No one's allowed to leave until they do."

"Who designed this torture?" she asked. "Martha Stewart?"

"Emily Post, I think." Then he looked toward the food table. His profile was just as rugged as the rest of him. "Oops. Here comes your date. I hope I see you later."

And then he was gone, before she could ask him if he was all right.

Howie was balancing three plates of food for himself. She had to help him set them down, and as she took her hands off her skirt, it popped up, nearly knocking him over.

"That thing could be used as a weapon," he said.

"Yeah," she said, "but if it is, it's a legal weapon."

"Requiring registration?" His eyes twinkled. So nice. So safe.

She smiled at him. "Nope. No registration. Just a huge down payment. And to think I could've gotten a house for this price."

"I'm pretty sure if you have to, you could use that skirt as a tent." Howie sat down beside her and dug into the food. She kept one hand on her skirt, and ate with the other. The food was delicious, even if it was mysterious.

She had planned to leave the dessert alone in favor of wedding cake, but her resolve wavered after she'd heard fifteen new toasts to the bride and groom. One more tribute to Brookie and Gerry's perfect union, and Tasha thought she'd down a bottle of champagne all by herself.

It took an hour to get through the meal and toasts, another half hour to cut the cake and get the pictures, and then it was embarrassment time as the single women lined up for the tossing of the bouquet.

Tasha didn't want it. Even if she believed in that superstition, which she didn't, she didn't want a basketball-sized grouping of roses, carnations, and baby's breath launched in her direction. And she knew that Brooke was going to aim for her.

So as everyone waited for the single women to gather like sheep for a sheering, Tasha blended into the background, as best someone dressed in a pink tent could.

Then her mother saw her. Tasha's mother, a petite blond who still had her girlish figure, raised her plucked eyebrows in a very familiar command: *Get over there.*

Tasha ignored it, so her mother left her father who looked bewildered at the edge of the crowd. Her mother moved quickly through the people, arriving at Tasha's side before she could make an escape, and grabbed Tasha's arm, pulling her none too gently toward the bevy of single women.

"It won't hurt you to try a little," her mother whispered.

"I am trying," Tasha said. "I'm wearing the damn dress."

"Don't curse. It's not becoming."

"Neither is the dress," Tasha muttered.

Her mother left her at the edge of the women, and then waited until Brooke noticed them. Brooke smiled and turned around. Tasha wanted to make a mad dash for the back of the bevy, but she didn't. Her mother was blocking her way.

Brooke may have been ladylike, but she had a hell of an arm. She tossed the bouquet directly at Tasha. The bevy of single women moved as one toward Tasha, and Tasha, keeping her hands at her sides, moved away from them like a quarterback making a desperation play.

The bouquet landed precisely where Tasha had been a moment before, caught by the eight-year-old flower girl who squealed with delight. The other women, many of them old enough to know better, moaned in disappointment. Tasha's mother glared, but Tasha pretended not to notice.

She was getting very good at pretending not to notice.

"Very deft. I didn't know a woman wearing eighty pounds of fabric could move that quickly."

Rick. He was right behind her again. Was he following her? The idea both thrilled and worried Tasha—especially considering that her mother was watching. Sometimes it amazed Tasha that she could manhandle convicted murderers, but she was terrified of her own mother.

"Anyone can move that fast with the right motivation," Tasha said, and then she headed toward the punch table, simultaneously hoping that Rick wasn't following her and praying that he was.

She passed the eight-year-old flower girl who was explaining to the four-year-old ring bearer—her little brother—that catching the bouquet meant she would get the man of her dreams.

"Daddy?" the little boy asked, obviously unclear on the concept.

"No," the little girl said, clutching the bouquet to her flat chest. "Prince Charming."

"The cartoon guy?" the little boy asked.

Tasha continued forward, grinning. Maybe the ring bearer wasn't as clueless as he had initially seemed.

"Tasha!" Her mother had found her and grabbed her arm. "There was no need for that display."

"Mom, abusing your daughter in public is a display. Dodging flying flowers is only common sense."

"Make fun if you will," her mother said, "but you're disappointing everyone."

Tasha stopped. Screw it. If her mother wanted a scene, she'd get it. "Oh? And just who would 'everyone' be?"

Her mother must have heard something in Tasha's tone because she pursed her lips. "Brooke has just had a marvelous wedding—"

"Yes," Tasha said softly, glad no one seemed to be looking in their direction. "And it's Brooke's day, not mine. I'm doing the best I can here, all right? Just because you would rather have had Brooke for a daughter than me doesn't mean you have to take everything out on me. I love Brooke and I'm pleased she's happy, and I wouldn't wear bright pink for anyone else. So get off my back."

Her mother teared just enough to moisten her pupils, but not enough to smear her eyeliner. "That's not fair."

"No, Mother," Tasha said. "You're not fair. And you're going to have to realize that no matter how hard you push, you are never going to have the daughter that you want. You're stuck with me, and I'm not changing who I am."

The tears had moved to the edge of the eyeliner. Tasha pulled her arm out of her mother's grasp and moved away before she committed the ultimate sin—ruining her mother's perfect make-up.

Instead of heading toward the punch table, now Tasha went to the open bar. Howie arrived a few steps ahead of her. He ordered wine for himself and for her, then handed her the glass.

"I always wished I could talk to my mother like that," he said.

She brought her head up. "You heard that?"

"Oh, don't worry," he said. "I was kinda standing guard so no one else could get close. I don't think anyone else even noticed except maybe that usher, the one who cut in on us—"

"Rick."

"Whatever. They've got stories about him, huh? Anyway, I just wanted you to know that I thought it was cool the way you defended yourself."

"Thanks." Tasha felt slightly confused. She wasn't sure if it was because of the supportive comments from Howie or if it was because of what he had said about Rick. Stories? What stories? She didn't really want to ask because she didn't want to seem too interested. Even though she was. Too interested, that is.

"I'm sorry," Howie said. "I embarrassed you."

"No." Tasha sipped her wine. She wished he had bought her something stronger, something she could just down. But she knew better than to do that. Drunk and disorderly at Brooke's wedding would be much worse than failing to catch the bouquet. "I don't normally talk to my mother like that either."

"Well, maybe it was time." Howie smiled at her. Then he pushed his glasses up his nose and peered over her shoulder. "The band's going to start up soon. I'm afraid we'll have to dance again."

"Yeah," she said. "Sorry about that."

He focused on her, surprise evident on his round face. "No, no. I didn't mean it like that—"

"I did," she said. "You're a good dancer. I'm not. I'm sorry you have to suffer through my klutziness."

He smiled. "You weren't klutzy the other day."

"You're being kind."

"No, I'm not."

Brooke and Gerald were hanging on each other, laughing, as they moved toward the dance floor. Even though Tasha had never wanted to be like her cousin, she did envy her cousin's easy grace and beauty. And the happiness that radiated from her face.

Tasha glanced to the side, and saw Rick standing at the edge of the crowd. He was the only person who wasn't watching Brooke and Gerald. He was watching Tasha, and she felt a little jolt of excitement.

She made herself turn back to Howie. "You said they told stories about Rick."

"Rick?" Howie sounded confused.

"The usher who cut in."

"Oh, him." Howie sighed. "The Marlboro Man."

"I guess," Tasha said, although she never would have thought of him that way. "Is that what they called him?"

"No. I do." Howie shrugged. "After he cut in. You two seemed like you knew each other."

"We met coming in late. We sort of bonded on our inability to make the family happy." It was her turn for a rueful smile.

"Well," Howie said. "Your family should be happy with you."

Tasha looked at him in surprise. "Thank you, Howie."

He shrugged, then glanced at Rick.

Brooke gathered up her train, and then to Tasha's surprise, detached it from the dress. She handed the long band of satiny material to one of the bridesmaids, who looked as stunned as Tasha felt. Tasha was suddenly glad she was by the bar, otherwise she probably would have been the fabric recipient.

Then Brooke stood on the dance floor, her skirt hiked up, and she peered at her shoes. For a moment, Tasha thought she'd take them off. Then Brooke giggled and shrugged. Gerald gestured and Tasha could almost hear him: *What does it matter if you have your shoes off?*

And Brooke gestured in return. Tasha could imagine that too: *It'll ruin the line of the dress.* In fact, that's exactly how Brooke's lips moved. Style before comfort.

"I guess he got some girl in trouble," Howie said.

"Hmm?" Tasha turned. She wasn't sure she heard him. She'd been concentrating on her cousin.

"Your usher friend. I guess he left Portland fifteen years ago in some kind of disgrace. He got some girl in trouble."

"Pregnant?"

"I didn't get the whole story. I do know she wanted to get married and he didn't. He ran off to Chicago. They said he's never held a real job and that he's not very reliable." Howie gave her a sad little smile. "I don't usually gossip, you know."

"I asked," she said. "Gossip can be an important way to find out things, and what you told me dovetails with what Brooke said."

"What did she say?" Howie asked, a little too eagerly.

"That Rick is a loser and a womanizer." Tasha sighed. She didn't want Rick to be a loser.

In fact, she wasn't sure he was. He seemed so solid to her. Solid and sad. Her perceptions usually weren't that far off. But then, she was usually judging thieves and rapists, not men she met at the Yacht Club.

"Well, he's got the looks of a womanizer," Howie said.

"What?"

Howie shook his head slightly. "A guy like me couldn't be a womanizer. I'm not good-looking. Women would laugh at me for even trying. But guys with looks like that, they can get away with anything."

"Do you want to be a womanizer, Howie?" Tasha asked.

He let out a small laugh. "No. Why?"

"You sounded a little wistful."

"I am." Then he grinned. "On that note, you wanna dance?"

"In the spirit of fairness, I should say no." She slipped her hand around his elbow. "But since I'm already wearing a pink tent and floppy hat, I may as well follow tradition all the way to the bitter end. But I have to warn you. I'm wearing spike heels. If I step on your feet, you may never walk again."

"You step on my feet," Howie said, "and I'm handing you over to the Marlboro Man."

Tasha laughed, but she was tempted to step on his feet. More tempted than she wanted to admit.

# CHAPTER 8

*Y*OU'VE BEEN KEEPING to yourself, Ricky." Rick's sister Jane, the mother of the groom, sat down across from him. She was a tall, slender woman, twenty years older than he was, with a cap of silver hair that made her look rich. Her shiny mother-of-the-groom dress only accented the look of wealth.

Since Gerald's Internet startup made so much money, he remained conscientious about sending money home to his mother. Rick had to commend him for that. Jane had raised Gerald alone. And with all the sacrifices she had made for him over the years, it was nice of Gerald to allow her to take an early retirement.

"I didn't want to get in the way." The glass Rick held in his left hand was warm. He'd been nursing that single beer all afternoon. He didn't want to lose control of himself. He had to be on his best behavior here, and when he got home.

He had to be prepared for anything at home.

Then he shook off the thought. He promised himself he wouldn't think of the Creep today. He would try to be the perfect wedding guest.

He had never done that, at least around his family. He used to party hard at wedding receptions, but that stopped when he moved to Chicago. Partying hard was something he never did any more.

Jane looked at him sideways. Her face had the look of their mother's now, the soft aging skin, the beautiful gray eyes. He wondered what their parents would have thought of this wedding—it probably cost more than their first house—and then sighed against the stab of pain.

"Why do you think you'd get in the way?" Jane asked.

Rick smiled bitterly. "You see that blonde over there?"

Jane looked at the dance floor. Tasha was struggling to follow Howie's smooth steps. "The maid of honor?"

Rick nodded. "I danced with her last night, did you notice?"

"Hard to miss you when you're attracted to someone, Richard."

He looked at Jane again. She was smiling fondly at him.

"Well, her cousin made it very clear that she's not to get near me during the wedding. I'm still dangerous, I guess."

"I have a hunch that Tasha Morgan can handle dangerous." Jane didn't sound surprised.

"Well, her family doesn't think so."

"Her family's old money—or what passes for old money in this town. They don't like anything."

"Her cousin didn't get that information out of the air." He took a sip of the beer. It was warm and flat. He tried not to wince.

"You did leave rather spectacularly, honey," Jane said. "It's not something people are likely to forget."

He sighed and watched Tasha. She really couldn't dance. It was surprising how well Howie handled her, considering. "Then why was I asked to participate in Gerald's wedding?"

Jane didn't answer. Rick turned to her. A slight frown creased her forehead. He recognized the look.

"You told Gerald I had to be part of it, didn't you?"

"Now, Ricky—"

"He never liked me. And the way I treated Teri only made it worse. He's doing this for you, isn't he?"

"You're family," Jane said. "And you've come home. We should acknowledge you. We should treat you better."

Rick wished the beer wasn't flat. He'd have to get up and grab another one. "I don't like being an obligation."

"You're not," Jane said. "Not to me."

He pushed the glass away. "You know, you're the only person who talked to me when I came home for Mom and Dad's funeral."

"It was a tough time for everyone."

He remembered landing in Portland, the way the clouds hung thick over the Columbia, the plane bouncing on the runway. No one met him at the airport. No one told him where the family was getting together before the funeral. He showed up at the funeral home and heard soft whispers following him everywhere. And no one met his gaze.

No one seemed to remember that the two boxes lying in front of the small chapel held his parents too. Parents who were too vibrant to be dead.

At least they had died together, just like they would have wanted. The obituary said they were found side by side in the remains of the Cessna, holding hands. They must have known the plane was going down, and they sought comfort in each other, even to the end.

The memory made his heart twist. Ten years had gone by, and the sharpness of the loss had never really dimmed.

"You should invite me to your home sometime," Jane said. "I don't like being strangers with my baby brother."

His parents had a picture of Jane holding Gerald in one arm and Rick in the other, as if they were twins. The photograph had stood on the top of their piano, with all the other family photographs. That, and his parents' fortieth anniversary photo were the only things he took from the house.

"The strangeness went both ways, Jane," he said softly.

She nodded. "I'm sorry for that."

He looked at her. She had a dear familiar face, and not just because it now resembled their mother's. Jane's eyes had never changed. They'd always looked at him with love, even when she had been angry at him.

"Would you like to see my house?" he asked.

She smiled. It made her look radiant. "I would love to."

They stared at each other for a moment, and then she broke the gaze.

"So," she said, "can you cook? Or should I bring dinner when I come on Friday?"

He hadn't planned on dinner. In fact, he'd just thought he'd have her over at some undefined future date, not Friday. He had forgotten how his sister used to roll over him like this, how she always got him to do something he hadn't planned on doing by giving him no choice.

He supposed he could say no. But he really didn't want to.

"I can cook," he said.

"Good." She held out her left hand. "Now dance with me. I hate being a wallflower at my own son's wedding."

# CHAPTER 9

THE DANCING HAD gone on for two hours before Brooke and Gerald snuck out. Tasha restrained herself and did not step on Howie's feet, but a half hour in, she did take off her own shoes, the line of the dress be damned.

Since she didn't have to worry about the sweaty-pawy part, the dancing was actually fun. She caught glimpses of Rick, who danced with several women—many of them older—and once he winked at her.

She couldn't help herself. She winked back.

The moment that Brooke and Gerald disappeared, Tasha decided she needed something to drink. She left the dance floor, and headed toward the punch table.

One of the members of the catering staff, a young woman wearing a white chef's outfit, tried to be as invisible as possible as Tasha approached. So Tasha smiled at her. The woman smiled back, then picked up the crystal ladle and began scooping punch into a crystal cup.

Crystal. It was a sign of her family's extravagance that the punch had to be served in fragile little cups that half the children in the room had probably already destroyed. It would have been much better to use a crystal serving bowl and paper cups, like most people did.

But her family never did things the way most people did.

Rick came up beside her, just like she knew he would. "Have they spiked the punch yet?"

"Haven't tasted it," Tasha said, then she took a tentative sip. It was good, made with some sort of fresh fruit and ginger ale to give it fizz.

"Well?" Rick asked.

"Could use a little more vodka," she said to the woman behind the table, who looked completely appalled.

Rick smiled. "I was hoping for a dance."

Tasha finished her cup of punch, giving herself time to consider. She had promised that she wouldn't draw the attention from Brooke (although she wondered if she had come perilously close when she fought with her mother), but Brooke was gone now and half the younger guests were already so drunk that they wouldn't know what was going on.

Tasha's mother was still in the room somewhere, but she wouldn't tattle to Brooke. She'd simply get angry at Tasha. Or angrier, as the case may be.

Tasha set the cup down, turned and smiled at Rick. "I dance like a truck."

"I know. I've been watching." Rick took her arm. "But I also know from personal experience that you can handle a slow dance."

She listened. The music had slowed down. The band was playing something soft and dreamy, with a bluesy feel.

"Afraid to go out there on something faster?" she asked.

"I'll leave that to Howie. He seems to be doing quite well."

"He's nice," Tasha said.

"Should I be worried?" Rick asked, and her heart rose at the question. It suggested the same kind of interest she felt.

"No. Howie and I discovered that friendship of the platonic kind is more to our liking."

"Oh, you tested out friendship of the non-platonic kind?" He was still bantering but his tone had changed.

"If you'll recall yesterday's episode, friendship of the non-platonic kind was being forced on us by all and sundry."

"Except me."

"Well, you were the guy gumming up the works."

"So to speak."

They had reached the dance floor. He took her in his arms and she sighed, feeling as if she had come home. Dancing with Howie had been fun. The conversation had been nice. But with Rick, she felt no need for conversation. She liked putting her head on his shoulder and feeling his strong arms around her.

She was never this comfortable with anyone she'd just met. She had no idea why she felt this way with Rick.

His face brushed her hair. "You've got to be the most beautiful woman I've ever seen."

"You say that to all the girls," Tasha murmured.

"No, I don't."

She raised her head. He was watching her, his blue eyes intent. He was very serious.

"What do you say we change into real people clothes and find a nice quiet place for dinner?"

Something in his eyes caught her—that sadness again. She'd seen it when he talked with his sister, too, and a wariness. She'd like to explore all of that.

She'd like to explore him.

"Dinner would be great," she said.

But neither of them left the dance floor. They kept their arms around each other and swayed to the music, their bodies moving as if they'd danced together a hundred times before.

Finally, the music stopped. Tasha felt as if she were waking from a dream. Rick took her hand and they walked off the floor hand-in-hand. She stopped to pick up her shoes. At that moment, her gaze met Howie's. She had to tell him that she wasn't riding back with him.

To her surprise, he smiled and waved at her, telling her without saying a word that he understood and approved. Behind him, she could see her mother, frowning. Tasha would pay for this later, but she suddenly found that she didn't care. She was an adult, and entitled to make her own choices.

"You look serious," Rick said.

"I was just thinking about the way these things make me get lost in my own past," she said.

"Me, too." He put a hand possessively behind her back. "Want to put on those shoes?"

"My feet have suffered enough," she said.

He laughed. They walked outside. The sun was still high, reflecting whitely off the bridges. It was only late afternoon.

Tasha felt surprised. She would have thought it was midnight.

She felt as if she had been in prison for a long time and was only now being set free.

"My clothes and car are at the church," she said.

"I'm sure it's locked by now."

She smiled at him. "You're really not familiar with my family, are you? If Reverend Brown locked the church while we still had possessions there, he'd suffer the wrath of one of the founding families."

"My," Rick said, "Gerald really did marry into royalty."

"More than you know," Tasha said. "Brooke was on the Rose Court."

"She wasn't Rose Queen?"

Portland's annual city celebration, the Rose Festival, had high school girls compete for the honor of Rose Queen every year. Those who didn't make queen became part of the entourage. It was, in some circles (Tasha's family circles), a Very Big Deal.

"Quite the scandal," Tasha said, only half jokingly.

"Were you on the Rose Court?"

"Are you kidding? Me?"

"That's not an answer."

She felt another blush building. "I headed the Rose Court for our high school. Brooke was in my entourage. *That* was the scandal."

"So both students and teachers liked you better."

"My grades were better," Tasha said as if that explained everything.

"The Rose Court isn't all about grades."

She looked at him. "You're a native Portlander?"

"How'd you guess?"

"Your knowledge of things Portland. Either that or you study the paper too much in the spring."

"Rose Queen was extremely important at my high school," he said.

"Where'd you go to school?" she asked.

"Lincoln. And you?"

She felt sheepish. "Marshall."

"Ah," he said. "The kids with the money for a good sports program."

"Privilege has its uses," she said, "as you can tell from my position as the head of a major Fortune 500 company."

His hand fell away from her back, and she suddenly realized he had no idea what she did. For all he knew, she could be telling the truth.

"I'm kidding," she said. "I don't even know what companies are Fortune 500 companies, let alone how to head one."

He stopped suddenly, staring at the parking lot. He looked a bit forlorn. She wondered if he'd heard her, or if he was still worried that she was someone he didn't want to be with.

"I didn't exactly come here in style," he said. "Certainly not in something that suits a tux and a pink chiffon whatever."

He wanted to impress her. That was the problem. He didn't think his car was impressive enough for the daughter of one of Portland's oldest and wealthiest families.

"That's all right," she said. "I may be wearing a pink chiffon whatever, but I'm barefoot."

He glanced at her, surprised, then grinned. "Oh, yeah. I forgot. All that talk of the Rose Festival, and I suddenly felt like I was in high school again."

"God forbid," she said. "Those are days I never want to relive."

"Me, either." He spoke quietly, as if there were more to it than simple teenage angst. "Well, come with me. Are you going to be okay barefoot on that asphalt, or do you want me to drive over?"

"My feet are tough," she said, although her nylons weren't. They were shredded. She wondered how bad his car was. She probably should discuss plans now, so that he didn't think she was trying to avoid being seen in his vehicle. "I tell you what. We probably should pick a place to meet. You can drop me at the church, and I'll drive myself over."

He nodded, as if he'd expected the caution. "I'm going to wait, though, to make sure that Reverend Brown knows the family rules."

"All right."

He led her through rows of cars to the most battered truck she had ever seen. Once upon a time it had been white, but that had been a lot of dents, mud and rust ago. She was glad she had spoken up when she had, otherwise he really would have thought she hated his truck.

Actually, she liked its lack of pretension.

"Well, here it is," he said. "My faithful steed."

"Does it have a name?"

He looked at her sharply.

She shrugged. "All vehicles with personality should have names."

He got a strange expression, then put a hand on the truck as if it were an old and good friend. "Porthos."

"Excuse me?"

"The truck's name. It's Porthos."

"I was expecting, you know, Hank or something."

He pulled his door open, and got inside. "Sorry to disappoint you."

"It doesn't disappoint." She waited for him to unlock her door, then realized that the lock was broken. It leaned haphazardly against the window. She pulled the door open, gathered her skirt as best she could, and stepped on the running board. The metal felt cool against her bare foot. "I like cars with literary references, especially references that suit."

"You know the *Three Musketeers?*" He looked pleased.

"Of course I do." She slid on the seat, then cursed. Her skirt rose in front of her like centerfold of a pop-up book. She wrestled the fabric down, then held it in place.

Rick was trying not to laugh. "I never realized clothing could be so much trouble."

"Oh, this is nothing," Tasha said. "You should see the dress my mother picked out for my confirmation."

He looked at her, then raised his eyebrows. "Um, Tasha. The shift is on the floor."

Buried in pink. She slid closer to the passenger door, thankful that the truck—although battered—was extremely clean. "Better?"

"Much." He started the truck. It roared to life, as if it had been waiting for the opportunity to leave.

"So," she said, as he drove out of the lot. "If you get a Jag will you name it Aramis?"

He glanced at her. He looked pleased. "How did you know?"

"Logical," she said. "Porthos is good-hearted but loud and uncouth. Aramis is cool and sleek and so handsome that no woman can resist him. But he's also a priest, so you have to get a car that's a religion. If you're going to carry this out, though, your Athos car will have to be dark and brooding and yet the perfect hero—which would be, what?, some kind of Mercedes, maybe? And I have no idea what kind of car you'd name D'Artagnan."

"Something that's a little bit country and a little bit rock n roll," he said, retracing their way to the church. The truck rattled as it bounced along Portland's streets.

She laughed.

"You're the first woman I've ever met who knew the reference," he said.

"You have to thank Richard Lester for that."

"The director?"

She nodded. "If it weren't for his movies, I wouldn't have read the books."

"Hardly anyone's seen the Lester *Three Musketeers*. They've only seen that John Malkovich abomination."

"The *Three* and the *Four Musketeers*," she said. "Perfectly cast. Michael York, Oliver Reed, Richard Chamberlain—"

"Raquel Welch, Faye Dunaway..."

She laughed. "See? You agree."

"Of course I do. Where do you think I found out about Alexander Dumas? It wasn't at Lincoln High School."

He pulled into the parking lot of the church. Her Mustang was the only car in the lot, and she suddenly worried that Reverend Brown hadn't gotten the memo.

"Is the Mustang yours?" Rick asked with something like awe. There weren't many classic Mustangs around any more.

"Yep."

He pulled in alongside it. "And does it have a name?"

"Lover Boy," she said, then clapped her hands over her mouth.

He raised his eyebrows.

"I usually don't tell people that," she said, letting her hands drop.

"It does imply an unusual relationship with your vehicle."

"A Mustang is a horse," she said. "Lover Boy is a horse name."

"You couldn't have gone with something classic like Secretariat?"

"My car is not a three-year-old," she said archly. "And he doesn't need to race to get his triple crown."

"I see," Rick said, then he shut off the engine. "I'm staying here until Reverend Brown lets you in."

"Don't worry," she said, opening her door. "The church isn't locked."

She sounded a lot more confident than she felt. She slipped out of the cab and onto the cool pavement.

"Where are we meeting?"

"Jakes?" he said.

"On a Saturday night? Maybe we shouldn't go somewhere so trendy."

"All right. You ever been to Stars in the Hollywood district?"

"Yeah," she said, smiling. Stars wasn't trendy, but it was good. It was a fairly new, undiscovered restaurant with excellent meals and even better desserts. "That sounds perfect. I'll meet you there in fifteen."

"You can't change in fifteen minutes, let alone get across town—"

"You forget. I got a Mustang." And then she slammed the truck's door closed.

The pavement here was covered with small rocks, and it took all of her dignity to keep from limping. She got on the grass as soon as she could, then went to the side door of the church, the door Brooke had sworn would be unlocked until the last bridesmaid picked up her things.

It was. Tasha heaved a small sigh of relief.

The truck started and pulled up alongside her. "Make it a half an hour," Rick said. "I've got to change too."

"I could have made it in fifteen minutes."

He shook his head. "I didn't want you to get a ticket."

"That's not likely," she said, but he was already pulling away. She watched the truck disappear down the road. Man, she liked him. She hadn't felt this good about anyone in a long, long time.

She smiled to herself and then went inside the church to turn into a person again.

# CHAPTER 10

*B*EEBE HEARD THE truck before he saw it: the roar of the old engine, the unmistakable sign of a muffler on its very last days. He knew the sound intimately—and could tell just from the volume of the roar how far away the truck was.

He had to get out of the garage and quickly. The last thing he wanted was Rick Chance to catch him trying to break into the house.

Not that Beebe was actually trying to break in. He knew about the security system—how could he not with the company's logo pasted on every door? Who would want a business logo all over his house, even if it was discreetly placed? Such things didn't ward off every burglar. Surely there were thieves as clever as he was.

Then again, maybe not.

He slipped out the side door and jogged to the neighbor's house. Fortunately for him, these people were never home. He'd used their rhododendrons as a stakeout more than once. And this afternoon, they would provide him cover until he could return to his own car.

He crouched on the mulch beneath the rhodies, and reached inside his shirt pocket. Then he removed the tiny binoculars he always carried with him.

Maybe this time he would see Jessamyn. She had to come out of that house sometime. Chance couldn't keep her imprisoned forever.

The roar of the truck seemed even louder than usual. Chance pulled into the driveway. He didn't even bother to open the garage door—unusual, since he seemed to be a creature of habit. Instead he shut off the truck and hopped out.

Chance was wearing a tuxedo.

How very strange. A tuxedo in the middle of the day. Something was going on.

Beebe rose on elbows, creeping forward just a bit. Maybe this day was the day Jessamyn would come out. Maybe Chance was going to take her somewhere special. The last time Chance had worn that tuxedo—in Chicago eighteen months ago—Jessamyn had been on his arm. She had been beautiful. Her red curls cascaded down her back, and she wore a blue dress that hugged her slender form.

But they hadn't enjoyed themselves that night. When they came home, she had her arms crossed and her make-up was smeared as if she had been crying. When she had gone into the house with him, she clutched her purse to her chest as if she were afraid someone was going to take it away from her.

Beebe had called from his cell phone—a brief call, asking for her, wanting to know if she was all right. And Chance had hung up on him, saying there was no Jessamyn in the house.

Chance had always stood between him and Jessamyn.

That would stop soon. As soon as Beebe got into the house, he'd get her out of there. And Chance would pay.

The front door opened, and Chance came out. He had changed into jeans, a polo shirt, and deck shoes. He locked the front door like he always did.

Someday Chance would make a careless mistake, but this wasn't the day.

Beebe sighed, and let the binoculars drop. He hadn't caught a glimpse of her. From this angle, all he'd been able to see was the entry of the house. He had to find a better place to spy. If he found that, he might even be able to see the code for the security keypad.

A shiver of delight ran through him. He should have thought of that sooner. All he needed was the code, and he could get inside.

He could free Jessamyn.

# CHAPTER 11

*R*ICK PULLED UP in front of Stars, wishing for the first time in years that he had a more respectable vehicle than Porthos. The truck had served him well, but it wasn't the kind of thing you drove a beautiful woman in, especially a woman who owned a classic Mustang.

The Mustang was already parked in the narrow lot. He shook his head as he got out of the truck. She still had to defy speed limits to get here. He'd never known a woman who could change clothes that quickly and still have time to drive across Portland.

But Tasha was full of surprises, and he found that he was enjoying them. He was pleased that she had decided to have dinner with him, but he was also worried about it.

The trip home had reminded him of the Creep. There weren't any new baskets or love notes, but he felt the Creep's presence all the same. All the way to Stars, Rick had been wondering if he should get involved with anyone before the Creep got caught.

Stars didn't seem that busy, even though it was early for a Saturday. It was on a tree-lined street just off the interstate. The restaurant had once been a supper club that the new owners had converted into a bistro. He had discovered it by accident. When he had been a boy, there had been a diner on this street, with the world's best hamburgers. He'd returned here shortly after he came back to Portland, hoping the diner was still around. It wasn't, of course, so he stopped in Stars. And he hadn't missed the diner since.

He stepped inside and inhaled the scent of fresh baked bread, coffee, and some delectable mix of spices that probably was the night's specials. Tasha was sitting at a booth toward the back, her chin resting on the back of her hand as she stared out the window. She had taken her blonde hair out of its fancy chignon and let it fall against her shoulders, and she had scrubbed the makeup off her face. She wore a T-shirt with the sleeves ripped out and the name of a local gym across the front.

She was the most beautiful woman he had ever seen. He hadn't lied to her about that.

Still, Rick hesitated. The Creep was ever present in his thoughts. What was he doing bringing an innocent into that? He'd have to tell her —if she was interested in anything more than a simple meal.

Tasha hadn't noticed him yet. She was still staring wistfully out the window. How little he knew about her. She seemed so solid, so strong, and so interesting. They had fit well together. He'd never clicked like that with anyone before.

"Sir? How many?" The hostess stood behind the cash register, hand poised on the stack of menus in their holder.

Busted. Tasha had turned in his direction and smiled. He smiled back.

"I'm with her," he said and crossed the restaurant to her.

She had an iced tea and was already halfway through it.

"How long have you been here?" Rick asked as he slid into the booth. The hostess had followed him, handing him a menu. He noted that she hadn't handed one to Tasha.

"Oh, fifteen minutes." She grinned.

"You have not."

"She has," the hostess said.

"I suppose she's ordered," he said.

The hostess shook her head. "Said she already knew what she wanted."

"Well, so do I," he said, handing the menu back.

The hostess took it. "Your waitress will be right over."

"Show-off," he said as the hostess left.

"I told you I could make it in fifteen minutes."

"That wasn't the point. The point was to get here safely." He winced at his tone. He sounded like her father.

He suddenly felt awkward with her, as if the banter since they met was a product of the wedding instead of being together.

She smiled at him. The smile warmed him.

"And here I thought the point was to escape that dreadful reception," she said.

He leaned back in the booth. It was padded and very comfortable. There weren't many people in the restaurant yet, and no one sitting close. He liked the privacy.

"I think most people would have thought that was a nice reception."

"Did you?"

"I'm not most people."

"I'm beginning to realize that," she said. "But it looked like you made up with your family."

"My sister," he said.

At that moment, the waitress, a college student by the look of her trim form and multitudinous tattoos, arrived. Both he and Tasha ordered and the waitress disappeared without a word.

"Your sister?" Tasha asked as if the waitress hadn't interrupted them. "The tall, stately woman?"

He nodded, remembering how nice it was to connect with Jane again. How much he had missed her.

"Were your parents there?"

He started. "My parents are dead."

"Oh," she said. "I'm sorry."

"Me, too." His words were soft. His parents had been a presence all day. Then, realizing he'd been abrupt, he added, "They died in a plane crash ten years ago."

"My god," she said. "One of those big crashes?"

"A private plane. In the Coastal Mountain Range."

"And here I've been complaining about my family to you this whole time. That makes everything seem very trivial."

"It's not trivial," Rick said. "I wish I still had them to complain about."

"Think they would have approved of Brooke?"

"Oh, I don't know. My parents were very adventurous people. Outdoorsy and athletic. They wouldn't have understood Gerald's business, I know that much."

"Really?"

He nodded. "I was a reader and my mother was constantly pulling books out of my hand, ordering me to go outside."

"Wow," Tasha said. "My mother was constantly trying to keep me inside."

He smiled. "Maybe we were assigned the wrong parents."

"Or maybe children are supposed to be different, just to keep parents on their toes." Even though Tasha's tone was light, her expression was pensive.

The waitress stopped at the table. She had two steaming earthenware bowls of clam chowder. She placed them on the table and ran, as if she were afraid she'd gotten the order wrong and didn't want to correct it.

Rick picked up his spoon. "Did you keep your parents on their toes today?"

"I yelled at my mother." Tasha folded her hands in her lap, like a child expecting to be slapped.

"About what?" He felt his back stiffen, hoping it wasn't about him.

"About the fact that I'm not Brooke." Tasha sighed. "I'm doomed to disappoint her."

"Brooke?"

"My mother. She wanted some dainty daughter who wore frills and she got a girl who fell out of trees and played varsity basketball."

"You were on the basketball team?" Rick looked at her in admiration.

"Yeah," Tasha said. "Just far enough into Title 9 to be able to participate in girls' basketball, but just early enough to miss all the scholarships. Although they did try to recruit me for the European tour."

"You were good."

"I was good." Tasha finally picked up her spoon.

"What stopped you?"

"The same thing that stops most young athletes. Injuries."

"Knee?"

"Shoulder. Screwed up my shooting. I still get twinges raising my arm over my head."

"I'm sorry."

She smiled. "I'm not. I don't think I was really cut out for the life of an itinerant under-appreciated female basketball player."

"That would have been way too much for your family."

"You got it," she said, and dug into her food.

They spent most of the meal talking about trivial things: sports, movies, favorite books. At the end of it, Tasha knew that Rick was the most pleasant dinner companion she'd ever had, but she didn't know much more. She couldn't figure out how to work the conversation toward his sadness.

And any more personal discussions would mean telling him she was a cop. And she wasn't ready to see that wary look in his eyes.

"You seem far away," he said.

The waitress had just brought them the cookie platter. It was a large plate filled with Stars' specialty: cookies of every shape and size. Some were frosted, others were old-fashioned favorites like raisin and chocolate chip. And all were the reason that most people came to Stars.

"Sorry," she said. "I was just thinking how pleasant this evening was."

He smiled. "It was nice, wasn't it?"

She nodded. "Maybe we could repeat it."

She couldn't believe how bold she was being. She usually let the man make the first move—laziness on her part, generally, although sometimes it was self-protection. No sense in being vulnerable if there was a chance she could get hurt.

The smile left his face. He suddenly looked trapped. "I don't know."

Tasha froze. Had she misread him? She thought they were enjoying each other. She thought they had both been attracted to each other.

Rick looked down at his long slender fingers. "My life is a little complicated right now. I'm not sure I should involve someone else in it."

"Oh?" she asked, then felt stupid. He was brushing her off. She didn't need more explanation than that.

He raised those magnificent eyes to hers. "I really like you, Tasha, and I'd love to pursue this. But I got some things going on in my life..." He stopped himself. "I'm sorry. It's hard to explain—"

"No need." She made herself smile, but the movement felt odd on her face. "I misunderstood. Just forget I said anything."

"Tasha, really—"

"It's all right, Rick." She glanced at her watch. "I should go."

"Tasha, I didn't mean to upset you."

She gave him a small smile. "It's all right, really. I enjoyed myself. Honestly."

How many times had she learned in interrogations to listen to the word "honestly"? It covered so many lies. She gathered her purse, opened it, and found her wallet. Somehow she managed to do so without her hands shaking. She hadn't been this embarrassed in years. Maybe ever. She pulled out a twenty and set it on the table for her share of the meal.

"I'd at least like your number." He was throwing her a bone.

She wasn't willing to take it. Her face flushed. The warmth coursed through her, making her even more uncomfortable.

She slid out of the booth.

"When things ease up for you, you can get it from Brooke and Gerald. They'll know how to find me." She was brushing him off now, letting him know that the bone wasn't necessary. It was probably rude of her, but she wasn't sure she cared—not when she was this embarrassed. And it wasn't like she'd ever see him again.

He was sliding out of the booth. She held out her hand, preventing him from coming closer.

"Thanks, Rick, for the fun afternoon. And for getting me out of that awful reception. I appreciate it." Then she turned her back on him and hurried out of the restaurant.

It was all she could do to keep from running to her Mustang. That was the first time her advances had ever been rejected by a man, let alone a known womanizer. Was she losing her edge? Or had he simply needed someone to hide behind at the wedding?

Or maybe he found her the most attractive woman there—the best of a small field that he no longer wanted to play once he returned to the real world.

Whatever it was, it had left her feeling young, awkward and unsettled. And more than a little angry. What right did he have calling her beautiful, flirting with her like that, asking her to meet him at Stars, dancing with her so closely, being near her through the entire wedding and rehearsal dinner, if he hadn't been interested? He had no business leading her on.

She could have had a very nice evening chatting with her new friend Howie, whom she had been very careful not to lead on. And he had appreciated it, dammit. He had appreciated it a lot.

Now she'd have to answer to her mother for leaving the reception early, and she had no excuse at all.

Somehow she found herself on Burnside, heading toward the bridge. She didn't remember pulling out of the parking lot or taking the back streets to get to Burnside. But here she was, the bridge looming tall before her.

It showed just how flustered she was. And how disappointed. She had never met a man like Rick before.

She hoped she never would again.

Rick stared at the plate of cookies for the longest time. She hadn't even touched them. Not a taste of the very thing she said she liked best about Stars. He was half-tempted to have them boxed and deliver them to her himself—except that he didn't know where she lived. He didn't even have her phone number, and there was no way to get it without disturbing newlyweds on their wedding night.

He wondered if Jane had it, and decided he didn't even want to open that door.

The waitress came by and poured him a cup of coffee that he didn't want. He was too busy berating himself to stop her.

*My life is a little complicated right now.*

*I'm not sure I should involve someone else in it.*

*I really like you, Tasha, and I'd love to pursue this. But I got some things going on in my life...*

*I'm sorry.*

She must have thought he was giving her the brush-off. That was what it sounded like. That was probably how he intended it. Subconsciously. He knew better than to bring someone he cared about into his life right now. That had been his biggest mistake in Chicago.

*I'm sorry.*

The thing was, he liked her more than he had ever liked anyone he'd ever met. He thought Tasha was stunning and she was great company. They liked the same books, the same movies, even the same parts of Portland. They seemed extremely compatible, and he had destroyed the evening with a few simple sentences.

*I'm sorry.*

He made himself take a chocolate chip cookie, but he couldn't force himself to eat it. This was the end. He wasn't going to let the Creep run his life in Portland the way he had in Chicago. Rick had left Chicago so that he would have a real life, so that he would be free to do whatever he wanted.

It wasn't working out that way.

He would get rid of the Creep, and then he would call Tasha. Somehow. He'd get someone to give him her number. Or he'd dig it up himself. How many Natasha Morgans were there in Portland?

He'd find her.

Just as soon as he was ready.

# CHAPTER 12

$\mathcal{T}$ASHA HAD THE crime scene photos spread across her desk. Desmond Pfeiffer lay naked on the hardwood floor of his living room, legs sprawled awkwardly, arms splayed. His head looked like a crushed melon, blood forming a pool around it.

She knew his brother had killed him. She just couldn't prove it. Something was missing. She just didn't know what.

"You should have those photos memorized by now." Lou sat on the edge of her metal desk, his cheap suit—the brown one—wrinkled from spending the afternoon in a hot car.

His desk was covered with notes from the Pfeiffer file as well. It was the only murder in Portland in the last three months—the murder rate was down for the first time in years—and they had been on the rotation.

Portland had ten homicide detectives, and the cases were passed through the department. Tasha had been on the squad for three years, and this was her twenty-fourth murder investigation. The others had been pretty straight-forward: a shooting in a convenience store, a few domestic abuse cases that had gotten out of hand, and several gang-related incidents. She had served on the serial killer task force her very first summer—and they had closed that case with incredible rapidity.

The FBI had damned them with faint praise by saying they had done good work, considering the killer had been ready to be caught.

The Pfeiffer case, though, was different. This time their perpetrator was smart, and even though she and Lou knew who the perp was, they couldn't find anything to pin the murder on him.

Cases were not prosecuted by hunches.

"I keep thinking I missed something," she said.

"What do you think, it's going to leap off the photo and grab you?"

"Maybe," she said.

"It doesn't work that way."

She sighed. "Well, maybe we're looking at it from the wrong angle. Maybe Damon didn't do it. Maybe someone else killed Desmond."

"Yeah, and my wife thinks I'm the second coming of Brad Pitt."

Tasha looked up at that. "Ah, come on, Lou. I'm sure she does. She stays with you, doesn't she?"

"Only because Brad's in a happy relationship, or so she tells me. I'm not sure how she knows." Lou pushed one of the photos aside and peered at the one beneath it. They showed the body from different angles, taking in different parts of the room.

Desmond Pfeiffer had been a former Nike employee who had invested his savings in something he had called "a wild hair idea." It was one of the first sports merchandise stores on the web, one that specialized in autographed shirts and cards and collectibles—long before anyone else had.

He'd pulled in close to two million dollars the first year, then, seeing that his idea wasn't unique and was about to fold, had sold the business to his brother Damon for a quarter of the business's on-paper worth. The problem was that the bottom fell out of the e-merchandise business —especially the sports stores—shortly after that, and Damon lost everything.

Even if the bottom hadn't dropped out, Damon might have lost everything. He was not the businessman his brother was. He'd invested in too much inventory, paid too much for it, and expected to reap huge profits, which he spent before he made them. Instead of coming out of the business rich, as his brother had, Damon found himself a half million dollars in debt.

"Why is a man naked at nine o'clock in the evening?" Tasha asked, still staring at the photos. The coroner had been able to put the time of death around nine—Desmond had come home at 8, talked to a friend at 8:30, and his body had been discovered at 9:30. He hadn't been dead long when the crime scene team had arrived.

"Tash, if you gotta ask me, your love life's going worse than I thought."

Tasha felt a blush build in her cheeks and she silently cursed it. A legacy from her dismal weekend. She didn't even want to think about it —especially the way she had run off after Rick turned her down. Later that night, she realized that if she had laughed and stayed, he wouldn't have known how interested she was in him.

The beauty of hindsight.

"The coroner checked the body," she said. "No sign of sexual activity."

"Could've been just starting," Lou said.

"And she hits him over the head?"

"Expectations," Lou said. "You know, maybe he wanted to and she didn't. Maybe he was trying to force himself."

"There was no evidence of a woman's presence."

"There's no evidence of anyone's presence. There's no fingerprints anywhere in that place."

"The housekeeper was there that afternoon."

"Yeah, and when he came home, he didn't touch the sink, or maybe the toilet, the refrigerator, a table, something? Come on, Tash. We know our perp's smart, so let's give him some credit here."

"That's a lot to wipe down in a short amount of time." She leaned back in her metal office chair. It squeaked. She needed to get some WD-40 and fix it, but she hadn't had time.

"How long does it take to bash someone's head in, huh? Maybe fifteen seconds. Two minutes if there's a struggle."

"But there's no sign of one."

"Who'd know?" Lou asked. "His brother's his only family, and

Damon says he never visited the place. You find anyone who's been inside that house?"

"No." She tapped her index finger against her mouth. "But that's it."

"What's it?"

"It was a Parade of Homes house."

"Yeah?"

"Sometimes people buy them already furnished."

"So?"

She looked at her partner. She loved Lou, but he wasn't strong on domestic things. "A man who buys a house already furnished isn't going to move the furniture around."

Lou grinned. "Oh, baby, this could be good."

"Maybe." She picked up the phone. "What year did he buy that house?"

"Last year, same as when he sold the business."

Ready to retire at the ripe old age of 35. Well, at least he'd enjoyed a few months before someone shattered his skull.

"Who are you calling?" Lou asked.

"A realtor friend," Tasha said. "I want to find out who handled the house. She should have that information at her fingertips."

"Think she's still got pictures?" Lou asked.

"Let's hope so," Tasha said.

Rick was in the upstairs den, working on his Internet computer. He'd bought the computer at the same time he'd bought the house, and put a DSL line into the den. The computer was the fastest available, and he appreciated it when he tried to download.

He had the television tuned to WGN so that he could watch the Cubs game, but the sound was turned off. He found the announcers annoying now that Harry Carey was dead. The radio was playing oldies, and a book lay open on the couch. This room was his play room—the couch, long enough to handle his six-four frame, was in the very center of the room. Toward the back was a recliner with a reading lamp next to it. The television was on a pedestal and could be turned so that it could be seen from anywhere in the room.

The only thing the den lacked was a phone. When he holed up in here, he didn't want to hear from anyone.

He was researching the latest surveillance equipment—something he should have done the day before. Instead, he had gone directly to Beaverton where all the electronic stores were and let sales people talk to him as if he were an idiot.

He wasn't quite an idiot, but he realized that all things electronic had advanced more in the past month than he had in years. Once upon a time, he knew everything there was to know about cameras and video, but that was five years before—the dark ages, in the electronics business.

So, instead of trusting the sales people, he went on the web to see what he could find. He wanted tiny cameras, the kind that could hide anywhere and be impossible to detect. He also wanted them to be motion activated, so the next time someone set off a perimeter alarm, he could see it and record it.

He wasn't even sure he could get the equipment he wanted in Portland. He knew that a few places in Chicago had them, but they were stores that gave him the willies—places that you walked into and instantly knew you were in Paranoia Heaven, with men who wished they'd been hired by the CIA but were probably too uptight to pass the exam. He'd like to avoid those places if he could, but if he needed to go to one to get state-of-the-art equipment, so be it.

Let the Creep follow him back to Chicago. That would serve him right.

The thought of the Creep made Rick reach for the window. The blinds were down, even though it was noon. He couldn't sit by an open window any more—he was worried that he was being watched.

Another gift from the Creep.

Rick lifted the slats of the blind and peered into the street. No cars. No people, except for the elderly woman across the street. She was sitting near her picture window, watching his house. He'd tried to talk with her to see if she'd seen anything unusual, but every time he went over there, she closed her curtains. He had no idea why she was afraid of him. Maybe she just didn't like company. Or maybe she worried about men who spent their days at home.

If that were the case, she was going to have a lot to worry about. The new economy meant a lot more men stayed home and telecommuted—especially in the Northwest.

Rick let the blinds drop and went back to his web search. Out of the corner of his eye, he saw stats appear on the TV screen. He grabbed for the remote and turned on the sound. The announcer's voices clashed with the Beatles who were singing one of Rick's favorites, "Paperback Writer," but he didn't bother to shut off the radio or even turn the volume down.

He wouldn't have the TV's sound on for long. Just for the at-bat.

One of the many things Rick missed about Chicago was spending his afternoons in Wrigley Field or even at Comiskey Park. Chicago had been a sports heaven. Portland, home of Nike, had only one professional sports teams to its name—the Trail Blazers. Rick liked basketball, but he wanted to spend hot afternoons in uncomfortable seats, drinking a cold beer, and watching men whack at a round ball with a big stick.

Maybe some day he could move back. When the Creep was gone, and he didn't have anything to worry about any longer.

A long fly deep into left field. Looked like it was going to go out of the park for a moment, before it did a sudden dive and bounced near the ivy-covered wall. It was a double.

Rick muted the TV and heard a chime. He frowned, turning toward the radio as if it could explain itself. The Stones weren't getting any satisfaction, and so far as Rick knew there hadn't been chimes in that song before.

Then he realized that was the sound of his doorbell.

He got up from the computer. He hadn't heard his doorbell since the day he and the realtor came to the house. She'd rung it to show him the lovely ringing.

It made him realize that no one had dropped in on him in the two months he'd been back in town.

He hurried down the steps, yelling that he was on his way to the door. He wondered how long his visitor had been there.

There was no way of knowing.

He was about to pull the door open when he remembered that he'd set the perimeter alarm.

"Just a minute," he yelled through the oak door. He punched in his code, undid the perimeter alarm, and then pulled the door open.

A man stood there, clutching a bouquet of flowers. He was small, nervous and balding, wearing a denim shirt and khaki pants. The bouquet—mostly roses and ferns—nearly hid his face.

"Is Jessamyn Chance here?" he asked in his nasal voice.

The very name set Rick's teeth on edge. He blocked the doorway. "Who the hell wants to know?"

"Th-These are for her," the man said. "I-I-I have to give them to her personally."

"Do you?" Rick stepped across the threshold, pulling the door closed behind him.

"Y-Yes." The man backed away.

Rick looked around him for a delivery van, hoping to see the logo of a florist shop on the side. But parked against his curb was a blue sedan.

He'd never expected the Creep to try the direct approach. But then, he hadn't expected the Creep to follow him from Chicago either.

He also hadn't expected the Creep to look so wimpy but then the police psychiatrist he'd talked to about this in Chicago said most of these stalker types appeared harmless in person.

"I-I-Is she here?" The man was holding his ground near the steps.

"Jessamyn Chance?" Rick said, putting the emphasis on the first name.

The man nodded, head bobbing like a nervous rabbit.

"You want to know if she's here?"

The man nodded again.

"Because you theoretically want to give her flowers."

The man nodded a third time. He wasn't taking his gaze off Rick.

Rick drew himself to his full height. He knew he could be imposing when he did that, and he used every bit of it. This Creep would have to know who he was messing with. "What is it about her that so fascinates you?"

"N-N-Nothing." The man's gaze flicked toward the house. "I j-j-just wanted to g-g-give her th-th-these."

Rick yanked the flowers out of the man's hands. "Consider them given," he said, and then he tossed the entire bouquet over the porch. They landed with a crash on the sidewalk below.

The man cringed. Rick grabbed him by the collar and lifted him against the porch's main pillar. The man was lighter than he should have been. Or maybe Rick was angrier than he should have been.

"For the past two years, you have made my life a living hell," Rick hissed, pressing his face close to the little man's. "I'm tired of dealing with you and your obsession. You want to get me out of the way? Fine. Now's your chance. Better defend yourself, because one of us is leaving this porch broken and bloody, and it sure as hell ain't gonna be me."

# CHAPTER 13

"K EY-RIST," LOU SAID, thumbing through the pile of real estate brochures on his lap. "Six-hundred-and-fifty thousand dollars for a five bedroom, four-thousand square foot home with a view of Mount Hood."

"Sounds low." Tasha was driving. They were in a city car—neither Tasha nor Lou had volunteered their personal cars for police department use, even though they did get a mileage and maintenance fee. No mileage and maintenance fee was worth the damage one year on the force could do to a car.

This car was a white sedan that still smelled new. But instead of a regular radio, there was a police radio squawking up front next to the new computerized information system complete with fax, and child safety locks so that the person in the back seat could not get out without the person in the front seat's permission. Not that Tasha would ever arrest anyone and put him in this car. It would be too easy to climb over the seat. But she appreciated the thought.

"Yeah, but look at this picture." He shoved the brochure toward her and she pretended to look. Driving in Portland had become a contact sport. If she took her eyes off the road for too long, she'd run the risk of being hit or worse. Things were worse in the small residential areas like this one. The realty office had been in a nearby strip mall, and Tasha had decided to take the back roads to the station instead of chancing the main arteries in the middle of the day.

"So?" Tasha asked.

"So?" Lou said. "All of the houses in this development look alike. You pay a kabillion dollars and get a large house that looks like every other house on the block. How much you wanna bet that you can only see Mount Hood from the upstairs window?"

"And only on a good day," Tasha said.

Lou glared at her. That part went without saying. Any clouds at all and the mountains went into hiding. "You're not taking me seriously."

"I don't know why I should. We're not interested in that house. We're interested in Pfeiffer's house. You didn't have to pick up all those other brochures."

"The wife wants to move."

"Then you should be having this discussion with her," Tasha said, wanting no part of it.

Lou sighed and dug through the pile until he found the brochure Tasha's realtor friend had given them. Inside of the brochure were lots of pictures of the models in that year's Parade of Homes, including some interior shots of the Pfeiffer home.

And, apparently, the realtor had taken some candid shots during the Parade of Homes. The images included various realtors and potential customers viewing the ground floor of the Pfeiffer home. It had been one of the main attractions of the Parade that year, and according to the media, it had been the most beautiful house on display. The realtor had copied those as well and stuffed them in the brochure.

"All right," Lou said. "Let's see what we got."

He started thumbing through the stack of papers, when the police radio squawked again. He started to turn it down and then stopped, listened to the call, and swore. "That's just a few blocks from here."

"We're not beat cops," Tasha said.

At that moment, the unit cars radioed in. The closest ones were ten minutes away.

"Tash, we should check it out."

She sighed. Lou believed they had a duty to respond if they were the closest. He always said that catching the bad guy in the act was the best way of preventing a homicide investigation.

"You know," she said, "I wanted to be promoted so that I wouldn't have to do domestic work any more."

"No one said it was domestic."

"In this neighborhood? Of course it is." But she turned on the siren and made a left, as Lou reached under the dash and grabbed the light. He slammed it on the top of the car as they headed toward the disturbance.

# CHAPTER 14

TO RICK'S UTTER dismay, the man slid down the post, put his hands over his head, and started to cry. Rick stood over him for a moment, fists clenched, feeling his anger build.

Why couldn't this Creep have the guts to fight? One good, knock-'em, drag-out and this thing would end.

Rick had expected the Creep to savagely attack him.

He never expected tears.

"Get up," Rick said tightly.

The man continued to sob.

"Get up!"

The man shook his head like a little boy protecting himself from an angry parent.

"*Get up!*" Rick finally reached down and yanked the man to his feet. Then wished he hadn't. The Creep's face was blotchy and tear-streaked. He looked pathetic.

Rick didn't want to feel sympathy for the person who'd ruined his life.

There were sirens coming closer. Apparently his little altercation with the Creep wasn't the only thing happening in his quiet neighborhood on this strange Monday.

"Just fight me," Rick said, even though he hated the tone. It sounded like he was begging. "One punch. Let's get this over with."

All that did was provoke another sob. The man wrapped his arms around his head again, and faced the pillar like it could protect him.

"Son of a bitch," Rick muttered. He had no idea what he was going to do. His fantasies of beating the little bastard bloody weren't going to work. He couldn't pound anyone who was crying. He just couldn't.

He wondered if the Creep knew that and was playing on it.

Of course not. How could the Creep know that? How could anyone?

The siren sounded close. Rick looked up and saw an unmarked car with a light on the roof round the corner. It was the answer to his prayers. He'd flag the cops down, give the Creep over to them, and tell them he was being harassed. Maybe they'd leave it at that. Maybe he wouldn't have to answer too many questions.

Even if he didn't press charges, they'd get the Creep's name and address. Maybe he was wanted for other stuff.

Rick grabbed the Creep's arm and hauled him down the front sidewalk toward the street. The elderly woman from across the way was standing in her front door, hands folded protectively near her chest, as if she were spying and praying at the same time.

The cop car pulled in front of Rick's house and stopped. Had they seen him? Then the siren and the light went off, and his stomach turned over.

The Creep wasn't fighting at all. In fact, he was a limp bundle that Rick had to drag down the sidewalk.

The car's passenger door opened and a beefy middle-aged man got out. He wasn't in uniform, but he looked like a cop. He wore a cheap brown suit that bunched over his considerable muscles. He had a badge in one hand and handcuffs in the other, and he was shouting, "That's enough! Let him go! Let him go!"

Rick stared at him for a moment, confused. This wasn't how he had planned it. The Creep squirmed slightly.

"Help!" The Creep's voice crackled and he sounded even more pathetic than he was.

"Let him go!" The cop said. His badge had disappeared and he was reaching for his gun.

The cop was talking to Rick! Suddenly Rick felt like he'd fallen into the rabbit hole. He let go of the Creep—who fell to the sidewalk with an audible thump—and raised his arms like he'd seen countless people do on television.

"Okay," the cop said. "Turn around."

The other cop got out of the driver's side. Rick caught a glimpse of someone tall and thin wearing a brown blazer before he turned to face his house. The cop hurried toward Rick, brought his arms down, and with a practiced movement, cuffed him.

It hurt more than he'd ever imagined it would. The cuffs were too tight around his wrists and his arms were in an awkward position. He could feel the strain on his shoulders.

"Officer, it's not what you think," Rick started.

"You shut up," the cop said. Then, in a more compassionate tone, he said, "You all right?"

Rick opened his mouth to answer when he heard the Creep say, "N-No. I was just—"

"Rick?" The voice was familiar.

He turned his head over his shoulder. Tasha was standing behind him. She wore a light brown blazer and her blonde hair was pulled into a severe bun which accented her delicate features.

"Tasha?"

"Oh, n-no," the Creep mumbled.

"What is this, Tash?" the cop asked.

"I have no idea." She sounded annoyed. "Rick, you wanna tell me what's going on?"

"He at-at-attacked me," the Creep said. "Th-Th-That's what's going on."

"Is that true?" Tasha asked.

Rick turned around. The Creep was still sprawled on the sidewalk, his face still blotchy and tear-streaked. He certainly looked like he'd been beaten up.

"He's been harassing me," Rick said.

"Th-Th-That's not true," the Creep said. "I've never s-s-seen him before."

"Who called this in?" It was that question that made him realize that Tasha was here in an official capacity, that she wasn't, for some reason he didn't yet know, traveling with the cop.

"You're a cop?" Rick asked.

Tasha rolled her eyes.

"Why didn't you tell me you were a cop?"

"Why didn't you tell me you beat people up?"

"You know him?" the other cop asked.

"He was an usher at my cousin's wedding," Tasha said.

"Hey," the Creep said. "Wh-Wh-What about me?"

"What about him?" Tasha asked Rick.

"He's been harassing me," Rick repeated. "This is the first chance I had to confront him."

"I was d-d-delivering flowers," the Creep said. "They're smashed beside the porch."

"I don't see a van," the cop said.

"I was s-s-s-stopping on my way home. The delivery was on my way. I was t-t-taking a half d-d-day. My wife is s-s-sick. Just c-c-call my boss. She'll c-c-confirm th-th-this."

"Who is your boss?" Tasha asked, whipping a cell phone out of her pocket.

"C&J Flowers," the Creep said.

"Tasha, how can you believe him?" Rick asked.

Her gaze was cold. "Because I saw you drag him across the front yard."

"*My* front yard," Rick said. "I was bringing him to your car so you could arrest him."

She turned her back slightly as she dialed information. Then she bent her head and requested the number for C&J Flowers.

"Are you all right?" the cop asked the Creep again.

"N-N-No," he said. "I've n-n-never been so s-s-scared in my life. N-N-Not even when I was a k-k-kid. I used t-t-to get beat up a lot you know. Because of the s-s-stutter. But nothing like th-th-this."

"I didn't touch you," Rick said.

"Except for the dragging across the yard part," the cop said. "Tash was right to ask. Who called this in?"

"I didn't," Rick said, "and obviously the Creep here didn't have a chance—"

"I'm n-n-not a c-c-creep," the man said. "I was just d-d-delivering flowers!"

"—but I suspect Old Lady Busybody across the street was the one who dialed 911," Rick finished as if the Creep hadn't said a word.

The cop looked over his shoulder. The old lady was still on the porch, hands clenched.

Another police car pulled in, followed by another. These were regular police cars, with sirens built into the top, Portland Police Department stamped on the side, and officers in uniform inside. What had that old woman said? That there was a riot going on here?

Tasha slipped her phone back in her pocket. "His story checks," she said to her partner.

"Whose story?" Rick asked.

"M-M-Mine," the Creep said, raising his chin defiantly.

Rick resisted the urge to growl at him, knowing that would make the Creep dissolve into tears. Again.

"They got an order to send flowers to this address and he volunteered to take them even though they weren't on his normal route. He was going to take the rest of the day off to spend it with his sick wife." Tasha delivered all of that news in a flat tone.

Oh, that was just beautiful. Rick closed his eyes for a moment, trying to contain the anger building in him.

"S-S-See?" the Creep asked. Or the Not-Creep, as the case may be. Either way, Rick could see why the guy got beaten up in school. And it had nothing to do with the stutter.

Rick opened his eyes. The Creep—the Not-Creep—was sitting defiantly, his arms crossed.

"Where's your goddamn van?" Rick asked. "I looked for your van before I even stepped out of my house."

"That's enough," the other cop said.

The uniforms were out of their car and headed Rick's way.

"Answer me," Rick said. He couldn't believe the mess he was in now. "Where's your fucking van?"

"S-S-See?" The Not-Creep shuddered. "He's t-t-terrifying."

Tasha glared at Rick as if she couldn't believe what she was hearing. He shook his head.

"Where *is* your van?" she asked the Not-Creep in a very gentle tone.

"I d-d-don't have it," the Not-Creep said. "I c-c-came in my c-c-car. I d-d-didn't th-th-think it would be a p-p-problem."

"Oh for god's sake." Rick couldn't keep the exasperation from his voice. "Why didn't you tell me this at the door?"

"You d-d-didn't g-g-give me a ch-ch-chance."

"I did too. I asked you a bunch of questions."

"And d-d-didn't g-g-give me a ch-ch-chance to answer th-th-them."

"That's enough." Tasha turned to the uniformed cops. "Take him." And from her gesture, she meant Rick.

"Hey!" he said. "This is my home. Doesn't a man have the right to defend his own property?"

"Against a flower delivery? Mr. Chance—"

"It was Rick this weekend," he said.

"Mr. Chance," she said again, this time more firmly, "we're taking you to the station where we can settle this. You'll have to come with us too, Mr.—?"

"Flegal," the Not-Creep said miserably.

"Mr. Flegal," Tasha said. "I'm sorry."

"B-B-But my wife—"

"Can she be alone a bit longer?" Tasha asked.

The Not-Creep wiped his eyes with the back of his hand. Could he be any more pathetic? Rick grunted and looked away.

"I guess so," the Not-Creep said.

"Maybe we don't have to take him," the other cop said, but by that time, two uniformed cops had taken Rick by the arms and were leading him to one of the squad cars.

He looked across the street. As his gaze met his elderly neighbor's, she grabbed her sweater tightly, and moved closer to her door. His frown deepened. He wasn't that frightening. Well, maybe he had been a little. He'd been trying to scare off the Creep—the Not-Creep—the Not-Creep whom he thought was the Creep. Anyone would understand.

The cops pushed him into the back of the squad car with a bit more force than necessary. He'd always wanted to ride in a squad car. He'd thought often of doing a ride-along, but he'd never gotten around to making the call.

He doubted he would have sat in back anyway, where there were no door handles and a plastic partition between him and the cops up front.

The radio squawked, reporting activity all over Portland. The configuration of the dash was slightly different than he had imagined it would be—and the back seat was a hell of a lot more claustrophobic.

He glanced out the window. Tasha was still talking to the Not-Creep, gesturing as she did so.

A cop. Why hadn't she told him? Was she undercover in some way? Was that why she wasn't in uniform?

But if she was undercover, why had she responded to a simple neighborhood argument?

He'd hated the look in her eyes when she saw him—the pure shock that soon became deep disappointment. Apparently she hadn't expected to be arresting him on Monday morning. It was probably lucky for both of them that he had turned down her offer to see him again. This wasn't what either of them had in mind.

He leaned his head back against the cracked leather seat. He was being arrested—arrested!—and all he could think about was the way it would change Tasha's opinion of him. His priorities were screwed up. Not to mention the fact that this was yet another way for the Creep to mess up his life.

An arrest. What would his family think of that?

Well, Rick already knew what they would think. They wouldn't be surprised. Although he was.

And the amount of anger he'd experienced when he was facing down the Creep—or the guy he'd thought was the Creep—worried him too.

If he hadn't been facing the world's wimpiest flower deliveryman, would he have pounded the guy into small pieces? Then he would have deserved this arrest. But maybe some other delivery guy would have arrived in a van—in some kind of floral uniform, even—or would at least have answered his questions.

The car moved forward and Rick closed his eyes.

He had no idea how he would get out of this one.

# CHAPTER 15

*T*HE PLAN HADN'T worked quite the way Beebe had expected it to. But he wasn't sure if it was failure or not.

He sat in his new hiding place, binoculars trained on Jessamyn's house. The delivery had made the husband extremely angry—he had never seen a more possessive man than Chance—but at no time did he touch the security keypad.

Perhaps he had used it before opening the door. If so, there would have been no way to see it.

Beebe kept the binoculars up, watching the police talk with the deliveryman. They had taken Chance away, and soon they would go away. Maybe, if he was lucky, the deliveryman would press charges against Chance.

Then Beebe could get into the house and rescue Jessamyn from her basement prison.

She would be so happy to see him. She would be startled at first—he was prepared for that—but she would be grateful. He knew from everything she'd written that she'd be extremely grateful. Being rescued was one of her many fantasies.

Being a hero was one of his. He'd never had a chance to be a hero before. When his father had imprisoned his mother—locked her in the basement, sometimes for days—he'd been too small to help.

He'd never even been able to find the key.

This time, though, he wasn't small. And he was smart. He knew about a lot of things. He was the only person who had figured out that Chance had imprisoned her.

Which made him the only person who could set her free.

Tasha stalked into the police station as far ahead of Lou as she could get. Back in Rick's neighborhood, she'd tossed Lou the keys to the car, and stared out the window, brooding.

But Lou wouldn't let it go. "You know that guy?"

"Not really," she'd said.

"He used your nickname."

"So?"

"You called him by name."

"Give it up, Lou."

"I'm just saying—"

"He was the uncle of the groom."

"Jeez, how old is Brooke's husband?"

Which led to a discussion of the wedding in all its horrors. Tasha wanted to think on the way back to the station, and instead, she was recounting the trials and tribulations of wearing a pink tent inside a BMW.

So she made Lou let her off outside the station and stalked in alone, to give herself a moment before she saw Rick again. And she was going to see Rick again. Nothing could stop that. Not rain nor sleet nor gloom of night. She was going to make that damn man explain himself if it was the last thing he ever did.

And it just might be.

"Hey, Tash!" the desk sergeant said as she passed.

"What?"

"Your guy's in interrogation. How come you're not letting the beat guys handle this?"

"Because I want to handle it," she said as she passed, heading toward her messy desk. The House was pretty empty—most everyone was on a case—and she was glad for it. Still she went into the lady's room to berate herself in private.

As she entered, she checked under the stalls for feet. Seeing none, she turned around and karate-kicked the metal trashcan behind the door. It slammed against the wall with a resounding bang, then landed on the floor with an even louder thud.

And it wasn't as satisfying as she wanted it to be.

She leaned on one of the grimy sinks and stared into the stained mirror. She wasn't mad at Rick—no, technically, she was mad at Rick but she was *really* mad at herself.

She'd been warned. Brooke warned her, her mother warned her, even Howie warned her, and she hadn't listened. She'd considered the sources and determined they were biased. Hopelessly biased. She had figured that they all wanted her with Howie instead of the most handsome man in the room.

And Rick was handsome. He had that square jaw and those rugged features and the wonderful twinkling blue eyes—which hadn't been twinkling at all as he dragged that pitiful delivery guy across his lawn. Then Rick's face had been red with anger—not that she'd been paying a lot of attention to his expression. She hadn't even realized it was Rick until she got out of the car. She was more worried about the pitiful delivery guy, afraid he was dead or beaten to a pulp or the victim of some serial killer.

Instead he'd been the victim of his own cowardice. He'd told them the story outside the house—or tried to. Whenever he spoke of Rick, his stutter got much worse. The guy—Flegal—had been terrified.

It sounded like Rick had gone crazy. One mention of this Jessamyn woman, and he'd started shouting and ranting. Since Rick was at least a foot taller than Flegal, in much better shape (gorgeous shape, if she was honest with herself), and obviously strong, the attack had brought back all of Flegal's memories of playground beatings. His stutter had gotten worse, and he hadn't been able to answer Rick's questions.

Tasha still wasn't sure what all of that meant, except that Rick was everything she'd been warned about. A handsome man who was extremely bad news. Violent, nasty, and abusive. So bad that his elderly neighbor spied on him. He'd only been in the house two months and already the old lady was afraid of him.

And Tasha had embarrassed herself by asking him out only two nights before. Fortunately he'd said no. But she'd spent all weekend brooding about it, wondering what it was about her that he hadn't liked.

Well, maybe he'd heard that she was a cop—no, that couldn't have been it. He'd been very surprised about it when he saw her and *why was she still making excuses?*

She gripped the sink even harder and would have ripped it off the wall if she thought it would make her feel better. Nothing was going to make her feel better.

Nothing except taking mighty Rick, sexy Rick, handsome, charming, gorgeous, twinkling Rick, down a few pegs.

Then maybe she'd be able to look in the mirror calmly. Then she might be able to forget the most galling part of the whole thing: that her family really had been right.

# CHAPTER 16

*I*F THE SQUAD car had made him feel claustrophobic, the interrogation room had made the feeling worse. Rick sat in a wooden chair, his hands still cuffed behind him. There was no window. There was a mirror which he knew hid a window. Someone could be watching him, even now.

There was a tape recorder on the table in front of him, a video camera on the wall, a table so scarred that it looked worse than the desks he'd had in school. The room had bland fluorescent lighting that made everything seem washed out. Even if the lighting hadn't been bad, the room would have looked terrible. Once upon a time, it had been painted a metallic green that had faded to the color of rotting avocados.

The room had a smell to it too. He couldn't tell if that smell was simply the cheap industrial cleansers that had been used or if it was a combination of ancient sweat, fear, and piss.

Come to think of it, the chair itself felt a little slimy. He scooched forward on it, then realized it was too late. If there was something on the seat—or something ancient embedded in the seat—it had already leached through his pants.

He'd been in this room hours. Or so it seemed. He suspected it had only been minutes.

The fact that they left him alone had him unnerved as well. They were giving him time to stew or to calm down. Or they thought he'd done something a lot worse than scream at a delivery guy.

And Rick wasn't quite sure how to handle this. His attorney was in Chicago. He had a good attorney, one of the best in the state of Illinois if not the country, but an Illinois attorney didn't know anything about Oregon law—and the last thing Rick wanted to do was to call his family to ask for help.

In their minds, this would be proof that he was exactly the man Teri had said he was all those years ago.

Teri. It was her fault he was in this position. Not this position exactly —not handcuffed in a police interrogation room—but in the position where his entire family would believe that he was a violent man unworthy of their time and help.

He glanced at the door. He wished someone would come to talk to him. He wasn't even sure if he'd been arrested yet. If they did arrest him, he would have to get an attorney somehow—just to protect his own sense of self-worth. He'd always complained about the way people on television answered questions without an attorney present. He didn't want to be like the characters he complained about.

Then he shook his head slightly. He had to stop thinking about characters and research and realize that this was his life, not a novel. He had to focus.

This was the first real mess he'd been in in a long time—which probably pleased the Creep to no end.

Then Rick frowned. What had the Creep been thinking of? He'd never used a delivery service before. Rick was willing to believe that the Creep would come to the door himself, but why had he sent someone else? And why roses and ferns? Why the front door in the middle of the day, when he'd known that Rick was home?

Had it been a diversion gone awry? Had there been something in those flowers? Or had he wanted to get the door open for some reason?

Rick slid back in his chair. He had to get out of here. He had to make sure the Creep hadn't done anything to his house.

Although, at the moment, the Creep was the least of his problems. If

Rick wasn't careful, he'd be spending more than a few hours away from home.

He might be spending years.

~

Tasha emerged from the bathroom to find Lou standing near the door, leaning against the wall, arms crossed.

"I was beginning to think we'd have to send a team in after you," he said.

"I'm all right."

"Yeah. That's why they tell me it sounded like World War Three in there. Who is this guy, Tash?"

"I told you. He was at the wedding."

"And you fell for those baby blues, right? The Paul Newman eyes."

"They're not Paul Newman eyes," she said.

Lou was silent for a moment. Then he said, "You want to let me handle this one, kid?"

He was trying to help her out. He was trying to take care of her. He rarely did that. She must have really looked bad.

"No," she said. "I'll do it."

"Look, Tash, if there's a conflict, then I have to handle it. You know that."

It took a minute for her to understand what he meant. And then she blushed. And then she cursed because the blushing mechanism, restarted by the evil Rick, wasn't shutting off.

"I didn't sleep with him," she hissed.

Lou held out his hands. "I didn't say you did."

"Well, I didn't."

"Good. So we don't got a problem, right?"

They had a problem. She had a problem, and Lou was her partner. He deserved to know.

"I danced with him a lot, though."

"Nothing wrong with dancing."

Oh, there was when it was cheek to shoulder, lost in the way two bodies moved together. As if they were made for each other.

Which Rick apparently had not believed.

Which still made her sore, and shouldn't have. Attraction was an ugly thing. She probably should let Lou handle this, but she wasn't ready to. She wanted to make Rick squirm.

"Is there something wrong with dancing?" Lou asked. Apparently her silence had gone on too long.

Tasha sighed. "I want to talk to him alone."

"Tash, I don't think that's a good idea."

"Good idea or not, I want to talk to him alone. Will you watch my back?"

"You want me to listen in?"

"I want you to shut off the intercom, but pretend like you're listening and if anyone else comes up to watch the interview, I want you to get rid of them."

"Tash, this is a simple case of assault. And the vic isn't going to press charges. It's a waste of time. We got the Pfeiffer case."

"He doesn't know that Flegal's not pressing charges," she said. "I want to talk to him first."

"Why?"

"I want to find out if he's done this before."

"Why?" Lou sounded like a three-year-old.

"Because then I might talk Flegal into those charges after all."

"Tash, if you got some vendetta with this guy—"

"What if he's a nut, Lou? What if he's a guy who'll attack anyone who crosses him? Shouldn't he be put away?"

"Did he strike you like a nut?"

"Not at first."

"You're the one with the famous instincts."

"Maybe they're not as good as I thought they were," she said not meeting his gaze.

"What happened with you and this guy this weekend?"

"I told you. We danced."

"You don't usually get so passionate about dancing with some guy."

"If you must know," Tasha snapped, "Brooke told me to stay away from him."

"So you courted the bastard all weekend."

Tasha started. She hated being that transparent.

"And?" Lou asked.

"And what?" Tasha said.

"And what else?"

"I told you," she said, "I didn't sleep with him."

"Wow," Lou said. "Three denials. How badly did you want to sleep with him?"

Enough that it kept her awake for the past two nights thinking about him. Fantasizing about him, and then berating herself for doing so. She had a hunch she was going to berate herself even more as the week progressed.

To her surprise, Lou put a hand on her shoulder. "Tash, let it go. I'll go in and tell him he's free to walk and you never have to see him again."

She shook her head. "I want to tell him that."

"So you don't need me to shut off the intercom."

"I do, though, Lou. I need to find out if he's everything Brooke said he was."

"That isn't what we do," Lou said.

She looked at him. "I can ask him a few questions, and then you can come advise him he's free to go."

"How about we keep this professional," Lou said. "You ask him about the incident. I'll listen. If he sounds bad, I'll search for priors while you go see Flegal and talk him into pressing charges. Deal?"

Tasha felt her cheeks heat up even more.

"If you didn't sleep with him," Lou said, "if you didn't even date him, then there can't be too much embarrassing information. And even if there is, Tash, it's me. Your partner. We've been together a long time. I've told you things I haven't even told my wife."

"I know," Tasha said.

"And I knew what you meant about Brooke. Our friendship's got to count for something."

"It does," Tasha said.

"I'll swear not to share any of the private stuff with anyone. And I'll keep any onlookers away. But that's all I'll do, Tash. The intercom stays on. I get to hear. Or you're not going in there."

She sighed. He was right. If Rick was as bad as Brooke said he was, and if Tasha found out that he had done things like this before, then she did want him off the streets. If she didn't follow the rules, she couldn't put him away.

"All right," Tasha said. "You've got a deal."

# CHAPTER 17

TASHA STOPPED IN the narrow hallway outside the interrogation room, and peered through the one-way glass at Rick. He looked uncomfortable, sitting there with his hands cuffed behind his back, but he didn't look frightened. Most people looked frightened when they sat in that room—even people who'd been there before.

His long dark hair brushed the edge of his collar and the position of his arms accented his broad shoulders. His tight jeans revealed the muscles in his thighs. He was as handsome and well-built as she remembered, maybe more so.

Then she shook her head slightly. She hadn't let good looks interfere with her investigations before. Good looks hadn't even informed her dating choices in the past. She had no idea why they were catching her now.

"Change your mind?" Lou asked.

"No," Tasha said and pulled open the interrogation room door.

Rick looked up as she stepped inside. Those blue eyes met hers—how could Lou think they were Paul Newman eyes? They were all Rick —and she felt a shiver of pleasure run down her back. A shiver she tried to instantly ignore.

"What's going on, Tasha?"

"I'll ask the questions," she said, as she took off his handcuffs. Somehow she managed to do it without touching him.

She put the cuffs in her belt.

"Tasha, there's no need to play bad cop with me. I know you—"

"Detective Morgan," she said.

"What?"

"I'm Detective Morgan."

He was silent for a moment as he rubbed his wrists. She stood over him, towering over him on purpose so that he'd have to look up when he faced her.

"So this is official, huh?" he asked quietly.

"Yeah."

"Am I under arrest?"

"No," she said. "I'm just asking questions."

"And if I give you the wrong answer, will you arrest me?"

She leaned on the table, sitting close enough to him that she could feel his body heat against her leg. Then she punched the recorder on.

"What happened back there, Rick?"

He sighed. "I'm being harassed."

"By whom?" She kept her voice soft.

He raised his head. He didn't look dangerous. He looked like the man she'd met at the wedding, the fun, flirty guy whom she'd wanted to kiss. If she hadn't seen him drag Flegal across the yard, she never would have thought him capable of violence.

"I don't know," he said.

"But you know you're being harassed."

"Yes."

"How?"

"He leaves stuff. He makes calls. He—"

"You're being harassed by a man?"

"Yes."

"Why?"

Rick looked away for the first time since he started answering questions. He was going to lie. People always did that when they lied—

except for the really good ones. They never broke eye contact. Either was an unnatural way to pursue a conversation.

"If I knew why, maybe I'd be able to stop him."

"Have you called the police?"

"No," Rick said.

"Why not?"

"I take care of my own problems."

Tasha nodded and stood. She glanced at the one-way mirror, wondering what Lou was thinking. Then she rounded the table and took the other chair. She scooted it back and put her feet on the desk.

"What does all this have to do with your behavior this morning?"

Rick shook his head. Then his gaze met hers, direct and personal. It was as if she could feel him touch her and she was all the way across the table from him.

"Look, you have to understand, Tash—Detective—why didn't you tell me you were a cop?"

"This morning," she prompted, as if he hadn't tried to get personal again. "What happened this morning?"

"This harassment's been going on for three years. It's the reason I moved away from Chicago. Apparently the Creep's followed me here—"

"Get to this morning, Rick."

At the sound of his name, he stopped and glared at her, obviously annoyed that she used his first name and wouldn't let him use hers. He was getting angry. Good. She wanted to see how out of control his anger was.

"I thought the delivery guy was him."

"Why?"

"Something he said."

"What did he say?"

"No one sends me flowers," Rick said. "The only flowers I get, the only presents I get, are from the Creep. Usually he leaves them on my doorstep. Today, when I saw the flowers, I thought he'd finally gotten enough nerve to ring the doorbell. I didn't see a delivery van and he wasn't wearing a shirt or uniform from the floral shop. So I thought he was the Creep. He kinda looked the way I thought the Creep would look, you know?"

Tasha knew. Rick kinda looked the way she thought the perfect man should look, so she knew very well. "And that made you hit him?"

"I never hit him."

"You dragged him across the yard. He couldn't get up."

"Because he was crying," Rick said.

"Because you hit him."

"I *never* hit him." Rick flung his head back in exasperation, nearly rocking his chair to the side. "I yelled at him, but I never hit him."

"You yelled at him?"

"Yes."

"Did you menace him?"

"Is that a legal term?" Rick asked.

It was. Menacing was illegal under Oregon law. "Just answer the question."

"I don't know what it means," Rick said.

"Did you threaten him?"

"I don't think it got that far." Rick let out a short breath. "You have to understand. I thought he was someone else."

"And that would have made it all right?"

Rick leaned forward as if he were trying to convince her. "I'm in my home, a home that has felt like it is under siege. Then the guy who is attacking me—I think—shows up at my door. I have the right to yell at the guy."

"But not beat him up."

"I didn't touch him."

"You did touch him," Tasha said. "I saw that. Your neighbor, Mrs. McGuilicuty, says you threw the flowers off the porch and then slammed him against the column so hard that he fell to the ground."

"I did throw the flowers," Rick said. "That scared him so badly he nearly peed his pants. He slid down without my help."

"And that made you angry."

"Damn straight it did."

"So you hit him."

*"I did not hit him."*

"Then why was he on the ground?"

"Because he was afraid."

Tasha let out a small breath. She had him pinned and she didn't want to. But she had promised Lou she'd do this by the book. "He was afraid of you."

"Yes."

"Because he thought you'd hurt him."

Rick's face flattened, as if he realized that he had trapped himself, but to his credit, he responded. "You heard him. He thinks the whole world wants to hurt him."

"And you obliged."

"I did not," Rick said.

"But you were angry."

"Yes."

"You said you were angry when he cringed."

"Yes."

"Why?"

"Because I thought he was the Creep and I wanted to beat the bastard to a bloody pulp and I couldn't do that if he was crying."

It wasn't the answer she expected—neither the honesty of it or the tone of it. "But he'd probably be crying when you were done with him."

"I would hope," Rick said, still rubbing his wrists. "But I couldn't do it when we started. I mean, that would make me a bully and I'm not a bully."

A bully? When was the last time she'd heard that term? She had to work at not looking surprised. "Oh, what are you then?"

"A man who is defending his home."

"Against flower delivery men."

*"I didn't know who he was."*

"The flowers should have been a clue."

Rick let out a loud sigh—an annoyed sigh. But he hadn't done anything with his hands, aside from rub his wrists, and he didn't seem like a man who could be pushed to the brink of control by the littlest thing.

"Do I need a lawyer?" he asked.

"You can have one if you want, Rick," she said. "But I haven't arrested you."

"Then I'm free to go, right?" he asked.

"Yes," she said.

He pushed away from the table and stood. "I can't say it was a pleasure."

"Rick," she said softly, "who's Jessamyn?"

He was almost to the door, but when he heard the question, his shoulders slumped. He did not turn around, but he didn't answer her either.

"Flegal said the flowers were for Jessamyn. He also said that you seemed pretty reasonable until he mentioned the name Jessamyn. Then he said you wanted to know what was going on with him and Jessamyn. Who is she?"

Rick still didn't answer. His head was down. Tasha wondered if Lou could see his face. It wasn't reflected in the mirror.

"Is she your wife?" Tasha asked.

"No," Rick said almost inaudibly.

"A friend?" Tasha's stomach had tightened. Part of her didn't want to know the answer. That was why she had held onto the question until the last possible moment.

"No."

"Then who is she?"

Rick turned around. He had a trapped expression on his face. Trapped and panicked and slightly sad.

"Rick? Who is Jessamyn?"

"Me," he said.

# CHAPTER 18

WHATEVER TASHA HAD expected him to say, it hadn't been that. She was glad she was sitting down. She stared at him for the longest moment, trying to imagine why he would call himself Jessamyn, and then not liking the answer she came up with.

Was this why he hadn't wanted to date her? Saying his life was complicated was a good way of deflecting questions about his sexual preference. He wouldn't have to explain himself in any way. And he hadn't.

That would explain his kindness too—what she had taken for interest had just been genuine kindness. But it didn't explain his anger at the person he called "the Creep" unless—

Unless Rick's Jessamyn persona was supposed to be secret and this Creep was going to reveal it.

Rick was staring at her expectantly. She was supposed to say something here, but she really was speechless.

She tried anyway. "What is it about your Creep friend that upsets you anyway? The fact that he knows your real identity?"

"He doesn't know," Rick said. "That's not even the issue—"

"Oh, so it's the fact he thinks you're a woman?"

"No, not really," Rick said.

"Then what is it, really?"

"I'm Jessamyn Chance."

She stared at him for a moment, letting the words reverberate in her brain. Jessamyn. Chance. She hadn't put the names together. It was like knowing a Rick Steele and then having him admit to being Danielle. She would have made the same mistake then, not putting the Danielle and the Steele together.

He let out an exasperated sigh. "I suppose you don't read anything published past 1940."

"No," she said.

"I run into people like you every once in a while. It's kind of a reverse snobbery. I mean—"

"I know who Jessamyn Chance is," she said. "I mean, I thought I knew who Jessamyn Chance is. I mean—you write romance novels?"

He didn't move. He looked like he was frozen in place. Then he said, "Yes."

She shrugged. She wasn't sure herself. "You don't look like a romance writer."

"What's a romance writer supposed to look like?" he asked.

"Barbara Cartland."

"I'll be sure to put on a pink peignoir the next time I see you." His blue eyes were flashing. He was angry now, and she didn't feel any violence from him. None. Just plain old fury. "And I don't write romance. I write contemporary romantic suspense."

"What's the difference?" she asked. "I thought romantic suspense is a subgenre."

"I thought you didn't read anything published past 1940."

"You said that. I didn't. I read all sorts of stuff. I've even read your novels." Then she blushed. She had read his novels. They were good, suspenseful, and extremely sexy. So sexy in fact that the last one—

Oh, she did not want to go there.

"What's wrong with my novels?" he asked.

"Nothing," she said.

"Then why did you stop?"

"I thought Jessamyn Chance was a woman."

"Everyone thinks Jessamyn Chance is a woman. If you tell anyone, I'm in deep trouble."

"Everyone?"

"Well, everyone but my agent and my editors."

She was still sitting. He was standing. The difference suddenly made her feel at a disadvantage, as if she were the one who was being interrogated.

"I'm the only one who knows?"

"You and whoever is outside that door," he said. "And whoever listens to the damn tape. You hold my entire career in your hands."

"I thought authors went on tours and TV talk shows."

"Jessamyn Chance is a recluse. Not quite as mysterious as J.D. Salinger. I've been seen at least. Not me, really, but my ex-girlfriends—"

"Girlfriends?"

"A reporter sees a woman and goes away happy. They can report on the way she looked—"

"So the girlfriends know."

He shook his head. "They acted confused whenever they approached because they *were* confused and why in the hell am I telling you this?"

Tasha shrugged. "Because I asked?"

He put a hand over his eyes and rubbed them. "I guess you could have a field day with all of this."

"I could blackmail you," she said.

He let his hand drop.

"If I weren't the law-abiding type." She grinned.

He didn't. "That's not funny."

"It sort of is, considering where we are."

"This is my career, Tasha—Detective Morgan. Romance readers don't like male names on their books."

"That's why *The Bridges of Madison County* did so poorly?"

"It's not romance," Rick said.

"I thought you don't write romance," Tasha said.

"Oh, for god's sake." He spun, reached for the door again, and then stopped. "Look, I know I'm in trouble with you. I also suspect that the delivery guy isn't pressing charges or you would have arrested me by now. Am I right?"

She didn't answer him. She hadn't expected him to know procedure that well.

He turned. "Am I right?"

"I wanted to find out how dangerous you are," she said sullenly.

"Then let me tell you." He came back into the main part of the room and sat in the chair across from her. His gaze fell on the recorder. "Do we have to keep taping this?"

She hit the stop button, and pulled the tape out, holding it in her hand. He stared at it like it was made of gold. "How dangerous are you?"

"I wrote science fiction and mystery novels under my own name," he said. "They were pretty mediocre."

"I don't want your literary history," she said.

He held up a hand to keep her quiet and to her surprise, she stopped talking. "A couple of those novels sold. Mid-list books, no great shakes. They appeared and disappeared."

She tapped the tape against her palm. He could justify himself later. Even though she was interested. But she wasn't interested as a cop. She was interested as a woman.

A woman who had felt a deeper disappointment than she wanted to admit when she thought Rick Chance wasn't interested in her—couldn't be interested in her, ever.

"Then my parents died, and as a kind of grief therapy, I wrote a book in which the couple—who weren't married—survived their plane crash, and found the person who tampered with the plane—"

"I read it," Tasha said softly.

"—and it was mostly from the woman's point of view, and the romance was central to it, because my parents were extremely romantic —" His voice cracked. He cleared his throat, and took a deep breath. "Anyway, as a lark, I sent it to my agent, who loved it. She told me to put a woman's name on it, and we sent it out. And then we sold it—to a romance market, not that big, really, and I realized that my family might read it, and if they did, then they'd see my folks in the characters and they were already upset enough at me, so we decided—me, my agent, and my editor—that Jessamyn Chance was a recluse who didn't do book tours which was all right, really, because we didn't expect the book to do any better than my other books."

"Then it became a bestseller."

He nodded. "My editor changed her mind and wanted me out there, but I wouldn't go. My agent tried to talk me into going out on tour too, but by then, I found out how freeing it was to be someone else, at least on paper, and I didn't want to lose that. So I said no. And I stuck to it."

"Well," Tasha said dryly. "I guess that makes you a very dangerous man."

He looked away. Then he placed his hands flat on the table and rose slowly. "Never mind."

She had hurt his feelings. She hadn't expected to do that. She hadn't even thought about it. This topic was very sensitive for him, for reasons she didn't understand.

"I'm sorry, Rick," she said, and winced. She'd lost all pretense of being a cop now. Now she was a woman, listening to him. "Sit down. Please. Go on."

He studied her for a moment, as if he were waiting for her to say something snide.

"Please," she said again. "Sit."

She wasn't sure why she was urging him. Something in his face, maybe, or that damned connection from the weekend. Or the way she wanted to touch his hand, reassure him that she was still here, still interested, despite his outburst, despite her earlier anger.

Or maybe she wanted him to come up with something so that she wouldn't keep thinking of the way he'd dragged that poor deliveryman across the yard.

Rick sat down. "I'm being stalked. Harassed by a man who thinks I'm the husband of Jessamyn Chance."

Tasha caught her breath. "He wants you out of the way."

Rick nodded.

"Has he threatened you?"

"He's been threatening me for the past eighteen months. He's the reason I moved to Portland."

Suddenly she was a cop again. "Didn't you report this to the Chicago police?"

"I did," he said. "Without telling them about the romance writing."

"How did you manage that?"

He rubbed his wrist absently. She could still see the red marks the cuffs had left. "I was dating a woman when all this started. Apparently, the Creep thought she was Jessamyn. He followed her, left flowers for her, chocolates, all sorts of things. Mostly at her apartment. She didn't tell me, and she really didn't think much of it. She thought he was leaving stuff for another resident who was named Jess—in fact, she'd take them to that apartment."

"How did you know that he was after your Jessamyn?"

"He approached her one afternoon, tried to take her to coffee. She wouldn't hear of it, and she left him as fast as possible. That night, she told me about it." Rick ran a hand through his hair. "Some of the things he did were right out of my books. Stuff that sounds romantic on paper isn't always in person."

"So you told her?"

He shook his head. "We called the cops, said we thought she had a stalker who was confusing her with someone else. They got a description of the guy, watched for him, but there wasn't much they could do."

"You don't have his name?"

"I've never even seen him," Rick said.

"Your girlfriend didn't get a name?"

He shook his head. "About a year into it, she got this job offer that was going to take her to France. Her apartment lease was up three months before she had to leave. Rather than look for a new place, she put most of her stuff in storage and moved in with me."

Tasha leaned forward, interested now.

"I guess he'd thought we'd been separated and then reconciled. I don't know. But he pulled her aside one afternoon in the Loop, had a conversation with her that was right of one of the books—about how you know your soulmate when you see them, and sometimes you're with the wrong person, so you have to make a choice. Anyway, it scared her. A lot. So we called the cops. They said there wasn't much they could do unless we knew who this guy was. We didn't."

"There's not much to do even if we know who the person is," Tasha said. "The law only protects you so far."

"I know that." Rick's tone was grim, and that sent a shiver through Tasha.

"What happened to your girlfriend?" she asked, not sure she wanted to know the answer.

"Oh, she went to France. We actually smuggled her out of the country. We—I, actually—bought her tickets on six different flights all leaving at the same time, and obviously, she missed all six of the flights."

Tasha frowned.

He nodded. "Then she went to the ladies room, put on a wig and some different clothes, and bought a new ticket to New York for a flight leaving immediately. We watched at the gate to make sure he didn't get on the flight. She didn't see him. She flew to New York with no problems, then took her already booked international flight to France."

"Did he follow her?"

"No. I don't even think he knew she'd left. He never thought of her by her own name, you know. Only as Jessamyn Chance. Apparently he wasn't following us that afternoon. So all that precaution was probably for nothing."

"And he kept harassing you?"

Rick nodded. "He got it in his head that she was in my house, and I wasn't letting her out. He started threatening me. The letters were nasty —although the ones to Jessamyn were filled with love."

Tasha stared at Rick. What a fantastic story.

"I did report all of this to the cops," he said. "They weren't able to do anything. They said—"

"The best thing you can do is move."

He glanced at her, then nodded. "I did. I came here. Then I started getting this creepy feeling that I was being watched. I kept telling myself that it was left over from before. I put in a security system, and thought I was safe."

"But?"

"He left a basket for me last week, and he set off a couple of perimeter alarms." Rick ran a hand through his hair. "Look, Tash, it got so bad in Chicago that I couldn't work. I kept listening for the phone, watching for him. I thought when I moved here, I'd finally get some peace."

"And you haven't?"

Rick sighed. "I did until I realized he'd followed me. I don't know, maybe he thinks I'm Bluebeard or something. I'm not, Tash."

She didn't care that he wasn't calling her Detective Morgan any more. "What did he do when your girlfriend came back from France?"

"She never did," Rick said.

"Because—"

"Because I stayed in touch. She knew that he hadn't gone away. She wasn't going to come back until she knew he'd been taken care of. And then..."

"Then?"

"She found someone else." He sounded bitter.

"You loved her?"

"I don't know. We didn't have a chance, really. Not with all of this." He raised his gaze to hers. "Now do you understand what I said on Saturday? Why things are complicated?"

She wasn't going to let this be about them, not yet. "You attacked a man today. If Mr. Flegal wanted to press charges, you'd be in jail for assault."

"I understand."

"I'm not sure you do." She leaned toward him. "Your actions today make you the dangerous one. You don't have a right to attack someone because they're giving flowers to your pen name. Do you understand that?"

"Yes," he said.

"Nor do you have the right to attack someone who is just standing on your porch, no matter what they've said to you in the past. Self-defense means just that. You have to defend yourself against imminent bodily harm. Whatever you thought Mr. Flegal had threatened, you had to know that he wouldn't have hurt you."

"He could have had a gun in those flowers."

"And if he did, you disarmed him when you threw the flowers over the railing."

Rick rubbed his eyes with his thumb and forefinger. "This has been driving me crazy."

Tasha studied him. He seemed to be telling the truth. She'd worked with other stalking victims before, and they all felt this combination of helplessness and rage.

"You need police involvement," she said, surprised that the words had come out of her mouth.

He raised his head, looking surprised. "Are you offering?"

Apparently she was, even though she didn't want to be. "I'm working on a major homicide right now."

Rick nodded, as if he expected her to back away from this. "All right."

"But I might be able to find out the identity of your stalker," Tasha said.

"How would you do that?"

"Let me see the basket he gave you. We'll check for fingerprints. That'd be a good place to start."

"I tossed it."

Tasha sighed. This wasn't going to be easy. Lou was going to be angry at her for offering. But she wanted to see if Rick was on the level.

She wanted him to be on the level.

"There should be other ways to find him," she said. "But even if we do, all we can do is get a judge to issue a restraining order unless your stalker breaks the law. Even if he gets convicted of whatever crime he commits, when he gets out he'll come back. They always do."

"I know the drill," Rick said. "The Chicago police already gave it to me. I moved on their advice, remember?"

So he said. But she didn't want to sound that cynical. "Can you give me your contact in the Chicago police department?"

"It's a Detective Stafford," Rick said. "I don't know his number offhand but I have it at home."

"Good," Tasha said. "The more he can tell me, the better. And maybe they can fax me their sketch."

"It looked like Flegal," Rick said.

"I'd like to see that for myself."

His gaze met hers. "You still don't entirely believe me, do you?"

"You threw a lot at me today," she said. "Your attack on Flegal, your profession, and then this story. You have to know how it sounds."

"I do," he said. "That's why I've been taking care of it myself."

"If taking care of it yourself means attacking the wrong people, then the only person you hurt is you." She stood. "Let me handle this. I'll see what we can get done. Otherwise, you might have to move again."

"And have him follow me again?"

Tasha was silent for a long moment. If Rick was telling the truth, she could completely understand his frustration. Moving was supposed to solve the problem once and for all, not make it worse.

"I'll do my best," she said softly. "I promise."

# CHAPTER 19

*R*ICK LEFT FEELING curiously upbeat. Even when he realized, as he stepped out of the precinct, that he had no way to get home, he didn't get angry. He felt as if a weight had lifted off of him. He hadn't realized how much his own silence had oppressed him.

He walked down the empty street toward a nearby convenience store. He'd use the payphone there to call a cab.

It was still mid-afternoon, but it felt like an entire lifetime had gone by. The anger that had flooded him when he saw the deliveryman—Flegal—had dissipated, leaving him spent. Then he saw Tasha, and realized that she wasn't who he had thought she was. No wonder her rich, snobby family disapproved of her work. It wasn't the kind of job a person got when she graduated from an Ivy League school. And it wasn't the kind of job a parent could brag about to her social climbing friends.

He wondered if Tasha believed him. He wasn't sure she did. She had been angry about his behavior, and he couldn't blame her. He was appalled to learn that this Flegal character was from a flower shop, and even more appalled to think that he might have beaten the wrong man senseless. In a way, he'd been lucky that Flegal had some sort of posttraumatic stress flashback to childhood. If Flegal had stood up to him, then Rick might have beat him bloody.

But of course, if Flegal had stood up to him, he probably would have identified himself and argued a bit with Rick before it ever came to blows.

Rick crossed the parking lot to the convenience store. A Chevy was parked out front, and a young attendant stood behind the counter, thumbing through the pages of the *Star*. The pay phone was just inside the door.

It was ironic, really, the way his life had turned out. He had all the money he needed from a job he couldn't admit to—a job he was embarrassed to admit to, if he told the truth—and because of that job, he'd lost a home, a girlfriend, and probably the chance at having another one.

He couldn't even really make up with his family—not if the Creep was going to threaten them too.

Maybe he should take Tasha's advice. Maybe he should move once more. But this time, maybe he should sneak off in the middle of the night, never to be seen again.

~

"Now, I heard everything." Lou was standing just outside the interrogation room. "He has the right to beat up on this guy because he thought this guy was stalking his imaginary friend."

"His pen name," Tasha said.

"Whatever. You read this Jessamyn Chance person?"

"The books have been on the bestseller list off and on for the past decade, Lou."

"Yeah? That's supposed to impress me?"

"No," Tasha said. "But you are supposed to recognize the name."

Lou shook his head. "You know I don't read that crap."

"Oh, yeah, I forgot," Tasha said. "You're the one who hasn't read anything published after 1940."

"Can I help it if my tastes in literature are more refined than yours?"

She frowned at him, then crossed her arms and leaned against the wall. "What'd you think of the interview?"

"I told you."

"You didn't believe him?"

"My hormones aren't the ones racing here."

"That's not fair, Lou."

He glanced down the hall, as if to make sure they were alone. "Look, Tash, you started out good. Call me Detective Morgan, and all that. But by the end, he's calling you Tash, and you're promising to help him. You'd gone in there thinking you might convince Flegal to press charges."

"You still think he's dangerous?"

Lou took a deep breath. "Here's what I think. We got problems every which way. Let's, for one minute, say this guy's job checks out. Then what he's doing is making up lies for a living, right?"

"Stories," Tasha corrected.

"I don't know about your family," Lou said, "but in mine, lies were always called stories."

Tasha knew better than to say anything. In her family, they were called stories too.

"So his job checks out," Lou said, undeterred by her silence, "and what are we left with? A guy who is so good at making up stories—lies —that people pay him for it."

"You're saying he lied to me?"

"How many people do you know come into that room and tell the truth?"

Lou was right about that. Hardly anyone did. Tasha kicked some imaginary dust with her right foot.

"He didn't have to say anything," she said. "He could have left. He was going to leave."

"Sure, he could have left," Lou said. "But he's a smart guy. He proved that when he said he knew that Flegal wasn't going to press charges just by the way you were treating him. Isn't it better to leave you thinking you need to help him than thinking you need to push Flegal to press charges?"

"So I go over there," Tasha said, "and he what? Lies to me some more? At some point, a farce of the nature you're suggesting falls apart."

"You go over there," Lou said, "and he capitalizes on those feelings you have for him."

Tasha straightened. "Are you saying that I'd forget I was a cop? That I'd forget why I was there?"

"Tash, you were soft with him."

"Maybe I believed him, Lou."

"Maybe you're thinking with your gonads."

She pushed off the wall. "You're out of line."

"Maybe," Lou said. "And maybe I'm the only one thinking clearly."

"All right," she said. "Help me on this one. If it turns out that Rick is lying, then you can push Flegal to press charges. But if it turns out that he's telling the truth, you owe me dinner."

"How come if I win I get extra work and if you win you get a free meal?"

She smiled and shrugged. "Payback for telling me that I'm unprofessional."

He didn't smile in return. Instead, his gaze fell to the tape in her hands. "So, Ms. Professional, what're you gonna do with that?"

She hesitated for just a moment. She had thought of destroying it in front of Rick, but she hadn't. "I'm going to save it."

"For what? A rainy day?"

"For the day we decide what to do with Rick."

"He asked for a lawyer."

"He wasn't under arrest."

"You shut off the damn tape before he told his cock-eye story."

"You overheard everything."

"Like that'll stand up in court," Lou said.

"I hope we're not going to go to court," Tasha said, and slipped the tape into her pocket.

"Yeah, me too," Lou said. "Too much paperwork. And speaking of, we have a murder investigation to finish."

"I know," Tasha said.

"It takes priority over your guy."

"He's not my guy," Tasha said.

"Still, let's stop thinking about your pretty romance writer and get back to work." Then Lou paused for a moment. "What kinda guy writes that crap, anyway?"

"I've been trying to figure that out myself," Tasha said. The question bothered her more than she wanted to admit.

# CHAPTER 20

*T*HE CAB LET Rick off in front of his house. His yard was covered with footprints. The roses and ferns were strewn along the sidewalk. He stood on the curb for a moment, staring at the mess.

Was Tasha right? Was he running the risk of making things even worse for himself?

Maybe he should move again.

He had thought he was safe this time. Stalkers usually didn't cross country to follow the objects of their obsession—although obviously, his had.

If Rick moved again, he'd have to do it stealthily. No moving company, no real estate agents. Simply a disappearance in the middle of the night—only his agent, his editor, and maybe Jane would know where he went.

The whole idea made his heart twist. There were only two places in the entire country where he wanted to live—Chicago and Portland. He couldn't live in Chicago, his first choice, so he had come back home. He had no idea where he would go from here.

He would give Tasha a few days. She had said she would help him. And if she didn't, maybe he could track a few things down himself. The floral shop might have a clue who ordered the bouquet. He would start there.

Rick glanced over his shoulder. Mrs. McGuilicuty was watching from her curtained window. He paused, thought briefly about crossing the street and asking her if she'd seen the Creep, and then changed his mind. After his display that morning, Mrs. McGuilicuty was probably terrified of him.

Her curtain moved slightly, and he got the sense that she had backed away from the window. He resisted the urge to wave at her, figuring it would only make things worse. So he turned around and headed up his walk.

A feeling of unease crept over him. Something was different—and it wasn't the roses spilled on the ground. It was something else.

That sense he'd had in the interrogation room—the sense that he had left himself open to some sort of attack from the Creep—returned full force. And he finally understood why.

He hadn't locked his front door. He had merely closed it. And the alarm was off. He had turned it all off just before he'd confronted the delivery guy.

Rick ran up the steps. The front door was closed as he'd left it. He'd been expecting to find it ajar. But the Creep was too smart for that. Rick reached for the doorknob and stopped, suddenly remembering all the research he'd done for his novels.

He slid his hand in his sleeve and used the cloth like a glove. He pushed the door before he touched the knob—he wanted to preserve any fingerprints that might be there—and the door swung open.

It hadn't been tightly latched.

He remembered pulling it shut, pulling it so hard that the doorframe had shaken.

Someone had been here. Someone had been inside.

The hair rose slightly on the back of his neck. His house, invaded by the Creep. He didn't see signs of the guy, but the air felt different, violated, as if just sharing it with the Creep had destroyed it somehow.

What if the Creep was still inside?

Rick's hands twitched. He didn't own a weapon—had always thought guns more dangerous in the hands of their owners than anywhere else. He thought of grabbing a knife, but that would show that he was afraid of the intruder.

Better to use his hands. He was a strong man. He could handle a single, cowardly stalker.

He hoped.

Little things had been moved. The picture of his parents which hung on the wall in the hallway was tilted. The book he'd been reading was face up and closed, left on the coffee table. He was about to check the bedroom when he saw that the door to the basement was open.

A shiver ran through him. He kept that door closed. His office was down there, and he didn't want anyone seeing that space. Not that he'd had any visitors to look at it, but still.

He snuck around the creaky parts of the floor and slid through the basement door. There were three stairs and then a landing before the stairs turned and went all the way down. He left the light off. This was the one part of the house he would be able to walk through in his sleep.

It worried him that the light was off. The basement steps were treacherous. Anyone who was unfamiliar with them would need some kind of light to make it to the bottom. He wondered if the Creep had heard him come in and was waiting at the bottom of the stairs for him to arrive—waiting to attack, waiting to get rid of his rival, as so many of his threatening letters had suggested.

Then Rick let out a shallow breath. The only way out of that basement was through a window, and those were set high in the walls. He had no accessible chairs down there and no ladders. The Creep wouldn't be able to reach the windows in order to get out.

Rick eased out of the basement door, back into the kitchen. Then, softly, he closed the door and locked it on the outside.

He went to the alarm and turned on its perimeter features. That would tell him if the Creep had somehow managed to open a window.

Then Rick went to the phone and called Tasha.

# CHAPTER 21

TASHA WAS FEELING a sense of victory. Desmond Pfeiffer hadn't changed the Parade of Homes interior decoration at all after he moved in. Even the cheap prints still hung on the walls. But when she compared the photos of the crime scene with the Parade of Homes photos, she noted that a Persian rug was missing. It should have been in the entryway, and it wasn't.

She pointed that out to Lou who was unimpressed. "Maybe he didn't like it."

"Or maybe the killer took it."

"Why would the killer take a rug?"

She slid out the Parade of Homes photos. The Persian rug ran from the entry into the living room, right near the area where Desmond's blood pooled.

"I bet our guy stepped in some blood, was walking along the carpet, turned to look at his handiwork and saw the footprints."

"Like he'd know we could use that to identify him," Lou said.

"Of course he'd know," Tasha said. "Remember all the OJ evidence about the Bruno Magli shoe? Not to mention CSI and all its clones."

"Like they're accurate."

"Still, I bet if we find the rug, we find the killer."

"What's the bet this time?" Lou asked. "If the rug doesn't lead us to the killer, I pull an extra duty shift. If it does, I buy you dinner?"

"Smart ass," Tasha said. "We could also check his shoes."

"Not without cause. He's not going to let us into his house."

Tasha was still staring at the photos. "There's something else missing. What is that?"

She shoved a Parade of Homes photo toward Lou and pointed at something round and shiny on the end table.

Lou picked up the photo and studied it up close. "Looks like one of those big glass paperweights."

He lowered the photo and looked at her.

She raised her eyebrows at him. "That's our weapon, isn't it?"

"Yeah," he said. "It probably is. I'll make a copy of this and we'll take it to the coroner, see what she says."

"She said a blunt object, rounded edges."

"It's size I'm worried about, Tash."

Tasha grinned. "Men usually are." Her phone rang and she grabbed it. "Tasha Morgan."

"Tash, it's Rick." His voice was low, so low she almost couldn't hear it. "I probably should have called 911, but after today, I thought it might be better if I called you."

"What's going on?" she asked.

Lou had started for the copier, but he stopped when she said that. She held up a hand for silence.

"I didn't lock my place this morning for fairly obvious reasons, and when I got here, it was pretty clear that someone had entered my house. The basement door, which I always keep shut, was ajar. I don't know if anyone's down there, but I closed and locked the door just the same."

"Are you still in the house?"

Lou frowned at her.

"Yeah," Rick said. "I turned on the perimeter alarm. I'll know if he gets out."

"Did you check all the other rooms?"

There was a slight hesitation. "I'll do that now."

"No, you won't. You'll get out."

"But the alarm—"

"Is there any way out of that basement?"

"The windows."

"Then an open window will tell us a lot more than your alarms will. Get out now. I'll be right there."

She hung up.

Lou was staring at her. "Let me guess. That was Tall, Dark, and Screwy."

"He thinks someone got into his house while we had him here."

"Nice ploy. Builds on your sympathy, gets you involved real fast."

"Lou, it's a call for help." She grabbed her suit jacket.

"If he was having trouble, why didn't he call 911?"

"And explain everything all over again? Plus the fact that he was down here for assault? Come on, Lou. Not even you would have done that."

Lou shook his head slightly. "I'm coming with you."

"Damn right you are. And if we find anyone, we're calling for back-up."

"You think we'll find someone?" Lou asked.

"You know," Tasha said, "I'm hoping we will."

# CHAPTER 22

*R*ICK STOOD ON his front lawn, shifting from foot to foot, feeling like an idiot. He was making quite a spectacle of himself for the neighbors—first the attack, then the arrest, and now this, standing outside doing nothing, like a lunatic. He wondered if Mrs. McGuilicuty was sitting near her window with her hand clutching the phone, just waiting for him to do something else before she called the police again.

Well, she'd be surprised when the police showed up.

It had been about fifteen minutes. He'd already walked the outside of his house. All the basement windows were closed. He saw no one inside. The other windows were closed as well.

He couldn't believe he'd failed to check out the other rooms. But he was convinced that the Creep had gone into the basement. That had been where he had tried to get in before. That had to be where he was.

While he waited, Rick had picked up the roses and put them in a pile beside the porch steps. He placed the ferns beside them, and then he collected the shards of glass, setting them near the destroyed flower arrangements. Oddly enough, he'd never found the card. The Creep always enclosed a card.

Had it blown away? Or had the Creep himself picked it up?

Or had the Creep staged this whole thing so that he could get inside. More and more, Rick was beginning to believe that was what happened.

But he wasn't going to tell Tasha. He already sounded crazy enough.

He was about to pace the grounds around his house a second time, when Tasha's white sedan pulled up. She parked just as haphazardly as she had that morning. And she wasn't alone. The older cop was with her, the one that had originally handcuffed Rick.

Well, what had he expected? Her to come alone, dressed in that spectacular green gauze?

"You think he's still inside?" Tasha asked as she got out of the car.

"He was inside or someone was." Rick walked up to greet her. "But is he still? I don't know. He's not trying to get out."

The other cop got out of the car, and glared at Rick. Rick decided this was the moment to take control. He extended a hand. "Rick Chance. We got off on the wrong foot this morning."

"And you still got that foot in your mouth, as far as I'm concerned," the cop said.

"Lou." Tasha sounded exasperated. "This is my partner, Lou Rassouli."

"Detective Rassouli to you," he said to Rick.

Rick let his hand fall. "Yes, sir."

"Tell us how to get to that basement," Tasha said, "and then we'll handle this."

"No way," Rick said. "I'm coming with you."

"Like hell," Rassouli said.

"It's my house. There's some creep inside."

"And if he shoots you, you'll sue the city. Not a risk I want to take." Tasha was all business, like she'd been earlier. He found he liked this side of her. "How do we get there?"

Rick told them. "I've got a pretty sturdy lock on my office door down there. If he got through that, and then barricaded himself inside, you'll have to come get me."

"Where's the key?" Tasha asked.

Rick stared at her for a moment. "I use an electronic combination lock."

She let out a small snort. "What? You afraid someone'll steal your next masterpiece?"

"No," he said. "I just didn't want anyone walking in there accidentally."

"You really are into this secrecy crap, aren't you?" Rassouli asked.

Rick felt cold. "You told him? I thought you weren't going to say—"

"You told him," Tasha said as she pulled out her gun. "He was outside the interrogation room."

Then she led the way to the house. The gun made Rick nervous. He had known this situation was serious, but to have two police officers enter his home, guns drawn, made it seem like something out of *Cops*.

He hovered near the porch steps, feeling useless. He didn't want to wait, but he understood the wisdom of it. Still, he knew it would take all his self-control not to follow them inside.

Rick's house was a revelation. Not as slobby as Tasha had expected and not neat-as-a-pin, but somewhere in between. There was a few days' worth of clutter—newspapers, some battered magazines—on end tables, and half-read books scattered throughout. An open and unfinished bag of popcorn leaned against the couch, as if he'd been eating it while he read something, and then forgot about it.

The furniture was comfortable and expensive. She wagered the wood frames were made of cherry. The end tables certainly were. He didn't have a television in his living room, but he had bookshelves— more books than she had ever seen in one place. The shelves went down the hall to what was obviously the guest bedroom.

It was empty. Lou checked the closet just to make sure, then he gestured to Tasha to follow him into the bathroom. It was old and one part of the house that hadn't been remodeled. It had a claw-footed tub and no shower, but there were no toiletries either. The guest bath. It had two doors. One of them led into the laundry room. That room was a mess of dirty clothes piled on the floor, clean clothes folded on top of the dryer, and wet clothes hanging from a peg behind the door.

This time, Tasha checked the dark places. Nothing. Yet.

Her heart was pounding, like it always did in these situations. She wasn't nervous. She was anticipating, knowing that at any moment, something—someone—could jump out at her, startle her, force her into an error. She had to be very alert to prevent that, and seeing Rick's stuff for the first time this way, made her feel slightly off her game.

The kitchen was spotless and stunning—a cook's kitchen, also made of cherry, with a flat-topped stove and a refrigerator that looked like it could fly all by itself. The room had a lot of light and no corners for anyone to hide in.

There was, however, a huge security keypad with a computerized screen that showed all parts of the house. Lou nodded toward it as he went by.

A confirmation, maybe, of Rick's story. Was that how Lou saw it? Or did he see it as part of the scam that he was convincing himself Rick was running? Tasha couldn't tell.

She found the basement door where Rick had said it would be. She showed it to Lou, who nodded. First, though, he wanted to check the upstairs. No sense going into the place where they could get trapped before discovering whether or not they were alone in the house.

Her stomach jumped at the thought. Would Rick come in and lock them down there? Was he that kind of nutcase? Then she shook the idea off. If he did anything like that, she had her cell phone and Lou had his. They could literally call for help.

She rounded the corner, went back to the narrow hallway and found the stairs leading up. They were broad, and made of polished wood. She glanced over her shoulder to make sure that Lou was following, then she went up.

Halfway up, she heard the faint murmur of voices. Her stomach jumped. She hadn't expected the Creep, as Rick called him, to be upstairs. She had expected him to be in the locked basement. She turned, gestured to Lou to remain silent, and continued up the steps.

There wasn't much of a landing upstairs—just a central space that had three doors leading off it, one to a bathroom, one to a bedroom, and one where the noise was coming from.

Tasha moved silently toward that room, noting that this house was in such good repair not even the floorboards creaked. The bathroom across from her was obviously the master bath. It had been completely remodeled. She could tell that from outside the room, from the tile, the size of the shower, and the partially visible sink.

Something reflected on the glass shower door, something from the room she was heading to. She kept her gun out, back to the wall.

The voices coalesced into familiar tones. Laughter, tinny and electronic. The voice of the guy who did most of Portland's helicopter traffic reports. She was hearing a radio.

That didn't make her drop her guard.

She waited until Lou was beside her, then she spun into the room, hands braced, finger on the trigger.

It was a den—and it appeared to be empty. A long couch with the indentation of Rick's body in the cushions, another half empty popcorn bag, and books scattered on the floor. The television was tuned to a rerun of *Full House*, the WGN logo in the lower right hand corner showing what channel the TV was tuned to. In the left corner, the word "mute" was displayed in prominent red.

A computer hummed near the shuttered window. The screen saver showed a slow-motion baseball game, obviously in progress. And the radio, now playing "It's My Party" not softly enough behind her, was not just any radio. It was a Bose. Spendy, like everything else in the room.

It looked like someone had been interrupted while working on the computer, and had not come back to anything, which would dove-tail with Rick's story about the flower delivery. But why would someone have a radio and the television on at the same time?

There was a small closet near the radio. She signaled Lou to watch while she turned the knob. The closet was dark and smelled faintly of leather. It was filled with suits and leather jackets. Ties of all design hung on the door, and expensive shoes covered the floor. She pushed the clothing back with her free hand.

Nothing. No one.

She let out a breath she hadn't even known she'd been holding. "Clear," she whispered.

That left the bedroom. A little shiver ran through her at the thought of it. Rick's bedroom. She had never expected to enter it like this.

Lou led them across that narrow landing and toward the bedroom door. This time he went in first, following the same procedure she'd used, back to the door, then turning in, gun out and ready. After a moment, he gestured her to follow.

The room was larger than the den, with windows that overlooked the backyard. The bed was made—ten points for Rick—and was covered with thick pillows. The spread was a simple tan with black lines. Very masculine.

The entire room was very masculine.

And it smelled faintly of Rick, a scent she was beginning to recognize, something akin to sunshine on a beautiful summer day.

Maybe Lou was right. Maybe she did have it bad. And it was distracting her. It was distracting her now. She couldn't take her gaze off that bed, thinking about him in it at night, in the dark, naked...

She wrenched herself away. Lou was opening the closet door and she was supposed to cover him. Her breath caught in her throat. If something had happened a minute earlier, she wouldn't have been paying attention. What if Rick's Creep had been inside? She would have lost her partner because she was ogling the bed of a man she'd nearly arrested that morning.

But this closet, filled with casual shirts, jeans and khakis, was as empty as the other one.

"Basement then," Lou said softly.

"Wait." Tasha wanted to check one other thing. She holstered her gun and went back to the den. Lou followed.

Once inside, she pushed the mouse beside the computer. With a melodic bing, the screen saver disappeared. Windows appeared—displaying the desktop in the background. In the foreground was an Internet website showing a stock graph that had frozen in real time. And in front of it all, was a notice that the user had been idle too long, and his modem had disconnected at 11:26 a.m., about ten minutes before Tasha had arrived that morning.

This room obviously hadn't been staged for her or Lou's benefit.

This was how Rick had left it when Flegal had come to the door. It also meant the perp hadn't come up here—or if he had, he hadn't touched the computer.

"Why'd you do that?" Lou whispered.

"Tell you later." Tasha made her way to the stairs. She went down slowly, making sure the front door was still closed. It was. And she hadn't heard anyone come inside. As she passed it, she peered through the frosted glass.

Rick was standing near the porch, hands in his pocket. He appeared to be whistling, although she couldn't hear him. Interesting. The house was built solidly enough to be somewhat sound-proof.

Then she turned away from the glass, got her gun out and headed for the basement door. When both she and Lou had reached it, she mouthed, "Ready?"

He nodded.

She unlatched it as quietly as she could. Three stairs went down to a landing, and then more stairs beyond that. They disappeared into darkness just like Rick had warned.

There was a small stick of wood on a shelf just inside the door, obviously meant to be used as a door brace. Beside the wood stood two industrial sized flashlights. She handed the brace to Lou, who pushed the door open as far as it could go and then shoved the triangle of wood into place. Tasha's hand hovered over the flashlights. Would it be better to turn on the light and give their perp some warning? Or would they be better off using the flashlights?

If Rick was right, the perp was either stuck outside the office door or in the office proper. If he was outside the door, then he could use the time that the warning gave him to put himself in a good defensive position.

Of course, if he'd already heard them walking around up there, the flashlight beams would make Tasha and Lou excellent targets, while making them unable to see the perp.

She flicked on the overhead light and listened for a corresponding movement below.

There was no sound at all from the basement. But the house was sturdy enough that she couldn't hear Rick whistling fifteen feet away. She might not be able to hear small movements in the basement either.

Lou was waiting for her to lead. She gathered herself, cleared any thought of Rick from her mind, and went down the stairs. These steps creaked. They were made of thick boards against slats.

All she could see at the bottom of the stairs was the concrete foundation, old and crumbly. No fancy remodel here. She made herself breathe shallowly, trying to be as silent as possible. Not because she wanted to surprise the perp, but because she wanted to hear him when he moved.

She heard nothing.

The basement smelled faintly damp, like most basements in Oregon did. As she came down the steps, she saw that the basement opened on her right into a cavernous and mostly empty room—one that had not been redesigned with the rest of the house. There was a pantry on one wall, so old that the boards had been leached of the color, and holding some rusted cans with the labels torn off. She doubted they belonged to Rick.

A dusty drain stood in the middle of the floor and old washing machine pipes stuck out of another wall. The pipes had been capped, the washing machine moved to the upstairs laundry room long ago, but the machine's outline remained embedded in the concrete floor like a memory that couldn't be erased.

The room seemed empty, but Tasha had learned not to trust those feelings. As an instructor had once told her at the police academy, sometimes those feelings came from what she wanted to be true, not from what was true.

Lou reached the bottom of the steps only a moment after she did. So far so good. No one had shot at them, no one had attacked them. And while they were coming down the stairs, they had been targets.

Tasha scanned the walls she hadn't been able to see from the stairs. Metal shelves stood against the back wall, with more rusted cans on them—probably paint that should have been recycled years ago. And beneath the stairs was a single, ancient toilet that looked like it hadn't been used in decades.

She didn't even see the room that Rick said housed his office, and that put her on edge.

"Tash." Lou was standing by the metal shelves. He nodded his head toward the side of the wall.

She went to him. In this space, anyway, there was nowhere for the perp to be hiding.

The basement was chilly. She felt goose bumps rise on her arms. As she approached Lou, she finally saw the room.

A fake concrete wall had been built across the back of the basement. It looked like the rest of the room until she got close to it. Then she realized the concrete wasn't crumbling. It was newer and had been painted to resemble the wall around it.

The door itself would have been invisible if it weren't for the tiny electronic display at shoulder level. Even the little keypad, which Rick had told her to expect, was painted a muted gray.

"Look," Lou said, pointing to the pad.

Beside it were gouge marks, and they were obviously fresh. The tailings from them littered the floor. Someone had been here, and had tried to get in without knowing the combination.

Or was that what they were supposed to think?

Tasha swallowed, checked the basement again. Empty. And she didn't hear anything upstairs.

"Think we should go in?" she asked.

"Yep," Lou whispered. "And this time it's me."

He watched the room while Tasha punched the combination Rick had given her into the keypad. She heard a soft click and the door eased open. She glanced at Lou. He gave her a goofy grin, then reached to the left as Rick had instructed, and turned on the light.

Lights. Maybe a dozen of them, making the room one of the brightest she'd ever seen. The office was huge—as big as the front part of the basement—and filled with desks and bookshelves, and framed artwork, which she recognized as the paintings which had adorned the covers of Jessamyn Chance's books.

Tasha felt some tension ease out of her shoulders. He wasn't lying after all.

"Shit," Lou murmured. "Where'd he get all this stuff?"

Tasha glanced at her partner. He was assuming that Rick had set this room up, like an obsessive would, with Jessamyn Chance's stuff. As if Rick were a crazed fan, and not the writer. Tasha felt a trickle of unease, but she willed it away.

She braced her back against the wall and stared at the unfinished basement. Her job was guarding Lou while he went inside.

She could hear him fumbling around, checking under desks, behind furniture. She hated this part—they were both so vulnerable.

"No one's here," Lou said.

Tasha stayed in position a moment longer. No one appeared at that moment, there were no rustling sounds. Only her and Lou in this weird basement, standing outside a secret room.

No wonder the Creep, as Rick called him, thought someone was imprisoned down here. That was what the door made it look like. Who would have thought there was such a comfortable space inside?

Tasha peered in. The bookshelves adorning the wall were cherry, just like the ones upstairs, only here, one wall of books was just Jessamyn Chance novels. Most of them were in English with various covers, but mixed among them were books in French, German, and Hebrew along with other languages she didn't recognize.

One desk in the far corner seemed to serve as a computer graveyard. She recognized an ancient Atari, an early IBM PC, and then a MacPlus. Apparently Rick didn't throw out any computer he had written on. A MacBook, screen dark, was open on a leather couch. And on the main desk a Power Macintosh hummed, clearly on.

Tasha went there. Beside the Mac was a yellow legal pad with barely decipherable scratchings—

*Need up-to-date listing of values for last set of Brooklyn Dodger cards*
*Why would a woman be a baseball historian?*
*Player won't care until he gets shot at.*
*What would he know that makes him a threat?*

She hit the space bar on the computer keyboard and the screen shuddered for a moment before opening. A half-finished letter faced her:

*Isabel Weidler*
*Weidler & Krause Literary Agency*
*1130 Avenue of the Americas*
*New York, NY*

*Dear Iz:*

*Still behind on the new book, but the move went well. I may have to take you up on your offer to have Jeremiah Canfield give me a tour of Dodger Stadium. Don't know when I'll be able to get to L.A., but I'll see what I can do to make my schedule match his.*

*Can you send me his number? Or give him mine? Don't know what you'll tell him about who I am. Maybe give him a list of the old Rick Chance novels, and tell him that this might be my breakout. Or just tell him I'm a client. As long as you let me know what role I'm supposed to play. And before you do this, you might want to find out if he reads Jessamyn Chance. If he does, he'll probably figure this out a year or two from now, and That Would Not Be Good.*

*Thanks for your willingness to do this. Didn't know how I'd get into that stadium otherwise. They were willing to give me the standard press tour, but there are a few places No One Sees, apparently.*

*On another matter, I got a check from your office with the usual paperwork missing, and on the stub this cryptic notation: British royalties. Since all of Jessamyn's books have been published in Great Britain, it would be nice to know whether this check was for the entire kit & kaboodle (which means I need statements from 3 different publishing houses) or whether it's for one. (As always, I'm hoping for the latter.) I'd call to straighten this one out, but I want the paperwork, so...*

The letter trailed off as if the author had been interrupted in the middle. Tasha touched the back of the chair. Rick spent a lot of time here.

Rick, whose alter ego was definitely Jessamyn Chance.

Lou had found a file cabinet. He had pulled a drawer open and was thumbing through files that were labeled in the same barely legible hand as the words on the legal pad. Lou pulled out one file and put it on top of the cabinet. Inside were papers with a publishing company logo, and below, lots of figures.

"Son of a bitch," Lou said. "He *is* a romance writer."

Lou sounded more shocked than Tasha felt. Somehow, standing in this room, made it all real. What kind of man wrote about mushy stuff for a living? She couldn't quite mesh the writer she'd read with the man she'd danced with.

The man whose anger had scared a deliveryman out of his wits.

"We don't have cause to be searching this stuff, Lou," she said.

"Sure we do, Tash. He gave us permission to come in here."

"To look for a stalker."

"That neither of us believed in."

"We believed in him enough to do a thorough search of the house."

Lou looked at her over the file cabinet drawer. Then he sighed and replaced the file, pushing the drawer shut. "This is legit, isn't it?"

Tasha nodded.

"We don't have time for it, not with the Pfeiffer case."

"Since when has time ever been a factor in our job?" Tasha could remember one February when they'd had five high priority cases, all of which should have been solved immediately. She doubted she slept more than eight hours a week for the entire month.

"I think we gotta hand this off to someone else. You're operating with your hormones, and I..." Lou's voice trailed off.

"And you?"

Lou touched one of the paperbacks sitting on top of a FedEx envelope. It was, Tasha noted, the newest Jessamyn Chance release. He didn't say anything.

"Lou?"

"It just doesn't seem right, you know." The words came out in a rush.

"You'd feel better if he was writing pornography?"

Lou set the book down. "Actually, yeah."

Well, she wouldn't. That much she knew.

"We're already on it, Lou," Tasha said.

"I know, but—"

"I'll do most of it, and I promise it won't interfere with the Pfeiffer case."

He looked at her. "It better not."

His response wasn't normal. Usually they covered for each other without any quibbles at all. "What's really bothering you, Lou? And don't tell me it's the time or Rick's job. Are you jealous?"

"Of him? Hell, no."

"I haven't been involved with anyone since we became partners."

Lou's back straightened. "I'm a happily married man."

"I'm not suggesting otherwise," Tasha said. "But we both know that partners have a special relationship. Are you afraid of losing that?"

"Tash," Lou lowered his voice to his confiding tone, "even if this guy checks to one-hundred percent legit, he's a nut. And you're gonna get hurt."

"By investigating his case?"

"By staying close to him. Attraction gets in the way, you know. It makes you blind."

"You were blind to Sylvie?" Tash asked.

"You know what I mean?"

"Yeah." Tasha moved away from Rick's desk and headed toward the door. "You mean you don't trust me to behave professionally in all circumstances."

"I didn't say that."

"Oh, Lou," she said softly, "I'm afraid you did."

# CHAPTER 23

*R*ICK SAT ON his porch steps, elbows on his knees, chin braced on the heels of his hands. He was staring across the street. There'd been a flash a block or so away, as if light had caught a mirror and reflected it in his direction. He couldn't see what caused it—probably some kid playing—but he had to admit it unnerved him.

Everything was unnerving him. If Mrs. McGuilicuty's blinds twitched one more time, he was going to go over there and rip them off her window. That would show her just how crazy her new neighbor was—and cement his position as the neighbor everyone wanted to get rid of.

The real problem was that it was taking Tasha and her partner forever to go through the house. How long was Rick supposed to wait? They hadn't given him a contingency plan. If something went wrong—if the Creep attacked them—Rick wasn't sure what he should do. His brain told him to go to one of the neighbors' and call for help, but his heart—his *macho* heart—told him he never should have let a woman like Tasha go in there in the first place.

Not without him protecting her.

And he knew that was totally ridiculous. His own heroines—if they had been living, breathing creatures—wouldn't have stood for an attitude like that. He knew Tasha wouldn't either.

He had wisely kept silent about it when she had decided to go into his house.

But he wasn't sure how much more waiting he could take.

Then he heard the front door open. He stood so quickly that he fell over. To his relief, Tasha came out, followed by her partner.

"No one inside," she said in that brisk professional tone she'd been taking with him.

"You been doing work on that electronic lock of yours?" Rassouli asked as he came down the porch steps.

"What do you mean?" Rick asked.

"Replace it recently? Try to fix it?"

Rick shook his head. His stomach was knotted.

"Well, there's gouge marks all around it, like someone was trying to disarm it or remove it." Rassouli was looking at Rick oddly, like he was trying to see through Rick.

"It was just installed two months ago," Rick said, "and the whole thing was designed so that you couldn't see it from across the room."

"You were right then," Tasha said. "He got in. I'm going to call over a forensics team and have them work it, unless you have objections."

"You think you'll find fingerprints?"

"Never know until you try," Tasha said. She seemed so cool, so remote. What had changed? Or was this the way she always was after searching a house?

"Did you go in the office?" Rick asked.

Rassouli looked down, as if what he had seen in there embarrassed him.

Tasha was the one who nodded. Although her expression became even more remote.

"Personally," she said, "I prefer windows. But it is a cozy space."

He would never have described that space as cozy. It was too large for one thing. But it was his personal place, and no one had ever been in it before—not here, not in Chicago. No one had even seen the private side of him. Ever.

He felt exposed. And that exposure had left him feeling rejected by both of them.

"He hadn't gotten in, right?" Rick asked.

"In the office?" Tasha clarified. "No."

Rick nodded, feeling relieved.

"But it looked like he made a concerted effort to get in. I wouldn't be surprised if he came back—or was planning to come back—with something that would open the door."

"Like what?" Rick asked.

Tasha shrugged. "Any number of things. If he saw what happened this morning, he might have thought he had time to figure out how to get in."

Rick ran a hand through his hair. He'd never thought about the Creep coming back. He figured the police would come, this would get solved, and he could go back to work.

Now he might have to move again. There might not be any other choice.

"I'm not sure you'll be safe here tonight," Tasha said. "Do you have a place to stay?"

It took him a moment to focus on her words. "I'll be all right," he said. "I'll batten down the hatches, turn on the alarm and dig in."

"Well, that alarm isn't going stop him from coming in if he wants to," Rassouli said crossing his arms over his chest. "And if what you say is true, that he's after this imaginary woman, he's gonna see you as an obstacle to getting her. He's never come in before, has he?"

"Into my house?" Rick asked. "No."

"Then this is an escalation."

"You ever think that the flower delivery was staged?" Tasha asked.

"To get me arrested?" There was no way the Creep could have known that would happen. That had to be serendipity.

"No," Tasha said. "To get him inside. He would have to have known that you would have had some sort of reaction. You might have left the door open for a brief moment and stepped away from it, giving him a chance to sneak in—"

"You think he was in the yard then?" Rick asked.

"It's possible," she said.

"Besides, your neighbor says you have a habit of slamming things into your garbage can," Rassouli said. "Maybe he thought you'd get the flowers, wait till the delivery guy left, and slam the flowers into the garbage can like you always do, leaving the door unlocked then."

"What good would it have done him to get in while I was home?" Rick asked, and then felt a shiver run through him. He already knew the answer to that question.

There was compassion in Tasha's green eyes. "The key is that he didn't get in."

"You think he would have tried to get me to open my office door."

Rassouli nodded. "If this nutball is what you say he is, this is how it would have played out. He would have got in, tried to free his lady love, failed, then come to find you. He'd've made you open the door. Now, if you'd refused, he'd've lost it and attacked you—probably killing you—"

"Lou!" Tasha said.

"—and if you had opened it, he would have made you take him to wherever the object of his dreams was hiding. And since she doesn't exist, that would've been bad for you. Either way, it's good that things turned out the way that they did. Now do you see why we want you out of the house?"

"Yeah, I do." Rick hated logic. Logic had made him move from Chicago in the first place. Logic was going to get him out of Portland yet. "If I leave, though, he'll just break in tonight."

"You batten down the hatches, as you say, turn on your alarms and if he breaks in, we have him." Tasha sounded enthusiastic. "Once inside, he's not going to go anywhere. He's going to try to open that door."

"My office." His haven. The most private place in his whole world. He had to risk that to catch this idiot. "You can't just station someone outside the house?"

"You do got a hell of an imagination, don't you?" Rassouli asked.

Tasha elbowed her partner. She had obviously tried to do it surreptitiously, but Rick saw it anyway. "We don't have the budget or manpower for that, Rick. Even if we did, all that would do is delay the inevitable. Your guy isn't going to show up if the police are here—and if he is crazy enough to show up, once it's dark our guys could miss him until it's too late. It would give you false security, and it wouldn't help us at all."

"So," Rassouli said. "You got some place to go?"

"I think there are enough hotels in Portland that I can manage," Rick said.

Tasha gave him a strange look. What had she expected him to do, go to his family? She should have understood after the weekend they'd just spent together.

"When you do leave, make a show of it," Rassouli said. "We want this guy to think you're gone, leaving your lady friend unprotected."

Rick nodded. He was actually queasy. If the Creep had tried to break down the door, it would only be a matter of time. And then he would destroy all that was precious to Rick.

He would have to take his computer files and the MacBook with him. Everything else he would have to trust to the cops.

To Tasha.

"Rick," she was saying, "do you have anything from this guy—notes, cards, anything?"

"Some early stuff in a file, I think," he said. "The Chicago police have more of it."

"Well, I can't call Chicago today, but I can see what you have." She put her hand on Rassouli's arm. Rick envied the casual ease between the two of them. "Lou, why don't you call for the forensic team? I'll stay with Rick until they show."

He knew it wasn't just kindness. She wanted to make sure he didn't damage any of the evidence they did have—destroy fingerprints, dislodge fibers—but he felt grateful just the same. He had never felt more alone in his entire life.

"We still got Pfeiffer," Rassouli said to her, his voice tight.

"And we'll be on it in a couple of hours."

Rassouli grunted and headed toward the car. Rick turned to Tasha to thank her, but she was already letting herself into his house.

~

Beebe sat in his car, the binoculars pressed so hard against his eyes that he was giving himself a headache. Damn, damn, damn them all. He'd almost freed her. Then Chance had come home. The police hadn't held him after all.

Couldn't they see how dangerous he was? He nearly killed that guy in his front lawn. God only knew what he was doing to Jessamyn, beautiful, fragile Jessamyn, locked in that hideous room with no way out.

Beebe had had a few moments of hope when the cops had shown up again. He'd thought they were coming to rectify their error, to arrest Chance once and for all. But they let him wait outside and they went in —and he'd suddenly understood.

Somehow Chance knew he had gotten inside. Had he seen the marks on the door? He wouldn't have told the cops about that, and they wouldn't have found that door. It had taken him nearly an hour to do so himself. Chance had planned Jessamyn's imprisonment for a long time —having that wall built in the center of that basement.

The man was evil. The police had to know that.

They should have kept Chance at the station, put him in jail, locked him away. Then Beebe would have been able to get to Jessamyn.

He fingered the axe on the bucket seat beside him. So close, and yet so far. Imagine if he had gotten in. He would have been chopping that door down when Chance got home. And then it really would have gotten ugly.

What if Chance had attacked him the way he attacked that poor deliveryman? Would Beebe have been able to defend himself?

His fingers tightened on the axe. For his Jessamyn, he could have. He would have had to.

## CHAPTER 24

*W*HEN RICK ENTERED the house, he found Tasha standing in his living room, her back to him. She looked like she belonged there. Her blond hair was coming out of its neat bun, tendrils falling on the back of her neck. Her willowy frame was outlined in sunlight coming through the picture window.

Each time he saw her, she looked more beautiful than the last.

She was holding a book in her gloved hands, and as he turned, he saw that it was one of the research books for his current novel, Roger Angell's *Boys of Summer*.

"I didn't know you were a baseball fan," she said.

"About as stone as they come," he said. "I was living in paradise before I moved here—a city with two teams, both of which had a long, although not necessarily glorious, history. I had hoped to spend my summer in Wrigley and Comiskey when I proposed this book. Now, as it turns out, I'll be lucky if I manage to see a single game."

Her green eyes held compassion. She set the book down. "You want to show me what he's done?"

"He did what you just did," Rick said.

She frowned, glancing at the table.

"That's one of the ways I'd known he was here. He'd taken the book I was reading, closed it, and put it on the table. He must have been looking at it."

"It wasn't the one I just held was it?"

Rick shook his head. "It was the one next to it."

She glanced at it. "*Demolition Angel*, by Robert Crais. A thriller. How come you don't write thrillers?"

"I do," Rick said. "It's just that I make the love story more important than the suspense."

"Is it all technique then?" She sounded disappointed.

"No." It was surreal, standing in his violated house, talking writing to a police officer he was so attracted to he could hardly keep his distance. "It's personal inclination, I think."

She nodded, as if that made sense to her. Then she squared her shoulders. He could almost see the mantle of duty fall on them. "Well, I suppose we should get to it."

"We're in luck," he said, not feeling particularly lucky. "The files are in my office—the only room we can be sure he didn't get into."

"As long as we don't touch the door going in, we'll be all right." She waited for him to lead the way.

The basement door was propped open with the doorjamb that the old owners used to use. He had only seen the door in the position once —the day he and the realtor had looked at the house. It seemed strange, another violation, or a reminder of the one that had happened.

This house wasn't his any more. Not in the way it had been. The Creep had part of it now, a part Rick wasn't sure how to get back.

He led the way down the stairs, wondering how Tasha had felt when she had come down here, looking for the Creep. Had she been nervous, frightened? Had she worried about protecting herself? Or was she one of those supremely confident police officers who never worried about anything?

He could feel her behind him, her breath in his hair, her warmth near his back. It reminded him of how it had felt to hold her while they were dancing, the way her head fit against his shoulder as if their bodies had been designed to be together. Women usually weren't tall enough just to rest their heads against his shoulder. Usually they leaned against his chest, or held themselves back so that there was just a bit of distance.

Tasha hadn't maintained any distance at all. Then, anyway.

When he reached the bottom of the stairs, he turned and felt a pang when he saw that his office door was open. He never left that open either. It was symbolic more than anything: his office—his writing—had become his secret. With the door open, he felt more revealed than he ever had in his life.

Tasha had already been in there, with that partner of hers, looking at Rick's stuff, seeing—maybe for the first time—that he hadn't lied to her. Seeing a room that no one else in the world had seen.

And now he was going to lead her in there again.

He walked his normal path to the office, still feeling strange. Normally, as he crossed this concrete floor, he was already thinking about what he would work on next—the way his characters would act in the upcoming scene or how they would get themselves out of the current jam.

He never used his office for anything other than writing. He did the rest of his computer work upstairs. His Chicago friends had always thought Rick made his money on the Internet—doing stock trades and buying and selling on eBay. He hadn't dissuaded them. He had increased his portfolio that way, and he did make his living on the computer, just not in the way that they had imagined.

Not even Rita, the girlfriend the Creep had confused with Jessamyn, had known how he'd made his living. During the tense three months she'd lived with him, he hadn't done any writing at all. Ostensibly, he'd been researching the next novel, but he'd been so upset over the Creep's constant attentions, he could barely think about anything else.

Rick went through his office door. The lights were still on. The upper drawer on the file cabinet was open an inch, and he wondered if Tasha or her partner had dug in there. Probably Rassouli. He seemed to have a lot of trouble believing that a man would write under a woman's name.

Tasha hovered in the doorway, apparently waiting for him to invite her. While it was polite, it ignored the fact that she'd already been here, pawing through his stuff.

"Come on," he said more gruffly than he'd intended.

She stepped across the threshold. It almost felt as if she were stepping inside his mind.

"It is a cozy room," she said again.

"It's too big to be cozy." He turned to the file cabinet, pushed the top drawer closed with his shoulder, and crouched, pulling open the bottom drawer.

There, in the back, was the Nutball file. Every major author had one, probably every public personality did. Rick got all his own fan mail, then forwarded it in a lump to a part time secretary he'd hired years ago in Chicago. She used a personalized form letter to answer most of it. Occasionally, he hand-scrawled a note and then sent it to her, with the original letter clipped to the back, so that she could type an envelope and mail everything out.

She was his biggest writing expense. Otherwise, he would spend most of his time answering mail, not writing novels. She even handled Jessamyn Chance's website and answered the e-mail that Rick forwarded to her from his second Jessamyn Chance account.

Not even his secretary knew who he was.

Now Tasha and Rassouli—and maybe the entire Portland police department—did.

"I've never been in a writer's office before," Tasha said. "Don't you get claustrophobic here?"

He thumbed through the files until he found the other one he was looking for. As he pulled out both the Nutball file and the file he'd originally kept on the Creep, he said, "When I'm in here, I'm not really here, if you know what I mean."

He stood. She was frowning at him. Apparently, she didn't know what he meant.

"I spend most of my time in my head, Tash. In an imaginary world. That one usually has windows. Or great outdoor views. And lots of adventure. Until the Creep showed up, the greatest adventure in my life was going to a Cubs game."

That wasn't entirely true. The greatest adventure in his life had been leaving home after the Teri debacle. But he wasn't going to tell Tasha that.

He handed her the files. "I never really checked to see if some of the early stuff in the crazy file was from him. I noticed him only gradually. Usually these guys send a one-shot letter, and then nothing else. But the repeaters come to your attention after a while."

"Mind if I sit down?" she asked.

He didn't want her—he didn't want anyone—in his chair. That was just too personal, in a way he couldn't explain at all.

"Take the couch," he said. Then he leaned over and grabbed the MacBook off of it. He'd left that on too. Which suddenly made him realize he hadn't shut anything off upstairs when he'd confronted the delivery guy.

It could wait. He didn't want to leave Tasha down here alone.

She took the files around his desk to the couch and sat there, looking like she belonged. A tendril of hair brushed her cheek, and he longed to tuck it behind her ear, then trace the firm line of her chin as he tilted her head toward his...

Oh, God. He wasn't used to curbing his imagination in this room. Usually, he allowed himself free rein to imagine anything. He didn't dare do that, not at the moment.

He made himself sit in his chair, and then he tapped the space bar. The sleep function went off the computer, revealing the letter he'd started writing his agent before the rehearsal dinner. He'd forgotten he'd even been writing it—that was how distracted he'd been lately.

He hit save and closed the file. Then he started backing up all his current work. He would transfer all of it to the MacBook so that he could work in the hotel.

"My god," Tasha said. "I didn't realize you got letters like this."

"It's not so bad," he said. "My stuff doesn't seem to bring out the kooks the way some of the horror writers stuff does. Usually I get very nice letters from people all over the country, telling them that my books have given them a few hours of pleasure."

He cherished those letters, too. They showed that what he did touched lives. It meant more to him than he could say.

The shrill ring of the phone made him jump. Even Tasha looked startled.

"You got a second line?" she asked.

"Upstairs," he said. "You think it's the Creep?"

"He calls, doesn't he?"

"Sometimes." The phone rang again. "If it's him, I'll put it on speaker. You can listen that way."

"All right," Tasha said, although she didn't sound happy about it.

He reached across his desk and picked up the phone. "Yeah?"

"Such a polite greeting," said the voice on the other end. "I seem to recall Mother teaching us to say, 'Hello, Chance residence' in that chirpy tone of voice. She'd chastise you for that abruptness, Rick, saying it wasn't very Northwest."

Jane. He'd forgotten all about calling his sister. "I haven't been chirpy for years."

Tasha tilted her head slightly as if she couldn't believe what he had just said.

"Maybe it's time to rethink that. Chirpy might make you seem a little less macho, a little more vulnerable. Women like vulnerable."

Then they'd really like him right now. "Chirpy would probably make me look ridiculous."

Tasha was frowning at him. He shook his head at her. She shrugged and then went back to the files.

"So," Jane said, "am I bringing food or are you cooking?"

He paused. He had no idea what to say to her. He had forgotten all about the meal, and he didn't know how to explain the predicament he was in.

"Look, Jane, something's come up..."

Tasha looked up at the mention of Jane's name. Did she know Jane was his sister's name? Or was she feeling just a little jealous?

"So Friday's not good," Jane said. "I've got Saturday free. Hell, I've got Thursday and Sunday free too. The life of a single woman whose only son has just gotten married. I really don't want to think about the fact that my baby is on his honeymoon right now."

"So spending time with your other baby is better?"

Jane laughed. The sound was normal and reassuring. He hadn't realized how much he needed that. "It's a regular tonic, Li'l Ricky."

His childhood nickname, from the *I Love Lucy* Show. He'd hated the name then. It warmed him now.

"How about we go out to dinner?" he asked.

"Out? But the point was for me to see your place."

"I know, but it's just not good for that right now—"

"What, are you burying bodies in the basement? I've seen remodel messes and if it's the everyday sort, I can handle that. I have a son, remember?"

"Jane, please..."

He heard her catch her breath. What had he done? Had some emotion carried through his voice, something that he hadn't wanted her to know?

"Are you all right, Rick?"

No. He wasn't all right, and he didn't know how to tell her what was wrong.

"It's been an awful day, Jane." The understatement of the year. "Let me take you to dinner and tell you about it."

Tasha stopped thumbing through the letters. She kept her head down, though, clearly listening.

"I can come over there now," Jane said.

"No," he said a little too quickly. "Let's still do Friday. That's all right, isn't it?"

"Yes. But, Rick, if you need something sooner—"

He let the warmth he was feeling toward his sister seep into his voice. "I know who to call."

"Please do, Rick. I meant what I said at the wedding. I don't like how far apart we've grown."

"I don't either, Janie," he said softly.

Tasha frowned slightly, as if the endearment bothered her. Or maybe she really was just studying the letter in front of her.

"Look, the next few days are going to be kind of strange. You might want to use my cell to reach me." He gave Jane the number.

"Rick, are you sure you're not in trouble?"

He never could put anything past his sister. More than his parents, Jane had been the one who watched over him and in some ways was more of a mother than his own had ever been.

"It'll be all right, Jane. I promise I'll tell you everything on Friday."

But as he hung up, he wondered if he would tell her anything. How would she react, knowing that her brother had a hidden life he had never told her, one that bared family secrets to the whole world? He wasn't sure he wanted to find out.

"Problem?" Tasha's voice was a shade too casual.

"My sister," Rick said. "I'd promised to cook her dinner on Friday night."

"Maybe you can do it at her place."

"I'm taking her out."

"And telling her everything." Tasha curled her legs under her, looking very comfortable. "Do you really mean that?"

"Better to find out from me than the cops, huh?"

"We're not going to tell anyone."

"You're not," Rick said. "But what about Rassouli? He never promised."

"He knows I'll kill him if he makes me break my word."

"And the tape? What did you do with that?"

She closed the file. "Are you interrogating me, Mr. Chance?"

"Just trying to see how much of my life I'll be able to preserve when this is all over."

"I don't know," she said softly. "And I don't think it's up to me or Lou or your family. I think it depends on when we catch your friend."

"I wish you wouldn't call him that."

"I don't know what else to call him," Tasha said. "You know, you've got some real interesting letters in here. I never realized sex offended so many people."

"It's just premarital sex that seems to upset them," he said.

"Really? What about this one here, complaining about the use of a condom?" Then she frowned at it. "Although it doesn't seem like a crazy letter to me."

"You mean you're against condoms?"

She flushed. He liked it when she did that. It made her seem more human somehow. "No. It's just the writer seems to have a point. You have a Catholic character having sex with his new wife—"

"A lapsed Catholic, having sex with his ex-wife. Apparently that letter-writer doesn't read very well." He leaned back in his chair. "Besides, that's not why the letter's in there."

"Why is it then?"

"You haven't gotten to the abortion stuff, have you?"

She thumbed through the letters, as if just by rifling them she could read them. "Abortion stuff? What do you mean?"

"In my fourth book, *Betrayal*, one of the characters says she was forced to have an abortion—"

"By her husband. I remember that." Tasha seemed excited to even be discussing the plot. "But that's not what the book was about. It was about the way people related to each other and what truth was—"

"I know," Rick said gently. "But in this culture, some words have become buzz words and abortion is one of them. I got a lot of hate mail on that book from people who obviously never read it. Some pro-life organization singled me out and I got hundreds of letters, almost all the same."

"If I remember right, the abortion didn't even happen," Tasha said.

"That wasn't the point," Rick said. "What they seemed to object to the most was a statement my protagonist made when she first believed the abortion story, that sometimes abortion was the only choice."

"You got hundreds of letters protesting a single sentence?"

He nodded. "One of the joys of being in the public eye. Even if I am wearing metaphorical drag."

Tasha gave him a gentle smile. "I have a hunch your letter writers wouldn't approve of that either."

"A man in drag?"

"Yeah," she said.

"I suspect you're right." He paused. "Do you approve?"

"I looked through your closets searching for the intruder," Tasha said. "I didn't see any dresses."

He said softly, "I wasn't really asking about a man wearing drag."

Her gaze met his, and then she looked away so quickly he wasn't sure what he had seen in her eyes. "I thought things were complicated for you right now."

She used his words from the restaurant, throwing them back at him.

"They are," he said quietly. "But you've found out about all the complications."

Her right hand was still rifling the letters, only now it was a nervous gesture. "I thought you were giving me the brush-off."

"I was."

She winced.

"Think about it, Tash. I had no idea you were a cop."

"Would that have made a difference?"

He nodded. "At least I would have known that you could take care of yourself."

She closed the file. "Don't make this my fault."

"What?"

"The fact that you blew me off. It's not my fault for failing to tell you what I do."

"No," he said, "it's not."

"You wouldn't have seen me anyway because of your secret identity."

"I dated while I was writing. It was the Creep, Tash. I don't know what he'd do to a woman I was dating. I was afraid he'd see her as some sort of rival for Jessamyn."

"Then why did you flirt with me?"

He ran a hand through his hair. "I thought he was gone."

"You said he followed you."

"The first basket appeared Friday night after the rehearsal dinner."

"But you flirted on Saturday."

He nodded. How to explain this? "Then I came home to change, and remembered how he'd terrified Rita."

Not to mention how that had unnerved Rick.

"I got to thinking about it on the drive to the restaurant and thought maybe I should wait before dating anyone."

Tasha took a deep breath, as if she were trying to grab ahold of herself. She set the files on the couch beside her.

"Tash?"

"How come," she snapped, "when a man has a secret identity in the movies, he's Superman or Batman or something really cool?"

Rick grinned. "I didn't say Jessamyn Chance was my only secret identity."

Tasha glared at him. "How many other pseudonyms do you have?"

"None," he said, "but I'm a writer. I can put one together fairly quickly. What do you want—someone who is upright and righteous like Clark Kent or dark and brooding like Bruce Wayne?"

"This doesn't look like Wayne mansion," Tasha said.

"Well, I'm not as rich as Bruce," Rick said. "But I can take your family on."

She turned toward him so fast, he thought for a moment she was going to lose her balance. She looked shocked.

He raised his eyebrows at her. "I may not use Jessamyn's name in my everyday life, but I do get to keep the money."

"My god," Tasha said. "I never realized—"

"Is that important to you? That I have money?" Rick felt a little chill run through him. He hadn't expected golddigging from Tasha. But then what did he know about her? Only what she had told him. And her job showed that she didn't have money after all.

"It's just so unusual," she said.

That wasn't the answer he'd expected.

She picked at imaginary lint on her pants. "You know about my family. Most of the men who know, know I'll come into money some-day. And that interests them."

"Are you sure?" he asked.

"It's usually pretty clear," she said.

"I think you probably didn't give them enough credit, Tash. You're a beautiful woman."

She kept her head down. "You said that before. At the reception."

"I meant it."

"Then you let me embarrass myself at the restaurant."

"It wasn't my smoothest moment, I'll admit. I was hoping that we could exchange numbers or something, so that once I got rid of the Creep, I could call you."

"You really thought you were going to get rid of him?"

Rick was silent for a moment. "I don't know what I was thinking. I just knew I couldn't put you in jeopardy. It wouldn't have been fair."

His cheeks flushed a little when he realized that he'd let her search his house for him, with the idea that the Creep was inside. But it was her job, and she was trained for it. The idea of the delicate Tasha was so far from his mind as to seem almost preposterous now.

"You are rather hopelessly macho, aren't you?" Tasha asked.

"If I were that, I would have come down here with you to search for the Creep, no matter what you said."

"Lou and I wouldn't have let you."

"You and Lou couldn't have stopped me." He spoke quietly. "But once I found out what your job was, Tash, I trusted you. I figured I would only get in your way."

"You would have." She sighed. "Things are complicated for me, now, Rick."

His computer clicked as it went into sleep mode. He hadn't touched it for a while.

"I'm working on a case involving you. Even if I wanted to, I can't—"

"It's all right," he said a bit too quickly. "I know that. I was just clearing the air."

But he wasn't sure that was what he had been doing. He had been apologizing, hoping that perhaps they could return to that easy flirtatiousness they'd had at the wedding.

"I'm sorry," she said.

"It's all right," he repeated.

"I just wanted you to know it's not—this." She glanced around the office. She had come all the way back to his initial question. "I find it kind of intriguing that you write as Jessamyn Chance. It makes me see the books in a whole new light."

"Re-evaluating them to see if the man got things right?" he couldn't keep the bitterness from his tone.

She didn't seem to notice. "Oh, I know you got them right. Maybe I'm the one who's sexist. I couldn't believe that a man was sensitive enough to have some of the attitudes in those books."

He was silent. In some ways, that had been the source of his fear of discovery—that his writing, his pen name, and his choice of material took something from his masculinity.

"Shows what I know, huh?" Tasha said.

"No," Rick said, "it's a pretty common attitude. It's one of the reasons that Jessamyn's still secret."

"What's the other reason?"

Rick paused. He'd mentioned it in passing in the police station, but he doubted Tasha had heard him—or at least had figured out what it meant in context.

"I'm a very private person, Tash," he said. "I liked having a part of myself that people saw but didn't understand."

"Liked?"

He shrugged. "I figure it'll get out now."

"Because of me."

"Because of everything." He touched the phone. "I'm going to have to talk to Jane sometime. She'll tell the rest of the family, and that'll be that."

"I'm sure we can come up with another explanation for Jane."

"Yeah," he said. "Let's tell her I have a pathological hatred of delivery men and instead of arresting me, you've put me in an outpatient treatment."

Tasha laughed. "Or we can tell her that you have a neighbor who is so nosy that whenever you need your privacy, you go to a hotel."

And then Tasha's face changed.

"What is it?" Rick asked.

"Mrs. McGuilicuty," Tasha said. "The way she spies on your place, she has to have seen your—Creep—at one point or another."

"You're right," Rick said, "but I can't approach her about it, not after this afternoon."

"No, but I can," Tasha said. "If she has seen him, she might be able to provide a sketch."

"She won't have to if he comes back tonight, right?"

"It's always nice to have backup," Tasha said.

"You don't believe he'll be back, do you?"

Tasha gripped the file tightly. "This one's smart, Rick. Think about it. How did he find you in the first place?"

Rick started. He hadn't considered about that. And neither had the Chicago police.

"He hasn't figured out who you really are, but he knew where Jessamyn lived. And then there was his ability to track you down after you moved, and to follow you here. Most people couldn't have done that no matter how dedicated they were. That's why we tell people to find somewhere else to live, and not to use a forwarding address."

"You don't think he'll be back?"

"He's smart enough to be unpredictable, Rick." Tasha set the file aside. "He got you out of the house long enough to attempt a 'rescue' of Jessamyn. I think, from the look of that door, he went away to get better tools. He was planning to come back. Whether he will or not is hard to predict."

"But if he does, you'll have him."

"If he does, I *hope* we'll have him." She kept those lovely green eyes on his. "But, like I told you before, we don't have enough manpower to stake someone outside. We could miss him. And if we do, we'll use your neighbor's prying eyes to help us."

Rick did not feel reassured. He sighed. Apparently that was all he ever wanted. Reassurance that this Creep would go away.

"You might want to try some of the other neighbors too," he said. "Who knows what they've seen."

Tasha smiled. "Already thought of that."

Rick's computer beeped. The large file dump he'd just done onto CD was complete. He hit the space bar, and used the mouse to drag the CD icon into the trash. With a whirl, the disk spit out of the extra drive. He shoved the CD into the laptop and started the download.

"This must be very hard on you," Tasha said.

For some reason, the comment irritated him. "Well, considering that I can barely work, I can't have a girlfriend, and now I can't stay in my own house, yeah, it's hard on me."

Tasha picked up both files. "Can I keep these?"

"For now, yeah," Rick said. "it's not like I'm going to reread them every day."

"For what it's worth," she said, "I do understand how your frustration bubbled over at that deliveryman."

"You didn't this morning."

"This morning, I had no idea what was really going on. And you did break the law, Rick."

"Maybe that was the Creep's intent," Rick said. "Get me out of the picture any way he could. He was probably happy when you hauled me away."

"He probably was," Tasha said quietly.

"And he'll be even happier when I leave tonight."

"As long as you do it with fanfare."

Rick didn't want to do it with fanfare. He didn't want to do it at all. But he'd been fighting the Creep on his own for too long and it hadn't been working. He'd try it Tasha's way for a while.

"Hey!" Rassouli yelled from upstairs. "Anyone down there? I got the team here."

"We're here," Tasha said.

Rick cringed. The forensics team. Time to turn his place into piles of dust and fibers. The laptop binged as it finished the download

"Well," Tasha said, "now we get to find out if our smart perp made his first major mistake."

"He probably didn't," Rick said.

Tasha smiled and stood. "Even the best of them forget something."

Rick stood too, packing up the laptop as he did so. His last hour in his most private place, a place that would never seem private again.

Chalk this up to another frustration caused by the Creep.

Rick almost welcomed the hotel room. At least there he had no expectations of being completely alone.

~

Through the passenger window of his car, Beebe watched as a police van pulled in front of the house. Four people got out, wearing uniforms with some writing on the back, writing he couldn't quite make out.

But it didn't matter. They were looking for something, and it had nothing to do with Chance's arrest that morning. Obviously Chance had realized he had been in the house. But how was Chance keeping them from Jessamyn? They couldn't know about her imprisonment, could they?

Beebe wiped his right hand on his pants leg, then repeated with his left, so that he never lost his grip on the binoculars. Maybe he'd done something, left some kind of trace other than the door. Maybe Chance knew he wouldn't have to show them the door at all. Maybe Chance was smarter than he gave him credit for.

Beebe let the binoculars drop for a moment, and leaned his head back against the seat and closed his eyes. He'd been underestimating Chance all along. He'd seen him as interference only, something to be gotten rid of. He hadn't seen how very dangerous Chance was.

That attack this morning showed him how violent Chance could be. The police's switch to Chance's side showed him how cunning Chance was.

And he had to be manipulative as well. In the early days, he'd allowed Jessamyn her freedom. They'd even separated for a while: Jessamyn had her own apartment, her own life.

But apparently she had done something to anger him. First she moved back home, and then she had disappeared—although Beebe knew she was still alive. She still answered his letters and his e-mails. And she still wrote her books.

Beebe didn't understand why Chance didn't just let her go. In a divorce, Chance would have gotten half the money. Maybe Chance was obsessed with her—Beebe understood that. Only Chance was obsessed with controlling her and Beebe was obsessed with rescuing her.

He should have gone to the police long ago, back in Chicago perhaps, before things got worse. But how could he tell them about her?

About the attraction between them, about the way she had looked at him, the fear in her green eyes when she told him that something between them just wouldn't work.

Fear of Chance.

Beebe had never realized that Chance would punish her for talking to him by locking her away. Her imprisonment was partly Beebe's fault, and he could never forget that. He owed her.

He owed her his life.

And somehow, he would find a way to pay that debt.

# CHAPTER 25

*B*Y THE TIME she reached the precinct, Tasha's stomach was growling. As she had driven there, Lou sullen and silent beside her, she had thought of taking the rest of the evening off, joining Rick down at the Old Multnomah Hotel and buying him dinner.

The feelings had been there between them again, strong and powerful, and this time she knew that he shared them. He had made that very clear. But he put her in more of a difficult position than she could describe to him.

Not only had he been a suspect just that morning, but he was now a victim too, someone that she had to think about protecting, not sleeping with. She had to keep her professionalism, especially after the way Lou had chastised her.

Clearly her attraction to Rick was obvious, and she had to prove, to both herself and Lou, that she could do a good job despite how she felt.

So Lou had left to get them some Burger King, and she settled at her desk to work on the Pfeiffer case.

"Hey, Tash," said Allen Stabos. He was one of the back-ups on the Pfeiffer case. He had been the person unlucky enough to take her place during Friday's garbage search. During a break in the afternoon's action, she had asked him to see if he could locate the rug.

"Hey, Allen." She really wasn't in the mood for pleasantries.

"Two neighbors say they saw the brother carrying an Oriental rug from the house."

Her eyes lit up. "You're kidding!"

"Think that's enough to get a warrant?"

"It might be." With that, the photos, and the bloodstain sliding from the body to the entry. "You want to give it a try?"

"It's your case."

"I know, but I have something else I'm digging in right now."

Allen gave her an odd look. "What was with that guy today? The arrest that you didn't complete."

"I'll tell you later."

"I've been hearing it's strange."

"Every case is strange," she said, trying to sound flippant. "Didn't they tell you that when you signed on?"

He grinned and nodded, then disappeared down the hall.

She let out a small sigh of relief, but she wondered how many other questions like that she'd get. She hoped not many. She didn't want to be the one who blew Rick's cover.

She leaned back in her chair. She should probably follow up on the new leads in the Pfeiffer case, but now even her sense of responsibility had disappeared. Her mind was on Rick's face, the bleak way he had looked at his home, the bitterness in his voice when he had told her all this incident with the stalker had cost him.

She got a sense that he had lost a lot before he'd met that stalker, and she wondered what that was. A man alone in a city far away from his home, a man who hadn't spoken to his family in years, a man whose family thought he was trouble, had more going wrong in his life than a simple stalker.

But Brooke had also told Tasha that Rick was a deadbeat, and he wasn't that, not if his comments about money were to be believed.

She sighed and decided she wouldn't get him off her mind if she didn't do some investigating. She had his social security number from the papers he'd filled out after his arrest. She went to the department's computer room and logged on, deciding to see what that 9-digit number told her.

It told her that he had never been late on a credit card payment— that he had a $100,000 limit on three of them, and he had a black AmEx, usually given only to people with exceptional credit. He owned his house outright—something she found odd (she'd never seen that before on a credit report) and he had more brokerage accounts than she had ever imagined.

The credit report also gave her bank account numbers which she decided she'd follow up on the following day.

He didn't have a single car payment—he hadn't had one in the past seven years, another thing she'd never seen—and he didn't lease. Some flicking through DMV records showed her he had five cars registered in Oregon: 2 Porsches, a Jaguar, an old VW Bug, and that horrible truck. She wondered where he stored the cars, and decided she'd wait until later to find out.

This was not the financial profile of a deadbeat. She stayed at the computer a few minutes longer, having the system search for his criminal record—if he had one. It came up negative. She double-checked Illinois, but he came up clean.

Then she went to an Internet search engine and punched in Jessamyn Chance to see if he'd been outed on the Internet. She got over a 100,000 matches, most of them more than 90 percent. It would take her hours to go through them. So she limited the search to Jessamyn Chance and Rick Chance and came up with nothing.

Finally she searched for Rick's name alone. He appeared in the society pages of the Chicago newspapers—he had been one of the city's better-known philanthropists—and in some of the early articles, there was a tall, slim redhead on his arm.

The woman was gorgeous. The papers identified her as Rita Colditz, one of the city's most prominent businesswomen. She was the CFO of one of Chicago's largest corporations, and her move to France had been big news.

Odd that the stalker hadn't seen any of this. Obviously, he wasn't a newspaper reader. And maybe didn't even get news off of television.

Tasha was still online when Lou returned with grease-covered bags that smelled heavenly.

Lou looked over her shoulder. "I hope this is about the Pfeiffer case."

"No," she said. "Although we've had a break."

She told him what Allen had found, and how Allen was going for a warrant.

"The Pfeiffer case just doesn't hold you, does it?" Lou asked.

Tasha shrugged. "I like a puzzle."

"So what are we working on now?" His tone told her that he already knew.

She didn't look at him. "I'm checking up on a few things Rick told me."

"Still don't trust him?"

"The more I learn the more I do trust him," she said. "But this stalker of his bothers me."

"That's taking empathy to an extreme." Lou hooked a chair with his foot and brought it to the computer. Then he sat down, putting the bags on his lap. "You'll have to get your own beverage. I spilled them in the parking lot."

She didn't care. She took the Whopper he handed her, partially unwrapped it, and bit in hungrily, letting the wrapper catch the drippy sauces.

"It's not empathy," she said around the food. "This is a guy who keeps everything about his job secret, right? So how did the stalker get close?"

Lou was eating a bacon double-cheeseburger. Tasha would have known that without looking—it was all Lou ever ate. But this time, she could see the little pieces of well cooked bacon peeking out of the bun.

"This is your puzzle?" he said around the food.

"Come on, Lou. You have to admit it's a good question."

Lou nodded. "Who did Chance say knew about his pen name?"

"His agent and his editor."

"And they were both women, right?"

Tasha nodded.

"I'm sure they got assistants who probably know," Lou said.

"I scanned that letter," Tasha said. "His agent is in New York. I'll bet his editor is too."

"The stalker guy traveled all the way here. He might have come from New York."

"Yeah," Tasha said, grabbing some fries, "but that doesn't fit. If his stalker worked for his agent or editor, then he'd know who Rick is. And the stalker didn't. It had to be someone else."

"Someone with access to Jessamyn Chance's address, but not her identity."

Tasha tapped the computer. "Maybe a hacker into his e-mail accounts."

"You gotta think that Chance is smart enough to use a dummy address on the web."

"Maybe," Tasha said. "But people are careless on the net."

"Tell me about it." Lou grabbed some of her fries. His were gone.

"It's worth checking out," Tasha said. "There had to be a way that this stalker zeroed in on him, and it wasn't because of the redhead."

Lou paused, French fry in hand. "What redhead?"

"The original stalkee, the woman. I found her on the net too. If our perp had just read the papers, he would have known she wasn't Jessamyn Chance."

"A hacker who doesn't read the newspapers, who has a thing for a woman who doesn't exist." Lou shook his head. "No wonder Chance had trouble dealing with this guy."

Tasha nodded. She finished the sandwich and crumpled up the wrapper, putting it back in the bag. Then she stuck her hand in the box of fries and found only the crisp ends. "Hey!"

Lou shrugged. "I gotta punish you for not working on Pfeiffer somehow."

She sighed. "All right. Let's go back to the desk and see what we can do."

"I suppose you'll want your fries back."

"You pocketed them?" she asked, then understood what he meant and grimaced. "Ew."

"I'll take that to be a no." Lou stood, picked up the bags and tossed them in a garbage can far from their desks. Garbage service in the precinct was slow. Better to have the food remains stink up a different part of the room.

When Tasha reached her desk, her phone was ringing. She grabbed it. It was the 911 dispatch. Tasha had had them call her if there was a hit at Rick's house, and apparently there had been.

The 911 dispatch spoke without preamble. "The alarm company says someone just smashed the third basement window on your house's west side."

Right near the hidden door. "Get someone on it," Tasha said.

"Already dispatched the nearest squad. They'll be there in five."

"See if they can get there in three," Tasha said. "We have to get this guy."

She hung up and cursed.

"A hit on the Chance place?"

She nodded. "Let's go."

Lou didn't have to be told twice. He led the way out of the precinct.

As he drove them to Rick's house, Tasha's heart was pounding. She could imagine herself telling Rick that they had caught his perp, breaking in. Oh, that would be beautiful. No stalking charge. They were always a bitch to prove, and in this case, it would blow Rick's pen name wide open. Not to mention being tabloid fodder for the next six months.

She mentally crossed her fingers the entire way there.

When they arrived on his street, it was ablaze with lights. Porch lights were on, living room lights were on, and people stood in the lawns, watching Rick's house. In front were two squad cars, their blue and red lights swirling, making an eerie glow in the neighborhood. Rick's front door was open and the interior lights were on.

Tasha got out of the car before it had completely stopped moving. She walked up to one of the patrol officers. "What've we got?"

He was young, but had experience lines in his square-jawed face. "Not a goddamn thing."

"What?" Part of her had expected this, but she hadn't believed it. She had wanted the perp to be inside, easily catchable. She'd wanted to end Rick's nightmare the same day she discovered it.

"This is how we found the place. Front door open, lights on."

"What about the basement?"

"Oh, that's a sight," the patrol officer said. "See for yourself."

She felt a chill. "You checked everywhere? All over the interior?"

"And two of our guys are walking the lawn. Nothing. Nobody running from the house when we arrived, either."

"They got him?" Lou asked, getting out of the car.

Tasha shook her head. "Have one of these squads check the parked cars on nearby streets. He can't be far from here."

"Beg pardon, detective, but he could be long gone."

"Oh?" she asked. "How long did it take you to get here?"

"Four and a half minutes from the time we logged the call," he said. "A lot can go down in four and a half minutes."

Didn't she know it. "What took you so long?"

"Driving from the Rose Garden. Personally, I think four and a half minutes is a fucking miracle. We're lucky there wasn't much traffic or our response would've been a lot longer."

He was right, but she wasn't going to tell him that. Instead, she walked up the sidewalk toward Rick's house. Even though she knew the stalker wasn't inside, she could feel her heart pounding. She didn't want to see what he'd done to the interior of the place.

Lou was beside her, looking grim. They went up the porch steps and inside.

The damage was a surprise. The patrol officer was right: it was amazing what could happen in less than five minutes. The end tables were knocked over, their contents spilled all over the room. The pictures had been pulled off the wall and shattered glass was every-where. Amazing that only the alarm company called 911. Couldn't the neighbors hear this?

The basement door was open just like she'd left it, but the lights were on. She went down the stairs quicker than she had that afternoon—this time she didn't need her gun out.

When she reached the bottom of the steps and turned the corner, she stopped in stunned surprise. The door at the far end of the basement was gone—well, not gone exactly, but chopped to bits. Someone had gone after it with an axe, then reached inside and pulled it open.

And then he had destroyed Rick's office. The computer, the desks, but—strangely—not the artwork or the books.

"Looks like he lost it when he figured out she wasn't in there," Lou said.

Tasha nodded. All the damage spoke of extreme rage. "We're going to have to call the forensic team back out."

"They're going to love this."

She walked toward the door. Rick wasn't going to be happy either. He'd been so proud of this place. And she had told him that this would work.

When she reached the door, she peered inside. Even the old computers in the back were ruined, thrown to the floor in a fit of rage. Their cases had shattered. Or perhaps they had been axed too. Even the couch bore slash marks.

"What's amazing to me is that he did all this and got out very fast," Lou said.

"You don't think he figured out a way to bypass the alarm, do you?" Tasha asked.

"And then reset it, and go out a broken window?" Lou shook his head. "Too much rage here. That's a finesse move, and at this point, he was beyond finesse."

Lou was right.

"It amazes me that he did all of this so fast," Tasha said. "He had to know that we were coming."

"Or he factored in the alarm."

"What do you think he would have done if he had found a woman in here?"

Lou gave her an odd look. "If she wasn't the woman he'd expected, he would have taken out his rage on her."

She suddenly understood the reason for the look. "I wasn't thinking of me. I wouldn't have considered staying here."

"Then I don't know what you're driving at," Lou said.

"What do you think his plan was? He broke down the door—he obviously thought she was in here, maybe even imprisoned in here—did he think he could get her out fast?"

"Sure," Lou said. "If our imaginary woman had been imprisoned against her will, then it would be logical that she'd want to run the minute she had freedom."

"You know that's not what would have happened," Tasha said. "She would have been scared by the axe, and scared of her captor's rage, and she wouldn't believe she could get out. She would take some convincing."

"It's all hypothetical, Tash. What's your point?"

"My point is," she said, "that he either hadn't thought that through, or he didn't know."

"I don't expect a stalker to understand human psychology," Lou said.

"I'm just trying to get a handle on his fantasy." She took a step deeper in the room. "I'll wager he thought she'd be happy to see him. I'll bet he even thought she'd run into his arms, and then they'd escape, to live happily ever after."

"So what if he did?"

"He's living a romantic fantasy," Tasha said. "Playing into that fantasy might be the best way to catch him."

"What do you have in mind?"

"Nothing yet," she said. "But I'll have something soon."

"You'd better." Lou sniffed. "Because we have one angry perp."

Tasha sniffed too. Urine. "Oh, god. He peed on everything."

Lou nodded. "It wasn't enough to destroy it. He had to show just how damn disgusted he was."

Tasha shook her head. "Well, at least we got a DNA sample."

"Now if we can only get a match," Lou said.

"We're a couple of steps ahead of ourselves," Tasha said. "We need a suspect before we can even think of a match."

She stared at the office. Poor Rick. She had no idea how she'd break the news to him—and how she was going to keep him away from here.

"We have another problem," she said.

"What's that?" Lou asked.

"Our perp's mad, right?"

"Right. He just found out that his dream lover doesn't exist."

"Oh, no," Tasha said. "He just found out that Rick's been fooling him, and he thinks that she's imprisoned somewhere else."

"Shit," Lou muttered. "He's going to go gunning for your pretty boy."

"Now more than ever," Tasha said.

"Chance can handle himself."

"Too well," Tasha said. "Our problems of this morning just got compounded."

"Tell him and he'll overreact to everyone. Don't tell him and lose him, and we got lawsuits like the department's never seen."

The idea of losing Rick made her heart ache. She didn't even think of lawsuits. "Let's see if we can get him protection."

"He's not going to take it," Lou said.

"Let's at least try." She turned her back on the ruined office.

"Hey, Tash," Lou said softly. "I was wrong about your guy."

"He's not my guy," Tasha said reflexively.

"You know what I mean."

Tasha raised her gaze to his. Lou was giving her his most sympathetic look.

"I gotta learn to trust your instincts," Lou said.

She let out a small bitter laugh. "I wish it were that easy."

"Let's catch this perp," Lou said.

"In a way that will stick," Tasha added. With no bloodshed. No bloodshed at all.

# CHAPTER 26

*R*ICK SETTLED ON the couch in the living room of his suite, and placed the MacBook on his lap. He would try to get some work done. It seemed to be the only thing he could do.

His room was gorgeous, square wood beams, high ceilings, and designs in the molding that showed the hotel's age. When he was a boy, the Old Multnomah Hotel had been one of the biggest, most beautiful hotels in downtown Portland.

Despite several remodels, it was still beautiful, and it still had that old-fashioned look to the lobby—lots of pillars and fireplaces and upholstered furniture.

Only now the lobby was filled with harried businessmen, most of whom worked for high tech firms. A lot of them, he had discovered, lived in the hotel during the week, and went home on the weekends.

If Rick were traveling, he would be comfortable here. The bedroom was as large as the living room, and the bed had a soft pillowtop over the mattress. There were television sets in both rooms, phones and fax machines and data ports. Even the bathroom had all the comforts of home and the shower was high enough to accommodate his six-foot four frame.

If he were traveling. But he wasn't. All he kept thinking about was his home, empty and vulnerable to the Creep. The Creep gave him no good choices. Rick had to listen to Tasha on this one, even though he didn't want to.

He had only been in this situation once before in his life and it had nearly ruined him. It was amazing how much damage a single person could effect on another person's life, given some focus and determination. He was still dealing with the aftereffects of Teri's wrath, years later. Friday night, when he met with Jane, he'd deal with the rest of it.

He shuddered, and stared at the computer screen in front of him. He'd opened the file for the third chapter of the novel, and he reread his notes.

The book didn't seem very alive to him at the moment. His heroine was a petite dark-haired woman who would learn, through the course of the novel, how to stand up for herself. But every time he thought of her, he saw a tall statuesque blond whom he would trust to guard his back.

He bowed his head and rubbed the bridge of his nose with his thumb and forefinger. If he wasn't thinking about the Creep, he was thinking about Tasha. And neither would help him meet his deadline.

Maybe it was time to be honest with his agent and editor, and ask them to push back the release date. He didn't want to think about all the problems that would cause—not just for him, but for the publishing house.

Best-selling authors were carefully positioned so that they had a chance of hitting the *Times* list at the highest possible point. Currently he was scheduled for his traditional May—the beginning of the summer season. If he delayed the book, he might get a worse date, or be delayed an entire year. His sales were good, but not good enough to go against the big guns of the fall.

Rick closed the MacBook. Maybe he was worrying about this too soon. If they caught the Creep tonight, he'd be able to get back to work. He'd finish in plenty of time.

His phone rang, startling him. He hadn't given the hotel room number out to anyone. He'd instructed everyone he'd contacted to use his cell phone. The only people who knew he was in the hotel were the police.

A shiver ran through him. The phone range again and he picked it up. "Yeah?"

"Lou and I are in the lobby." It was Tasha. Her voice sent a different kind of shiver through him. He ran his hand on the back of the MacBook. "We're coming up. What's your room number?"

He gave it to her and she hung up without saying good-bye. He set the MacBook on the table, picked the complimentary USA Today off the couch, and glanced around to make sure everything was in order.

Then he grinned at himself. She wasn't here for a date. She was here on business.

That thought sobered him immediately. She had some kind of news, and he hoped it was good.

Three crisp raps on the door made him turn. He peeked through the hole, saw Rassouli shifting from foot to foot, Tasha behind him staring down the long hallway. Her distorted features did not look happy.

Rick undid the chain lock and the deadbolt, pulling the door open. "Come on in."

They did, Rassouli first. Tasha closed the door behind her.

Rick couldn't stand the suspense. "What's happened?"

Tasha glanced at Rassouli. Rassouli raised his brows at her, as if encouraging her to speak.

"Just tell me," Rick said.

"He got in," Tasha said. "But he got out before we got there."

"There's a team going through the house now."

Rick went very still. He wanted to slam his fist through a wall. Instead, he clenched his fingers. The anger welled up quickly and powerfully. It was ten times worse than what he felt when he attacked the delivery guy. "I thought you said this would work."

"I said it was the best shot we had," Tasha said.

"Great." Rick turned around, and headed for the window. The hundred year old brick buildings across the street looked sturdy and secure. Below him, the narrow tree-lined sidewalks of downtown Portland were filled with pedestrians, probably heading to a performance at the nearby Arlene Schnitzer Concert Hall.

"He got into your office," Tasha said.

Rick let out a small breath. "Then he at least knows that Jessamyn doesn't exist."

"I don't think so." Her voice was soft.

Rick felt his shoulders stiffen. "What do you mean you don't think so?"

"There was some damage."

Rick stopped breathing. His place. His private place, damaged. "What kind of damage?"

"It looked like he went into a rage." Rassouli spoke with a lot more authority than Tasha was. Rick recognized the tone. It was the we-have-bad-news-and-I'm-going-to-get-through-it-fast. "He smashed some things."

Rick turned to them. "The art?"

It was the only irreplaceable stuff in the room. He had his novels backed up off premise and the current work was in this room. He could live without his files, and get duplicate copies of the published books, but the art was all one of a kind.

"Anything that looked like it belonged to Jessamyn, he didn't touch," Tasha said.

"That's not entirely true," Rassouli said. "He got the computers."

"Jesus." Rick sat down. "Is there any part of my life this asshole isn't going to ruin?"

They didn't answer him. Both cops stood awkwardly in the center of his hotel room, looking like they wished they could be somewhere else. Hell, he wished he could be somewhere else. Somewhere with the Creep's neck between his hands, somewhere where he could legally choke the life out of the man and not suffer any consequences.

"I suppose he didn't leave a business card," Rick said.

"We have people canvassing the neighborhood," Tasha said.

"Shouldn't you be doing that?" That sentence came out harsher than he intended. Or maybe not. Maybe he was even angrier than he thought.

"Usually." Tasha pulled out the other chair beside the table and sat down, resting her elbows on her thighs. It was a masculine way to sit, a way he'd never have any of his heroines sit at all, and yet he found it attractive—and he didn't want to.

He didn't want any of this.

"So what's different?"

Rassouli took the final chair, and leaned it back on two legs. "What's different is your guy's escalating."

"Now that we provided him opportunity." Rick took a deep breath, stifling the rest of what he wanted to say. The blame, the vicious words. Tasha didn't deserve it. Neither did Rassouli. They had warned him that this might not work.

Rick had understood it intellectually. Apparently, he hadn't understood it emotionally. Or he hadn't wanted to.

"No, Rick." Tasha leaned toward him. "All of today was an escalation. The flowers, the first break-in, now this one. He seems to be feeling some time pressure."

"I don't see how it would matter now." Rick looked at her. "He's got to know Jessamyn doesn't exist."

"No, that's not what he believes."

"Come on, Tasha. The evidence is there. Anyone with half a brain would know."

"It's not his brain that's the problem," she said. "It's his obsession. That's what I was trying to explain to you before. Just because Jessamyn wasn't in that room doesn't mean that she hadn't been there before."

"Oh, come on," Rick said. "I understood it when the room was blocked off, but it's clearly an office. No one could live in there. There isn't even a bathroom."

"I don't think he saw it that way," Rassouli said.

"He saw the office," Tasha said, "where she writes her books."

"Then why would he destroy the computer?" Rick asked. "It would be her computer."

"No. It's the computer you made her use."

Rick shook his head. "That's crazy."

Tasha just stared at him.

Rick stood up and went back to the window. The traffic was thinning. The downtown had settled into its quiet evening mode. All the nine-to-fivers were home, and the concert goers were happy in their theatrical worlds. The diners were eating something wonderful and discussing their petty problems.

Not thinking about how quickly—and easily—they could lose it all.

He sighed. "He thinks I've got her somewhere, huh?"

"Yes," Tasha said.

"Or worse," Rassouli said. "He thinks you killed her."

"Why would I do that? It makes no sense."

"We're not dealing with a rational man." Rassouli's voice was quiet. This was the kindest the man had been to Rick. Was it because he perceived Rick as a victim now? Or because he finally believed him?

"So he'll be looking for her, right?" Rick said. "He'll leave me alone."

"On the contrary," Tasha said. "He'll be going after you."

Rick leaned his forehead against the cool glass. "Why? Jessamyn's the one he wants."

"And you're the barrier toward getting her. Only you know where she is."

"Okay. I'll watch for someone following me."

"It's not that simple." Rassouli again. Were they doing a subtle good-cop/bad-cop? Was Rassouli playing the kind role just because it was unusual?

Rick stood and slipped his hands in his back pockets. "You just said he's going to use me to find her. Well, he can't do that without following me."

"He can torture it out of you," Tasha said. "And given the condition of your office, I wouldn't put it past him to try."

"But I am Jessamyn."

"And if you tell him that, he'll flip," Rassouli said.

"He'll think I'm lying?"

"No. Because deep down, he might know you're telling the truth."

"Jesus." Rick sat down again. He had always thought the Creep hazardous to his work and his peace of mind, but never to his health. He knew the Creep had threatened him, but he'd seen that as a way to get to Jessamyn, more than anything else. He'd even thought the Creep might try to hurt him, but Rick knew he'd be able to take most anyone in a fight.

He hadn't expected something lethal.

From all the reading he'd done, he thought stalkers only got lethal with the object of their obsession, not with someone who got in the way.

But that was what Rassouli had just told him. The moment the Creep figured out—even subconsciously—that Jessamyn was Rick's pen name was the moment Rick's life was in danger.

"You think he knows already," Rick said.

"As you said, how could anyone see that office and not know Jessamyn doesn't really exist?" Tasha was watching him closely. "We're pretty sure it's not conscious."

"And that's supposed to relieve me?"

"No."

"Then what do you want me to do?"

They didn't respond, just watched him, as if he already knew what they wanted. And, in reality, he did.

"Oh, for crissake. I already moved once. He followed me here. What's to stop him from doing it again?"

"Don't use a forwarding this time," Tasha said.

"I didn't the last time."

"Don't buy a house. Don't be visible. I'm sure you have enough money to live a peripatetic lifestyle for a year or so."

Usually, he would have been ecstatic that someone he was interested in knew how to use peripatetic in a sentence. Right now, though, it annoyed him.

"I can't live that way," he said. "Ultimately I have to be trackable."

"Come on," Rassouli said. "You can pretend to be a girl, but you can't keep where you live secret?"

Rick clenched his teeth. "First of all, I don't 'pretend' to be a girl. And secondly, my job, while I do it at home, requires a lot of back and forth. Every day, it seems, I'm doing some piece of business, by phone, fax or e-mail. Not to mention all the mail and the UPS and the things that have to be done yesterday. If I am hard to find, then I lose control of my career."

"If you are easy to find," Tasha said, "you may lose your life."

"We don't have a budget for protection," Rassouli said. "We're a small department without enough manpower, and the threat on your life at the moment—at least according to department procedure—is mostly imaginary."

"It doesn't feel imaginary," Rick said.

"It's not imaginary," Tasha said. "But we need something we can prove before we go the expense of 24-hour police protection."

"Why don't you guard me?" He couldn't believe the words had come out of his mouth. But they had—and he couldn't take them back even if he wanted to.

"I'm a homicide detective, Rick."

He glared at her. "You're telling me it's not your job?"

Rassouli had tilted his head toward the window as if the view of the building across the street had suddenly gotten very interesting. He seemed to be fighting to hold back a smile.

Tasha opened her mouth, then closed it again. "I just told you that this case doesn't fit our guidelines for protection."

"But you also told me I should be protected."

"I told you that you should move."

He let out a small breath. "I can't just move tomorrow."

"Why not?"

"Because if I do, Tasha, he'll come after me. Then he'll be some other police department's problem. I'll have to explain to them who I am, what the scenario is, and why I'm letting this Creep follow me from place to place."

"There's no guarantee he'll do that."'

"There's no guarantee he won't." Rick threaded his fingers together. "And if he's tracking me through my job somehow—and I have to believe he is—he'll find me again, just like he found me here."

"I agree," Rassouli said, putting his chair down on all fours. "But he's not too close. Otherwise he'd know who you are."

Rick nodded. He'd thought of that too. "If that's the case, moving isn't going to do me any good. In fact, it'll put me in even more danger. Imagine how long it'll take to convince another set of detectives that the threat is serious. You can't even convince your department."

"That's not what I said." Tasha's green eyes flashed at him. "I said we can't get you protection. It's a different thing."

"But you could offer me protection."

"It's not my job, Rick."

He didn't take his gaze off hers. "You'll let me be a sitting duck?"

She let out an exasperated breath and then looked at Rassouli. "Explain this to him."

"You're on your own, Tash."

"Lou, we have the Pfeiffer case."

"It's nearly wrapped and you know it."

Rick got the definite sense that Rassouli was enjoying Tasha's discomfort. He wondered what had caused that. "I think having you as protection is a good solution."

"It's a terrible solution." Tasha frowned at Rassouli. Rassouli grinned and shrugged. Then she turned that green glare back on Rick. "Either I babysit you or I find your stalker. Which is it, Rick?"

"I'm a cake-and-eat-it guy," he said. "I think you can do both."

"Not if I'm sitting here all day."

"Why not? I have Internet access. I'm not tied to the room. If you need to investigate something, I can come along."

"And sit outside your house while I interview Mrs. McGuilicuty? I don't think so."

"I thought you have people talking to the neighbors."

"Got ya," Rassouli said softly.

"You're no help, Lou."

"Didn't know I was supposed to help," he said.

"You didn't want me on this case," Tasha said to Lou. "Want *us* on this case."

"That was when I thought it was simple assault." All the humor had left Rassouli's face. "But that bastard outfoxed all of us tonight. I want him as much as you do. And frankly, if we leave Mr. Chance alone and he faces the perp on his own, we're as responsible as if we gave out the address."

"You think the protection idea is a good one?"

"Unofficially, I think it's the best option we got," Rassouli said.

"And officially?"

Rassouli turned to Rick. "You're on your own, Mister."

Rick leaned back in his chair and watched them both as they discussed this. He wanted their help. He was glad they were considering it.

He had handled this on his own for too long.

But he was willing to compromise. "Tash, it doesn't have to be you, you know."

"It ain't gonna be just her," Rassouli said. "Sometimes you'll get me. I know I'm not as pretty, and I'm probably not as much fun to dance with—"

"Lou!"

"—but I can guard with the best of them. And besides, I figure you might know more about this perp than you realize you do. A few hours together, we might figure out how to find this guy."

Rick was beginning to like Rassouli. He wasn't sure how he had felt after the interrogation room that morning—and Rassouli certainly knew more about him than he wanted, but it didn't matter. The man seemed to have a clear head on his shoulders.

"What about the Pfeiffer case?" Tasha asked.

"Allen's handling it. If there's blood on the shoes, we're through. Hell, if he has the paperweight, we're through." Rassouli picked the hotel notepad off the table, and flipped through the pages. "I think a day or two won't make a difference."

"You think you'll find the Creep in the next two days?" Rick asked.

Rassouli's gaze met his. "I think we got to."

The chill Rick had felt earlier returned.

"All right then. Obviously you boys settled this without me." Tasha turned to Rassouli. "You get the night shift. You want me to call your wife?"

"I'm perfectly capable of calling my wife," he said.

"I don't think someone has to be at the hotel," Rick said. "I wasn't followed here. If he'd known where I was, don't you think he would have been here by now?"

"How do you know he hasn't been?" Tasha said.

"We're staying," Rassouli said. "Or at least one of us is. Can I use your phone?"

"Sure."

Rassouli got off his chair and wandered into the bedroom. Apparently he wanted to speak to his wife in private.

Tasha looked at the back of her hands. Rick longed to take them in his own. Instead, he said, "I won't bite you, you know."

She raised her head quickly. "Excuse me?"

"I know you need to be professional. I won't compromise that. That wasn't why I suggested you act as my protection." It was a little lie. He did want her, not Rassouli, beside him. But he wouldn't have touched her. He wouldn't have interfered in anyway.

Unless she wanted him to.

"Then why did you suggest it?" Tasha asked.

"Because," Rick said, "whether you approve of it or not, I'm going to find this guy. And I have a hunch you'd rather know what I was doing."

"You can't get involved, Rick."

"I am involved. All of this is aimed at me, and I'm not the kind of guy to sit quietly on the sidelines failing to defend myself. I did that once and damn near lost my entire family. I'm not going to do it again."

She frowned. "What do you mean you lost your family? The plane crash?"

He shook his head. He'd said more than he meant to. "It happened long before the plane crash. I was already gone from here by then."

"But you were stalked?"

He let out a shaky laugh. "Not quite."

"What does not quite mean?"

"You read *Betrayal*, right?"

"I told you I had," she said.

"Well, the woman in the book was my fiancée for fifteen minutes, until I found out that she was lying about being pregnant. Only she told my family that I forced her to have an abortion that she didn't want—

even though there had been no baby at all—and my parents, my family, believed her."

"That's why you went to Chicago," Tasha said softly.

"That's why I went to Chicago."

She studied him for a moment. He stiffened, wondering if she was changing her opinion about him.

"I always thought that novel was devastating," she said. "I'm so sorry that it actually happened to you."

"Well," he said, "if you can't change it, write about it."

Tasha nodded. Then Rassouli came into the room. He looked serious.

"Tash—"

"Oh, come on, Lou," she said. "Don't do this to me."

"Do you have a hot date?"

She flushed. Rick scooted back and watched.

"No," she said sullenly.

"Well, I do. At least, I do if I go home."

"That's more information than I wanted, Lou."

Rick suppressed an amused smile. He had a hunch these two always bantered like this. He liked the affection it showed—and the respect between them.

"Tash, we have tickets to the Santana concert tonight."

"Yeah, right. And I'm having dinner with George Clooney."

"Really?" Rassouli sounded surprised.

"Lou, if you had Santana tickets, you would have been bragging for weeks."

"They were a surprise, Tash. Friday's my birthday, or have you forgotten?"

Rick crossed his arms. Tasha closed her eyes and moaned. "Birthdays are not fair."

"Looks like you and the writer get to spend the night together." Rassouli grinned at her. "If I were you, I'd get him to tell you how he does all that research."

"Lou!"

Rick's gaze met Rassouli's, trying to figure out if this was a set-up.

He doubted it.

"And you," Rassouli said. "No matter how flip I'm being, you asked us here for protection, and that's all it should be."

"I know," Rick said. "I already promised Tasha that."

"Good." Rassouli looked at both of them. "I gotta get home or I'm a dead man. I'll have my beeper if you need me, Tash."

"You owe me for this," she said.

"No, I don't. This is payback for garbage duty."

Tasha moaned.

"I'll be back. Eight a.m. sharp. And you," Rassouli looked at Rick, "be ready to do a ride-along."

"Yes, sir," Rick said.

"Night." Rassouli grinned at both of them as he let himself out the door.

"Son of a bitch," Tasha mumbled. "How does he always manage to do that to me?"

"I thought you don't do protection," Rick said.

"Stake-outs. He manages to get out of those, too."

"He'll have me tomorrow," Rick said.

"Yeah, a ride-along. That'll be difficult. Me, I'm stuck on a hotel couch." She sighed.

"I'll sleep on the couch," Rick said.

"No, you won't," she said. "The couch is near the door. I'm not going to cross two rooms to confront someone who's broken in."

"Better hang out the do-not-disturb," he said. "I don't want to know what you'll do to the housekeeper if she doesn't knock loud enough."

Tasha glared at him and stood. "We gotta go out."

"And here I was thinking of dinner in."

"You shouldn't be enjoying this."

His good mood suddenly vanished. "I'm not, Tasha. I'd much rather be home, in my office, meeting my deadline."

"Sorry," she said in a tone that implied she wasn't. "We still gotta go out."

"Why? This hotel has room service."

"Well, right now I have no change of clothing," she said, "and Lou just took our car. So you have to drive me home."

"How about we get dinner on the way?"

"Sounds fine by me," she said. "As long as we stay away from your neighborhood."

Rick sighed. "He's going to find us, isn't he?"

Tasha grinned. It was a confident, strong grin. "Not if I find him first."

# CHAPTER 27

*T*HEY WALKED TO the parking garage and were about fifteen paces from Rick's truck when Tasha stopped.

"Damn," she said.

"What?" Rick asked.

"That truck of yours. It's a neon sign saying, 'Find me.'"

"What's wrong with my truck?"

"Besides the dents and the missing muffler? Oh, let's try the non-existent paint job, and commemorative license plates."

Rick looked at his truck. It was parked kitty-corner in the stall so that it wouldn't get any more dents. The sides were a bit rusty, the paint a bit strange, but he loved that truck. It was more dependable than all his other cars, and it carried stuff—a lot of stuff—without complaint.

"I thought you were without a vehicle."

"I am," she said. "But we can get to my vehicle rather easily. Then we follow our evening's plan."

"Okay," he said, and let her lead him back across the street into the hotel. He found himself watching everyone to see if they were watching him. Men especially. If they looked the slightest bit suspicious, he glared at them, hoping the intensity of his look would scare them away.

"You know," Tasha said, "it's better if you let me keep an eye out for us. You're drawing attention."

"I'm not doing anything."

"You've got hotel security watching you."

Sure enough. He looked toward the front desk. A man wearing a uniform, a name tag, and a walkie-talkie stood near the pillar with his arms crossed. He was staring at Rick.

Rick grinned. "At least I've got the good guys looking out for me."

"I wouldn't say that." Tasha headed toward the concierge desk. "I think you're just making yourself memorable, and if our guy shows up and asks about you, maybe fifty people can tell him you're here."

"You sure know how to dampen a man's mood."

"My job is not to entertain you. It's to make sure you survive the next couple of days."

"I thought it was to catch the bad guy."

"That too," she said.

She leaned across the concierge desk and asked them to call her a cab. The concierge obliged. Rick stood back with his arms crossed. This was so different from Chicago. There, they would have stepped outside the door and had the valet hail one of the passing cabs.

"Come on," Tasha said. "Let's go outside."

He waited until she had started, then slipped a tip to the concierge, who gave him a grateful smile. There was a group of people on the sidewalk, along with a pile of luggage. He and Tasha stepped around it.

The air was getting cool as the skies grew dark. When he had been in Chicago, this was one thing he had missed about the Pacific Northwest. The temperatures cooled down significantly at night. Sleeping was always good here.

Within a few minutes, a cab had rounded the corner, and skidded to a stop in front of them. Tasha got into the back without hesitation, and Rick followed, hoping they were trusting their lives to a driver who knew what he was doing.

Tasha gave the address, which Rick instantly recognized as the precinct. He had thought they were going to her house first, and he said as much.

"I'm parked there," she said rather tersely and leaned back in the seat, staring out the window at the passing scenery. Her position made it clear she wasn't interested in conversation. Rick settled in too, and hoped the drive would soon end.

The driver obviously hadn't realized that they were going to the police station because as he pulled up, he said, "This can't be right."

"Oh, it's right," Rick said, reaching for his wallet.

"I got it," Tasha said.

But Rick had already paid, taken the receipt and slid out of the cab. He stood on the curb, staring at the building.

The first time he lived in Portland, he'd managed to avoid this place, and now he was here twice in one day.

"Let's go in," Tasha said.

"I thought we were just coming for the car." Behind Rick, the cab driver gunned his engine and then sped off, as if he didn't want to be in front of a police station any longer than necessary.

"I want to check a few things first." Tasha passed him and headed for the door.

Rick sighed. At least he was going in the front door this time, and he wasn't handcuffed. That was a step up from the morning.

The station wasn't as busy as it had been earlier in the day. There were fewer uniforms walking around, and almost no one in the waiting area. Tasha strode past the main desk without saying hello to the desk sergeant. The man didn't look up as Rick passed either.

They stepped into an area filled with desks and files and phones. A few detectives huddled over those desks, staring at files. Tasha's desk was near a wall with a large window in it, a window that looked into someone else's office. Shades blocked the view.

Tasha didn't even seem to notice. "I hope you're not that hungry."

He was a little. The area smelled of cold pizza—two boxes were open on a table that also housed the coffee maker. "Why?" he asked.

"Because this may take a while."

"What are we doing?"

"Come with me." She led him into a tiny room that had once been an office. It had four computers, all of them more than a year old. She sat at one, jiggled the mouse, and the police department logo appeared on the screen.

"You can log on from my system," Rick said. "And we could have had room service while you were doing it."

"I have access to information here that we can't get off your system," she said.

He doubted that, but he let her believe it. Besides, he wasn't sure he wanted a police officer—especially this police officer—to know he could illegally find his way around cyberspace.

"All right," he said, pulling over a chair. "What are we trying to find?"

"Tell me again who knew you were moving to Portland. Your family?"

"No," he said. "They didn't find out until I'd arrived."

"Who else?"

"My agent. My editor. Some of my Chicago friends, but none of them know I write."

"Someone who has at least part of the connection," Tasha said, "is your secretary."

"She doesn't know anything about me. I told you that."

"But she knows you moved."

"She knows Jessamyn moved. She got the address change about a month before I moved so that she could help me with the transition."

"Help *you* with the transition? Or Jessamyn?"

"Jessamyn," he said. "But my secretary believes that Jessamyn is married to Rick."

"Bingo," Tasha said.

"Before you go any farther," Rick said, "my secretary is a woman in her sixties who has worked for me for the past ten years. She's been steady, reliable and never given me a spot of trouble."

"I'm sure she hasn't," Tasha said. "But does she have any relatives who might?"

"I don't know," he said.

"Give me her name," Tasha said.

"I don't think it's her."

"Her name." Tasha's tone was flat. He decided not to argue further.

"Miranda Foyt."

"Relative of A.J.?"

"I doubt it."

"You never asked."

"I've never met her in person," Rick said.

"Then how do you know so much about her?"

"You see, there's something called a resume—"

"Oh, cute," Tasha said. She opened a database and typed in Miranda Foyt's name. "Where is she located?"

"Chicago," Rick said. "You know, I have all this information on my computer."

"Including her social security number?"

"No," Rick said. "That's at home."

Tasha grunted. They both knew they weren't going there. Not tonight at least.

"What are you doing?"

"Seeing if she has a sheet."

"Miranda Foyt? She's a grandmother."

"So was Ma Barker."

They waited a minute as the already outdated system tried to access information. "Nothing," Tasha said.

"If it were that easy, I could solve it myself," Rick said.

Tasha frowned. "There's no way of knowing relatives or anything else."

"I doubt it's her, Tash."

"Humor me." Tasha closed that screen and opened a new one. "Let's figure out who else has access to your information."

Rick put his hand over hers. It was like touching a live wire. Her gaze met his. She had felt it too.

"Let's do this differently," he said. "Let's get some dinner, you get your clothes, and then let's come back here. This building never closes, right?"

"Yes, but the sooner we do this, the sooner we get the Creep off your back."

"I know," Rick said. "However, I'm dying of hunger and you can quiz me at the restaurant."

"That's not the most efficient way of doing things." Tasha wasn't looking at him, but she hadn't removed her hand from his.

"No," Rick said, "this isn't the most efficient way. Once we have your car, we can even stop back at the hotel if we need information."

She smiled at him, then she moved her hand. "I hope you know I need to resolve this quickly."

"Not more than I do," he said.

~

Beebe's fury hadn't dissipated by the time he reached his apartment. But he had to be careful. He didn't want his neighbors to see.

He parked the car in its spot, and tossed the axe under the seat. Then he grabbed his binoculars and got out of the car.

The apartment building was thirty years old. It had windy wooden staircases that sagged under extreme weight, and thick concrete between the entrances. On the so-called decorative sidewalk were shrublike evergreen plants he'd never seen before and hoped to never see again. They smelled faintly of cat pee. At first, he'd thought one of the many strays sprayed the damn shrubs, but then he sniffed the plant himself and realized that horrible smell was native to it.

What was worse was that some idiot had planted it outside a place where people lived.

His apartment was on the first floor, with an outdoor access under the stairs. He rarely saw his neighbors, unless he was getting his mail or doing his laundry. Then he tried hard to be nice. He didn't want them to notice him. He didn't think it was appropriate. He wouldn't be here that long anyway.

He let himself in, not stopping to pick up the circular flyer that had landed on the mat left by the previous tenant. He hated this apartment. It was dark and cramped. The entry was small—there wasn't even enough room for the table he always placed near the door—and the tile was a brown so dark that it never felt light here.

The living room was square and opened onto a U-shaped kitchen.

The refrigerator groaned, and the stove didn't heat evenly. When he stood at the sink, he could look out his window, which had a great view of the slime-covered pool or if he turned around, he could see into the apartment's only bathroom—a tiny thing that had room only for the essentials—a toilet, a sink and a small shower.

The bedroom was dark and indistinct. He kept the only window shuttered. Most of his stuff was in there, and he didn't want anyone to see it.

He slammed the door closed with his foot and leaned on the plaid couch he'd bought at Goodwill. Maybe it was better that Jessamyn hadn't seen this. All of his good furniture was still in storage in Chicago. After that home of hers—of Chance's, really—this would not have impressed her.

Where was she? Was she even still alive?

Beebe couldn't imagine that Chance would kill her. He'd have no reason to, right? Unless he felt he'd finally gotten enough out of her.

Beebe kicked the box he'd been using as an end table. It slid across the room and slammed into the thin wall beneath the living room's only window—a view of the sidewalk behind the buildings.

He hurried over and closed the curtains. No sense having someone peek in. His neighbors were problem enough, all chatty and interested, even the twentysomethings who lived upstairs. They were thin, but they walked like they weighed three hundred pounds. When he spent a day indoors, they drove him crazy with their thud-thud-thudding. He thought about complaining to the management, but realized that would draw too much attention. And he hadn't planned on being here that long anyway.

Although it looked like he'd be here longer than he wanted to.

Damn Chance. He'd squired her away, and no one was the wiser.

Maybe he hadn't even moved her from Chicago.

That thought sent panic through Beebe's stomach. He hurried into the kitchen, pulled open the refrigerator and grabbed a beer. Then he made himself set it down. No alcohol until she was safe. That was a promise, one he'd keep. He knew how she felt about drinking. Her books had told him. Alcohol in moderation was good, as a celebration or a simple accompaniment to a nice dinner. But as a cure-all it was bad. It would only lead to bad things.

He set the beer back in the refrigerator, and took out a piece of chicken instead. He'd bought a bucket of cold fried at the grocery store the day before and had only eaten a piece. In fact, that was the last solid meal he'd had. He'd eaten a banana for breakfast before heading over to Chance's house to watch for the flower delivery.

That felt like it had happened days ago.

Beebe's stomach churned, but he forced himself to bite off the crunchy skin. If she was in Chicago, she was dead. He couldn't accept that. She had to be here. Chance had to be hiding her. But where? He rarely left the house, and when he did, he went to the same old places.

Except this weekend, when he'd been gone for nearly two days straight. Beebe hadn't investigated where Chance had gone because it had seemed unusual—and the tuxedo implied an occasion of some sort. Instead, Beebe had used the time to figure out how to get into the house.

But what if Chance had done all this to lead him off the trail? What if Chance had been tending to Jessamyn all weekend, while Beebe was trying to talk to her through the basement windows?

He made himself finish the piece of chicken, then washed it down with some orange juice. He felt a little clearer after that, not quite as shaky.

He had to think.

He'd watched the house after Chance had left, hoping to rescue Jessamyn. He hadn't thought to follow Chance. It probably would have been Beebe's best, easiest route to Jessamyn.

He'd go back in the morning, and catch Chance in the predawn hours. The man always slept late anyway. Then he'd make Chance tell him exactly where Jessamyn was.

# CHAPTER 28

*I*T FELT LIKE a date. Tasha had to keep reminding herself
that it wasn't. She had picked the restaurant because she
wanted to go to a place Rick didn't frequent. They ended up at a trendy
hotspot that Rick said he'd never been to.

Tasha picked it because it had high booths which made for private
dining. She didn't want any casual eavesdroppers to make the wrong
kinds of connections.

She had changed out of her work clothes into a loose cotton top and
a pair of jeans. She wore running shoes, figuring she might need them.
She brought a jacket to cover her gun holster, and made sure her badge
and cuffs were in her purse. In the car, she had two other changes of
clothing and her overnight bag. She wasn't sure when she'd get
home again.

Rick had smiled appreciatively when she had emerged from her
bedroom. He'd been investigating the books she had in her wall-to-wall
bookshelf in the living room.

She had been embarrassed to bring him inside; the place hadn't been
cleaned in weeks. It showed all the signs of a busy single woman's life, a
crumpled blanket on the couch in front of the television, empty pop
cans on the coffee table, and shoes strewn all over the place.

At least she was neat enough to drop her clothes in a hamper in the bathroom and to hide her dirty dishes in the dishwasher. But that was about it. Living alone had been quite an adjustment, especially for a woman who'd never learned domestic chores. Her mother had always said that's what maids were for. Once Tasha had cooked a meal—an assignment for the home economics class she had taken rather defiantly as a teenager—and her mother had refused to eat it. *You've practiced, dear, now let's let Elsie cook something proper for dinner.*

Tasha shuddered. She didn't know why that had come up—probably because she rarely let people into her house. She understood Rick's need for privacy perhaps better than he did. She'd had the same need since she was a little girl.

"Chilly?" he asked.

Maybe she liked his voice the best. It was deep and sexy and warm all at the same time. But those eyes were wonderful too—so dark and mischievous. Not to mention the mustache which added dimension to his face, or that square jawline that most men wanted and never had.

"No," she said, managing to keep her voice as cool as possible. "I'm fine."

She'd been brusque with him all day. It was the only way to keep this professional—and even that wasn't working. She was not looking forward to spending the night in his hotel.

Lou had known that, dammit. Even if there were a concert—which she doubted—he would have stayed if he felt he needed to. Instead, he'd made Tasha do it, perhaps as punishment for dodging the Pfeiffer case, perhaps as a way of proving to her that her attempts at professionalism were fooling no one. Least of all her.

If she had to, she'd stay up all night tweaking the police database and using their account to access FBI files. She'd find this creep just to prove to everyone she could do it—raging hormones or no raging hormones.

"Well, you look like you're concentrating pretty hard." Rick had one hand around a sweating water glass. The other rested on the very edge of the table.

The waitress had brought some sourdough bread and olive oil, then had made a show of teaching them how to dip the bread in the oil.

Personally, Tasha preferred a thick slab of butter if she was going to smear extra fat on her food, but she didn't say anything. Rick didn't seem to mind the unusual topping. He'd torn through half the loaf, then offered her a piece in mild embarrassment.

Apparently, he had been as hungry as he had said he was.

"There's a connection, Rick. We just have to find it."

"You know, Tasha," he said, "I'm convinced we will find it. But we are going to spend the evening together. It's okay to relax just a little bit and talk about something else."

"No relaxing, Rick. At least for me." Not just because she was his protection, but also because if she relaxed, the date feeling would get even worse.

And then she wouldn't be responsible for her behavior in that hotel.

He grabbed another piece of bread. She noticed he wasn't dipping either.

"All right," he said, "let's leave my secretary out of it for a bit. Let's think about who else knew I was moving here."

"Moving company, real estate agent." Tasha reached for a piece of bread before Rick ate all of it.

"This started long before I hired any of those people," Rick said.

"Did you use the same company when you moved to Chicago?"

He laughed. "I lived out of my car for the first month. I couldn't afford to hire a moving company, and even if I could I wouldn't have."

"Why not?"

"Because I wanted to get out of here fast, and I drove until I felt like stopping." His tone was bitter. He set his piece of bread down.

She let out a small breath. He clearly didn't want to talk more about the rift with his family. And she could understand it, especially after all of the things that they seemed to believe about him. "All right. How about everyday people you dealt with?"

"Me, myself and I mostly," he said.

"But you mentioned your agent—"

"No one in New York would have done this," he said.

"Not a disgruntled former assistant?"

"Why go for Jessamyn when they all had to know she wasn't real?"

He shrugged. "It's a tightly guarded secret, but I'm sure that there are a number of professionals there who know I'm the writer."

At that moment, the waitress brought their meals. Tasha's was grilled pork in marionberry sauce, and Rick had the ahi tuna special. Tasha's meal was purple. The sauce had even leached into the garlic mashed potatoes. It was pretty, but not all that appealing.

Still, she dug in.

Rick cut into his tuna. "Oh, this is rich."

"The tuna?" she asked.

He shook his head. "I meant, after today."

"I'm sorry," Tasha said. "I'm not following."

"The only people I can come up with are delivery people. You know, package services and—god forbid—postal employees."

"I thought you didn't use any forwardings."

"I didn't," he said. "But sometimes I get special delivery packages."

"And they'd be addressed to Jessamyn?"

"They'd be addressed to me. But sometimes there are giveaways. You know, something in the memo line on an air bill or even on a box of books."

"What do you mean?"

"Stamped on the side of a carton of books is the name of the book and its author, and usually the ISBN. It's a system for bookstores—they can see what's in the box without opening it. But those are the boxes I get for my own books, and I'm clearly not a bookstore."

"You don't get anyone else's books that way?" she asked.

He shook his head. "Most of my other packages come from the same publisher. If the Creep is smart—and you keep telling me that he is—then he would have been able to put two and two together."

"So your subconscious was telling you to attack delivery people?" She couldn't resist the question.

He stared at her a moment, apparently to gauge whether or not she was serious, and then he smiled. "I guess so. I'm so smart I'm ahead of myself."

"Or behind yourself as the case may be."

"Cruelty thy name is woman." He took another bite of the tuna. It was mostly gone.

Tasha was having trouble finishing her meal. It was all right—not nearly as good as the restaurant critics had made it sound. There was too much sauce and the marionberries were tarter than usual. The pork was good, but not spectacular, and there was too much garlic in the mashed potatoes.

Or so she told herself. The problem with finishing her meal might have been the Whopper she'd had only a few hours earlier.

"Delivery people," she said, "could transfer pretty easily."

"Or quit one company in one town, and apply to another in a different town without attracting any suspicion."

"But he's been watching your place."

"We don't know how many hours he's there," Rick said. "Besides, wasn't there some kind of flap a year or so ago about delivery services making most of their employees part-time so that they wouldn't have to pay benefits?"

Tasha set her fork down. "You're right. How do you remember things like that?"

"It's my job," he said. "The more trivia I know, the better my books are."

"There must be logic in there somewhere," she said.

"Oh, there is." He finished the tuna and shoved his plate aside. "That's how Jessamyn gets her ideas. She puts one piece of trivia with another, and voila! a book."

"As if it were that easy," Tasha said.

"If it were that easy, everyone who won on *Who Wants to Be a Millionaire* would be a novelist."

"How do you know they aren't?" she asked and then felt her grin fade. "Don't tell me you watch that?"

His smile was sheepish. "A person has to do something between writing sessions. I prefer *Jeopardy!*, but I take what I can get."

She shook her head. She was enjoying this too much. It was feeling date-like again. "I don't know how we'll track the delivery guys tonight. That'll take phone calls bright and early tomorrow."

"Oh, I don't think so," Rick said.

He had an odd look in his eyes. She frowned. "Why not?"

"Well, detective. If I had certain skills that allowed me to do certain things with my computer that would get us certain types of information quickly, would I get in trouble for doing it in front of a police officer?"

"You aren't suggesting what I think you're suggesting."

"I probably am," he said. "But since you made it clear that any other suggestion of, say, a more suggestive nature, would be the wrong kind of suggestion, well, then I simply had to suggest something else."

"I can't believe you said that."

"What?" he asked. "My first suggestion, my allusion to a suggestive suggestion or the fact that I can use suggestion ad nauseam in a sentence?"

"The latter."

He grinned. "Words is my business."

"I remember that from the wedding." She instantly wished she could take the sentence back. She hadn't wanted to mention the wedding or anything surrounding it.

His grin had faded. "I told you I wrote at the wedding?"

"No, but I noted several times that you were good with words. It always seemed to disturb you."

"When people say things like that, it feels like I'm giving myself away."

Tasha pushed her plate away. "I don't think most people would look at you and think Jessamyn Chance."

"Thank God for that," he said. Somehow he had already managed to take the check. He slipped a credit card in the little folder and put it outside her reach at the end of the table.

She wondered which credit card it was—the black AmEx with no limit or the platinum Visa which he could charge up to 100K.

She wished she could ask him. She hated knowing more about him than he knew she knew.

And then she shook her head. He even had her thinking in word play.

"You didn't answer me," he said. "About my ability."

She was so deep into flirtation that for a moment, she didn't follow what he was asking. And then she remembered how this little playful interlude started. He was telling her that he could hack into systems.

"However did you learn that skill?" she asked, letting the playfulness go—a bit more reluctantly than she wanted to admit, even to herself.

"I was a teenage boy raised in the Northwest. If you didn't know how to break into a few systems, you weren't cool."

"I thought only nerds knew how to do that."

He grinned. "Guilty as charged."

"I trust you haven't done it in years." God, she sounded prim. Almost like a schoolmarm.

"Trust what you like," he said. "All I did was ask you a simple question."

"You're putting me in an ethical quandary, Mr. Chance. Do I allow the committing of a crime in order to stop a criminal, admittedly a more dangerous one? Or do I go by the book?"

"No one would get harmed."

"Except our case, if someone found out." She could just imagine what Lou would have to say about it.

"The information I'd get would be the same information you'd get from a phone call. You can make the calls as backup later. No one would have to know."

"Except me, Rick." She shook her head. "Let's forget we had this conversation. I'll be on the phone bright and early tomorrow."

"It gives him a chance to get away."

"He's not leaving. He has to find Jessamyn."

"It gets you off this case faster."

She frowned at him. "I'm not an ends-justify-the-means girl."

Amazingly, he smiled at her. Then he took her hand, and kissed the inside of her palm. "You know, that's the most romantic thing anyone has ever said to me."

She pulled her hand out of his. "This is not a date, Chance."

"I know," he said. "If it were a date, we'd have taken my truck."

## CHAPTER 29

TASHA AND RICK arrived back at the hotel just after dinner. She couldn't think of a reason to go back to the station—unless she let Rick practice his illegal magic tricks.

So it felt even more like a date than it had. Only it felt like the kind of date she'd never been on before. The kind that ended up in a man's hotel room for a one-night stand.

Rick unlocked the door and Tasha went in first, her hand on her gun, making sure the three rooms were empty. They were. The newspaper cluttered the table, Rick's laptop was still sitting on the couch, and the bed—which dominated that bedroom—looked untouched.

She beckoned Rick inside. He closed and locked the door behind himself.

And stood there, hands at his side, like a little boy who expected someone else to take his mittens off.

"Now what?" he asked.

"What do you mean, now what?"

"You and me, what happens next?" He shrugged. "I've never been protected before."

"I haven't done much protecting," she said, going to the window. The street was dark except for the amber glow of the streetlights. A teenage couple smooched in a doorway. A white car drove past. Other than that, the street was empty. "But it seems to me that you should go about your business and I try to make sure no one harms you."

Rick remained near the door. "You don't honestly think the Creep is going to break in here tonight."

Tasha closed the sheers and then the heavy drapes. "He broke into your house," she said, and winced. She hadn't told him that part, and she didn't want to get stuck on it, so she added quickly, "But he doesn't seem like the breaking-in type to me. If he finds out where you are, he'll come to the door, maybe posing as a member of the hotel staff or someone who has the wrong room. People answer the door for that sort of thing all the time you know."

"And if I were to open it, he would—what?—shoot me?"

She turned. Rick had moved to the couch, his legs on the coffee table and crossed at the ankle. His hand rested on his laptop as if it were a lifeline.

"Possibly," she said. "More than likely, he'd find a way to get in here, and then he'd torture you until you told him where Jessamyn was."

"He'd have to be a lot bigger than me to do that." Rick's forefinger tapped on the computer's top.

"Not necessarily," she said. "A gun does a lot of talking."

"So." He tipped his head back, leaning it against the pillows against the wall. "You don't have to be eternally vigilant."

She stiffened. He *was* good with words. He'd backed her into a verbal corner. "I should be ready for all contingencies."

"I suppose," he said. "But wouldn't eternal vigilance in this case merely be an overreaction?"

She knew where he was going, and she didn't like it. "Rick—"

"Tasha." He sat up suddenly, all pretense at relaxation gone. "There's something between us and it's time we stop pretending it doesn't exist."

She stayed by the curtains. "It seems to me you were the first one to pretend that it didn't exist."

"And you've been punishing me ever since—when you remember."

"Punishing you? I thought you were some kind of assailant this morning."

"And tonight?"

She sighed and sank into one of the chairs by the table. "Tonight I'm on duty."

"Really?" He stood. "Serve and protect and all that."

His expression was warm, his tone belonging to the Rick she'd met at the wedding. And she thought she saw desire in his eyes. "I think you're taking that out of context."

"Hmm." He was nearly to her chair. "Protect. That's what you're here for, right?"

"Rick—"

"And serve? I'm a taxpayer, right. You're in service to me."

"I don't like the sound of that," she said.

He put his hands on the arm of her chair, his face a few inches from hers. Those blue eyes of his were gorgeous and deep. She could get lost in them.

"Tasha," he said softly, "how about we forget all the other stuff, just for one night?"

"And have our Creep come to the door? Rick, that's—"

He kissed her. He tasted faintly of the coffee he'd had after dinner and something else, something as good as his scent, something indefinably Rick. In spite of herself, she leaned into the kiss, tilting her head back, and enjoying the feel of his mouth on hers, the way he tasted her as if she were a fine wine.

When he pulled away, ever so slightly, their lips no more than a millimeter apart, she heard herself groan in protest.

"See?" he said softly. "We can't just ignore this."

No, they couldn't. This time she bridged the gap between them, her lips brushing his. He didn't touch her anywhere else, his hands still gripped the arms of the chair, his body was a discreet distance from hers. And she wanted to close the gap. She wanted to touch him more than she'd ever wanted anyone.

She slipped her arms around his neck, and this time it was his turn to groan. He pulled her against him, stood her up, and continued kissing her, all in one long fluid motion. Now they were leaning against each other as they had been when they were dancing, and it felt as right as it had then, holding and swaying to a music that only they could hear.

His fingers brushed the hem of her cotton shirt and she started out of the fog that had held her. She caught his hands in her own.

"Wait," she said against his mouth.

She stepped away, took off her gun, and set it on the table, hoping she wouldn't regret that, hoping she'd been right about the Creep. Out of the corner of her eye, she checked to make sure the chain was on the door. It was, and the safety lock button had been pressed. If hotel propaganda was to be believed, no one could get in—not without an axe.

The memory of Rick's office door—shattered with a few measured blows—made her shudder.

"Stay with me," Rick said, and slipped her into his arms again. He kissed her—oh, the man knew how to kiss. How to be gentle and demanding at the same time; teasing and provocative; warm and enticing. His hands had stayed on her back, and yet she felt desire course all the way through her—desire built simply from the kisses, the way he held her, the way her body fit against his.

This time, it was her fingers that tugged at his shirt. She wanted to feel his skin, to see if it was as smooth and muscled as it looked. She yanked the shirt up, trapping his arms. He laughed and pulled away, letting her drag the shirt over his head.

She let the shirt fall as she slid her hands across his flat stomach, around his side and to the muscles in his back. He tugged at her shirt now, but she stopped him again, reaching for his belt. She unbuckled it, then unzipped his jeans, pulling them off him. She wanted to see him— all of him—to know everything about him. She had wanted that from the moment she met him, only days ago. Days. It felt like weeks.

It felt like her entire life.

He bent down, slipped the jeans off, somehow managing to get his shoes off at the same time. Then he stood before her, nude.

She'd seen perfect men before, in calendars and magazines, but she'd always thought them airbrushed and carefully photographed. She never realized they could exist in real life—strong square shoulders, tapering down to narrow hips and muscular legs.

She took him in her hand, and he moaned. Then she leaned over and replaced her hand with her mouth. He reacted as if she had lit his entire body on fire.

His hands were in her hair, touching her neck, reaching for her breasts. "Tasha," he said, "Tasha, please."

She smiled and let him go long enough to say, "Serve and protect, remember?" and then she continued.

"Oh, God, Tash, I didn't mean that." He clung to the table with his right hand. She could feel him struggling for balance, balance and control. He tasted good, felt good. She ran her hands along the insides of his thighs, touching him everywhere she could reach.

Finally, he grabbed her arms and pulled her up, clawing at her shirt.

"You're wearing too many clothes," he said.

She tugged off her jeans, happy to be rid of them, then pushed him back toward the sofa. He tripped on his shoes and nearly fell, but she caught him, easing him down. Then she slipped over him.

He fit inside her. No one had ever felt like this, as perfect as he had when they danced together. But she didn't savor the moment. Instead, she started to move.

"Tasha—"

She bent over, her hair forming a cloud around them, and kissed him. Her hands on his shoulders, his hands on her breasts, caressing, stroking, touching. Moving to their rhythm. Fast and wonderful and powerful.

She'd never felt like this, as if her skin were alive. Every place she touched him sent desire flaming through her. Every place he touched her did the same. It built, until she thought she couldn't take any more.

Then he moved quickly and suddenly, his arm wrapped around the small of her back, holding her against him. Her shirt bunched up, and the rough fabric of the couch scraped her skin and he was on top of her, making everything even more erotic. Her hands were in his hair, his mouth was on her neck, and suddenly she was gone, gone with him, exploding in a thousand ways, like she never had before.

He was with her, every step, as if they'd planned it, his body pulsing with hers, his moans mixing with hers, until there was nothing but warmth and sensation and love.

~

"I'm crushing you," he said a moment later, sounding remarkably calm given what had just happened.

"No, you're not," she said. But she had become aware of her shirt, gathered in a knot behind her shoulder blades, the slight charley horse in her left leg, and the fact that her right foot was wedged against the coffee table.

"You know, this couch was not made for tall people," Rick said, "and my knees will never be the same."

"They'll recover," Tasha said. "In about twenty-five minutes, the same time it'll take me to recover."

"Oh my God," he said in mock horror, "a never-ending cycle. I'd read about women like you!"

"And?"

"I've been praying they existed." He propped himself up on one elbow and eased the hair off her face with his finger. "You are beautiful."

"You keep saying that." She smiled. "One would think you do it to have your way with me."

"I think it was the other way around," he said.

"You started it."

"Yes." His finger felt warm and gentle against her skin. "And then I lost control of it pretty quickly."

Her smile widened. "Not that quickly."

He eased off her, then helped her to her feet. He wobbled as she pulled. She could barely rise. That had taken more energy than she thought.

"Next time," he said, "the bed."

"Are we going to try for every room in this suite?"

"Good idea." He grinned. His cheeks were still flushed, and his eyes twinkled. He was even better looking than he had been before. Handsome. Movie-star handsome, just like she had noticed that first day. "But how about a little food first?"

"It's all about satisfying needs for you, isn't it?"

He raised his eyebrows in mock innocence. "Isn't it that way for you too?"

"Actually, yes," she said, and kissed him. He wrapped his arms around her and made the kiss deeper.

"We could do this all night," he said after a moment.

"And then I really wouldn't be doing my job," she said.

"Promise me," he said, slipping his hands under her shirt, "that when this is over, we'll do what we want for an entire night."

She smiled. "I promise."

He laughed, and let her go. She felt the loss of his warmth. He gathered his clothes and headed for the bathroom. He looked as good from the back as he did from the front.

She watched him until he disappeared through the door. She was falling in love with him—or maybe she had already fallen. With a man who had a penchant for writing books under another name, and a stalker who was trying to kill him.

Tasha smiled gently to herself. Maybe Brooke had been right after all. Maybe Tasha always did get involved with the wrong man.

But no wrong man had ever felt this right before.

She pulled off her shirt and followed him into the bathroom, hoping that their friend the Creep would give them a few more hours alone.

# CHAPTER 30

*T*ASHA HAD INSISTED on sleeping near the door. They had taken the extra blankets and the pillow they'd found in a drawer, and made up a makeshift bed for her. She slept in her T-shirt and jogging shorts—just in case she had to chase someone into the hallway, or so she said—her gun and badge beside her on the coffee table.

Rick stood over her for a moment, watching her sleep. Her face, in repose, was softer. The active intelligence, the animation that was so much a part of her, enhanced her features, but hid them also. She had classic cheekbones, a narrow chin, and a small nose—the very features that most women would accent. Tasha didn't accent them at all. She never wore make-up and she didn't seem to care how her hair flowed around her face.

He liked that about her. In fact, he liked everything about her, including that slight furrow in her brow as she slept.

He longed to touch it—to touch her again—but he didn't dare. She needed her rest. He still wasn't ready to sleep. The stresses of the day haunted him, and as much as the evening had relaxed him, it still hadn't removed the anger that nestled inside him.

Tasha had helped him manage to block out the Creep for nearly two hours. But after that, the Creep returned, bringing with him all the anger Rick had tried to suppress—suppress for years.

He would find this son of a bitch, and then he would make him pay.

Rick bent down beside the couch, moving as silently as he could—he didn't want to startle a woman with a gun—and then grabbed the MacBook. He carried it into the bedroom, and plugged it into the DSL line the hotel provided.

Then he logged on, turning the sound down so low that Tasha couldn't hear it in the living room of the suite.

She had made it clear that she didn't want to know if he had broken the law to find the Creep. She didn't want to be party to it. But he had to know if their brainstorming this evening was a dead-end or not. He didn't want to waste the morning tracking something by phone that he could download in the space of a few hours.

He started with the delivery service he used the most, then hacked into the personnel records at their Chicago office. He would sort by year, then by route, then by employee, and see if any of the people who'd had his route had quit about the time he moved to Portland.

Then he would cross-reference with the Portland office.

If that didn't work, he'd find the next company and start all over again.

The alarm cut through Beebe's sleep, distant, pinging, shrill. The freshly laundered covers—laundered the day before in anticipation of Jessamyn's arrival—were wrapped around his legs. He'd been exhausted, but sleeping fitfully. The dreams were back, haunting him.

The dreams of Jessamyn the last time he had seen her, her red curls glinting in the sunlight, her eyes begging him for help. Sometimes that was all he could see of her—her green eyes and her red hair. He was beginning to forget what she looked like.

Just like he had forgotten his mother.

Pinging.

He opened his eyes. His bedroom was dark, so dark he could barely see. But his computer screen was on—the screensaver off and the windows display like a beacon of light in the dark room.

There was activity.

Beebe hauled himself off the futon he'd been using as a bed and walked barefoot across the room. He grabbed his robe off a peg before sitting in his chair. Then he shut off the notification alarm.

His program's window was already open. Someone using Chance's account had been online for five minutes. Chance's account, usual log-in number, new website.

Chance was checking delivery services.

His hands grew clammy. So close. So very close.

Beebe was a ghost in the server, unseen, a lurking witness to all that Chance did. Only right now, he didn't want to watch. He wanted to find, just in case Chance was logging on from Jessamyn's hiding place.

Chance had gone through a number of servers to get to his. All Beebe had to do was find the place where connection originated.

That took a few minutes. He had to trace backwards, but he did so, finally ending up with an I.D. on the original server. The Old Mult-nomah Hotel. He called up the address, had the computer pinpoint it on a map. He still wasn't as familiar with Portland as he wanted to be.

Downtown on Third and Alder. Now all he needed was a room number.

And a plan.

# CHAPTER 31

*A*T 3 A.M., Rick had a list of over fifty names from several delivery companies—people who had been fired or laid off or transferred to the Pacific Northwest. People who had retired or quit for any reason. People who were no longer on the payroll, the reason for their disappearance unclear.

His back ached and his eyes were dry. He rubbed them, set the MacBook aside, and broke into the room's fridge. It would cost him way too much money to drink the Diet Coke inside—much more than a Diet Coke was worth, no matter how tired he was—but Tasha would pitch a fit if she found out he left the room without her.

She was still sleeping soundly on the couch. She hadn't moved at all. He envied her the ability to sleep like that—his tired body would give anything to stretch out on the bed—and he also wondered how effective she would be if someone crashed through the door. Would she sit up, bleary with sleep, and not know what was happening? Or was she one of those people who could be wide awake instantly, completely alert and functional?

He didn't know, and he very much wanted to find out. He wanted to find out everything about her. Maybe that was why he had told her so much about himself.

He hadn't told anyone about Teri before. About the way she'd used him, the way she'd convinced his parents before he'd even had a chance to defend himself. The way she'd wormed her way into his life, and then destroyed it.

And Tasha had understood. She'd read his book and she'd understood.

The Diet Coke can was cold against his hand. It felt good. His right hand ached from manipulating the mouse with his thumb. He hadn't been sitting in the proper position, and he would pay for it later.

He brought the can up to his forehead, letting the condensation cool him. He hadn't even told Rita about Teri. Rita. He had thought he might fall in love with her, given time. He'd actually wondered quite often if he had been on the precipice of it when the stalking started. Then their relationship had changed. The relationship had become about the Creep. Every conversation was about him, and how to avoid him, how to live with him, how to find him.

By the time Rita had moved in, they weren't even sleeping together any more. He had given her space in his home solely for her convenience, and because he was feeling guilty about the Creep. Not guilty enough to tell her that Jessamyn was his pen name, but guilty all the same.

Then, of course, things got worse. He'd been happy when Rita had gone to France, and he'd wondered why he hadn't felt more when he discovered that she had met someone new.

He rummaged in the refrigerator for more food, found some kind of energy bar thing, and then went back to the bed. He'd pulled back the coverlet, and had bunched up the pillows, but not even that was making him more comfortable. If anything, it made him want to curl up and go to sleep.

But he couldn't. He needed to find this guy. If the Creep had escalated the way that Tasha said he had, then things could get a lot worse.

The sooner Rick was back into his house, the sooner the Creep was gone, the better off they'd all be.

So Rick grabbed the last pillow, put it high enough for his head to rest against it, and continued his search.

~

Beebe sat in the hotel's lobby on a comfortable oversized chair that leaned up against a pillar. His seat gave him the best possible view of both the elevators and the front door, but a fern blocked the front desk's view of him, even though he could see the desk.

A large tour group provided extra camouflage. They had been trickling down all morning, piling their luggage near the concierge, giggling and laughing about their trip to Spirit Mountain Casino and then the coast beyond.

Casinos. A waste of time and energy. He wondered if Jessamyn liked them. She never mentioned them in her books. He used her books as a blueprint for all things. He knew what kind of restaurant to take her to (French or Continental cuisine only), what kind of flowers to put in her hotel room (daisies, catching the light), and how she liked to be seduced (sudden, quick, and impulsive).

He had been studying her for years. And soon he would find her. He would save her.

And she would be his.

He would be her perfect man.

He picked up a section of the *Oregonian* one of the tour members had tossed onto a nearby end table and pretended to study it. So few people noticed a well-dressed man reading a newspaper in the lobby of a hotel. The key was to make sure he looked like he belonged.

That was easy. No one looked exactly like they belonged in a hotel. No one at all.

Beebe was watching for both Jessamyn and Chance, although he had a hunch Chance didn't let her out of the room. After all those years of imprisonment and abuse, Beebe wagered that Jessamyn probably didn't fight Chance on anything. She probably wouldn't even tell housekeeping she was in trouble.

If Chance even allowed housekeeping inside.

Beebe wondered if he'd been studying the page too long. He was trying to control his body. The worst thing he could do was fidget. But he wanted to go to the room. He had found the number during his late night search, and what he wanted more than anything was to go there now, break down the door, and snatch Jessamyn away from Chance.

But Beebe knew better. Hotels were filled with security cameras and watchful guards. A hotel's reputation was based on the way its guests were treated. The last thing the hotel needed was a news item about a man who broke into a room—even if it was to rescue an imprisoned woman.

Beebe loudly turned the page in the newspaper, and resisted the urge to touch his gun. Normally, he didn't like guns, but he was good at them. He'd spent a lot of time at the range with his father when he was a boy. His father had told him to never take a gun anywhere unless he planned to use it—and never to point it at anyone he didn't want to shoot.

His father had pointed that gun at his mother. His father had wanted to shoot her.

And he had.

Beebe shuddered, willing the memory to go away. He didn't want a gun anywhere near Jessamyn, but it was the only thing he could think of. Chance was bigger than he was, and appeared to be stronger, and whether or not he wanted to admit it, Chance's attack on the flower delivery guy the day before had frightened him.

Beebe had spent half the night imagining what would have happened if it had been him.

The thing he kept reminding himself of was that he needed to be strong for Jessamyn. He was her only hope—had been her only hope for years. And yesterday, he had come so close to failing her.

Chance was moving her again, and that was a bad thing. Chance was tiring of her, and when men like that tired of women, they didn't divorce them.

They shot them.

# CHAPTER 32

"*D*id you stop at the station before you came here?" Tasha asked Lou.

He was seated at the table near the window, his gaze taking in the mess the room had become. Tasha almost felt as if he could see everything that had happened here in the past twelve hours. She tried not to blush as he stared at the couch.

"No, I came straight here." He threaded his hands behind his head. "Looks like you had a long night."

"It wasn't what I expected." Tasha sat down across from him, blocking his view of the couch. Her stomach was growling and she wanted a shower.

"Oh?" Lou looked a little too interested.

"He didn't show. He didn't make contact in any way. He's quiet, and I don't think that's good."

"Our perp?"

Tasha frowned. "Who'd you think I was talking about, Rick? I was with him the entire time."

"And how did he take to captivity?"

She could feel the blush start to heat up her cheeks. "Well enough, I guess. But he's sick of this whole thing, and who can blame him."

"Not me." Lou let his arms fall, resting his elbows on his knees and leaning toward her. "Okay, I'll be honest. I want the rest of the dish—"

At that moment, Rick came out of the bedroom. He looked exhausted, as if he hadn't slept at all. He had changed into a polo shirt, a pair of jeans, and tennis shoes. If it weren't for the bags under his eyes, he would look like a man who didn't have a care in the world.

"Anyone for breakfast?" he asked.

"I'm starving," Tasha said, "but I'd like to shower. What if I meet you and Lou in the restaurant?"

"Good idea," Lou said.

Rick smiled at Tasha. His look was so warm that it heated her blood. The blush that had been threatening finally hit. "So," he said teasingly, "I'm Lou's responsibility now?"

"I'm afraid so," she said. "Get him to tell you about the concert. He won't say word one to me."

"You don't tell a woman about a Santana concert," Lou said, pulling himself out of his chair. "It's just too mystical."

Lou seemed to be ignoring that blush—or maybe he would tease her about it later. She tossed a pillow at him. "Get out of here."

"My pleasure," Lou said.

"Want me to order you anything?" Rick asked.

"Coffee," Tasha said. "An entire pot."

"Your wish is my command," he said, and bowed slightly. She wished he would stop, that was what she wished. If Lou hadn't already figured out what had happened, he would shortly.

"Go," Tasha said.

Rick rose and headed for the door. Then Lou grinned at her and waggled his eyebrows. So he had figured it out, dammit.

"I said go." She sounded testier than she wanted to. "The sooner you leave, the sooner I get my coffee."

"Yes, ma'am," Lou said. He followed Rick out the door.

Tasha ran a hand through her ruffled hair. It felt odd, suddenly, to have Rick out of the room. She had been hyperaware of him—partly because she felt responsible for him, and partly because she was so attracted to him, even now, after all that had happened the night before.

She had been horribly unprofessional. The terrible part about it was that she didn't care. Lou, she had finally realized, had expected it. Maybe he had set up his departure the night before to prove to her that she couldn't fight her attraction. After all, he had moved from disliking Rick intensely to rooting for the man all in the same day. She wouldn't put anything past Lou.

She glanced at her clothes, still spread out along the sink. She had opted against a shower when she had realized what time Rick had awakened her, wanting to at least be dressed and presentable when Lou arrived. She had managed that—barely. But he had still given her a slight knowing grin which had annoyed her.

Rick had left the shower stall door open. She reached inside and turned on the water, then felt a prickle of unease run down her back. What had caused that? She couldn't tell. She went back into the main area, and saw nothing.

Hyper vigilance had its price in paranoia. Still, she was glad she had come back out front. She had been about to make a rookie mistake.

Her gun sat on the coffee table where she had left it. She picked it up and carried it into the bathroom with her. Rick didn't strike her as the type to play cowboy, but if he were, she didn't want to leave temptation there for him.

Then she closed the bathroom door, pulled off her clothes, and checked the shower's water temperature. She adjusted the hot slightly, and stepped in.

~

The tour group was loud and obnoxious, swarming about Beebe like bees around a hive. He thought of moving, but didn't want to give up his view of the lobby and elevators.

Voices, laughing and talking, covered the soft mood music being piped in from the speakers above him. It seemed like the decibel level had risen in the past half hour. He could barely even hear the loud ping of the elevator doors as they opened.

He had been staring at the sports section for nearly five minutes now, pretending to be an avid fan. Surely avid fans read every line in the sports section. Although he wasn't reading. He was staring at the elevator around the side of the paper.

Mornings were hectic in the Old Multnomah's lobby. And apparently, there was some kind of conference going on here because the line outside the restaurant doubled all the way back to the gift shop.

Milling people everywhere. They made him nervous. He set the newspaper down, brushing his forearm against the gun hanging from his hip. The suit coat concealed it. He almost wished it didn't. He wanted to point it at the ceiling, shoot out a tile or two, and shout for quiet.

But he didn't. He would go through with his plan. All it took was patience.

Then the elevator door opened and a crowd of people got out, dragging suitcases on wheels. More of the damn tour group. They marched to the front desk and got in line. He was so busy watching them that he almost missed the last two people to get off the elevator.

A burly, familiar-looking man, and Chance. They were talking and laughing. The big man was all eyes, sweeping the room as if he were looking for something. Finally, he pointed at the restaurant. Chance frowned at it and shook his head.

Together they marched toward it, looking purposeful.

This was Beebe's opportunity.

He almost got up and ran toward the front desk. But he made himself wait. They might be here for just a moment. They might be ordering room service or getting muffins to take back to the room. He had to make sure they were not going back, at least for a while.

Chance spoke to the hostess, who traced her finger down a sheet before her. Then Chance looked at his watch. The woman shrugged. It looked like an apology.

Chance went back to the burly man, and they conferred. They went to the main doors and slipped outside.

Now Beebe was ready.

Carefully, he folded his newspaper and set it on the end table beside his chair. Then he went to the front desk.

The line was ten people long. All of them were dragging suitcases and all of them were chattering and laughing like the people who had been surrounding him. Hadn't anyone heard of automatic checkouts? He was in a hurry, and he didn't want to wait for a group of idiots to complain about a five dollar phone charge on their already overpriced bill.

He buttoned his suit coat and shifted from foot to foot, careful to keep his right arm over the bulge in his jacket. He should have bought a shoulder harness. He knew it, but he hadn't done it. And now he would have to be very careful not to reveal his gun.

Three extra hotel employees took spots at the check out desk. Two others finished with their customers, and suddenly, the line shortened by five.

He stared at the backs of the departing guests, willing them to hurry. One was an elderly lady who seemed to want every charge explained to her. Another was a young man who was having some sort of dispute over parking.

Beebe glanced over his shoulder at the main doors. No sign of Chance. Then Beebe scanned the lobby once again. The elevator doors opened, and he felt a stab of panic. He should have been watching them.

What if Jessamyn had come down on her own?

After all the years that Chance had beaten her down, she probably wouldn't have hurried across the lobby. She would have hesitated, looked rabbit-like and fearful.

She hadn't come, at least not yet.

Three of the hotel employees had finished with their guests and beckoned others. Four people walked to the counter. One of them was a couple. He felt blessed. Only one more person ahead of him, and he would be able to get to Jessamyn.

Finally, the last of the original customers, the old lady, moved. The person ahead of him, a middle-aged woman wearing a shirt one size too small, took her place at the desk.

Beebe glanced at the elevator doors. Still no Jessamyn.

"Sir?" The voice came from the front desk. A perky looking woman, no older than thirty, smiled at him. "May I help you?"

"Yes." He didn't have to work at sounding breathless and panicked. It came naturally today. "My name is Rick Chance. I lost the key to my room, and I need a duplicate."

"What's your number?" she asked.

"Four-fourteen." A hard-won number, found through a lot of database searching and ingenuity.

She punched some keys on the hotel's computer system. He rocked from foot to foot, hoping he had gotten it right. So much had gone wrong the last few days, that this might too.

Oh, well. If it did, he had his gun.

He shuddered. Using it here would make it that much more difficult to get to Jessamyn. He should have had a back-up plan. One more sign that he was getting careless. He usually had a back-up plan.

"Here it is," the front desk clerk said. Then she grabbed one of those white plastic room keys with the magnetic strip, put it in her little machine, and handed him the key. "Do be careful with this one, Mr. Chance. If you lose too many keys we have to charge you."

Beebe smiled at her. "I'm sure this will be the last one I'll need."

# CHAPTER 33

$\mathcal{T}$ASHA FINISHED TOWELING her hair, then peered at herself in the mirror. The hotel-provided blow dryer seemed to work only on fry mode, and she didn't want her scalp to peel off. So she'd have to go to breakfast with wet hair. There were worse crimes.

Still, she sighed. She was really gone. She wanted to look as perfect for Rick as possible. Her cousin Brooke would approve.

Tasha put on her clothes, put her gun in the harness, and slipped it under her left shoulder. Then she put on her jacket, praying it wouldn't be too hot today. She hated the stares she got when she peeled off the coat. Even if she explained to people that she was a police officer, she still got odd looks. And that was the last thing she needed today.

Her shoes were missing. She went into the living room, and didn't see them anywhere. She knew she had to have taken them off here. That was where she and Rick had... ignited. She grinned at herself. There was no better word for it. Except maybe erupted.

She checked the bathroom. No shoes. How could she have misplaced them? Shoes weren't something she normally lost.

Finally she went into the bedroom. Her shoes were on the messed up sheets, flanking the open MacBook.

Her heart lurched. Rick had set them there, knowing she would look for them. He wanted her to see something on the computer.

She cursed softly. No wonder he'd had bags under his eyes. He'd been up all night doing illegal things. She could ignore them, she supposed. She could take the shoes and not touch the MacBook, going downstairs and meeting his questioning gaze.

Or she could see what he left. Maybe it was just a simple note, like a love letter.

She hoped.

She hit the spacebar and the computer whirred out of its sleep mode. The screen shimmered twice and then came into focus. She wasn't staring at a webpage, as she had expected.

Instead, what she saw was a Microsoft Word document. A letter, as she had hoped.

Beautiful:

I have names for you. Do not ask me how I got them, because I won't tell you. Ever.

These may save you a few phone calls.

Have I told you that I've fallen in love with you?

Rick

Her breath caught. She stared at the last two lines again. *Have I told you that I've fallen in love with you?*

"No," she whispered to the machine, "you haven't."

She wanted to pick up the damn computer and clutch it to her chest. The man was an incurable romantic. Of course. How else could he have gotten his job?

She ran a finger along the screen. Such a message deserved an answer. She longed to type out her feelings as well. Instead, she scrolled down. Rick had divided the names into categories: Possibles, Unlikely But Worth Mentioning, and My Number One Choice.

Under My Number One Choice, he'd written *Herbert Beebe:*

His company photo matches the description Rita gave the police. It also matches my memory of the sketch the police artist did from her description. The dates match up. He was on my route from the publication of the second Jessamyn novel until February when he took an early retirement. He put all of his possession in storage, then moved to Portland. The address listed as his now is in an apartment complex that rents furnished places. It's way below his means. (He invested well after the crash of '87. He's got enough money to live—has had for years. Could have retired long ago, but didn't. In fact, his personnel file says he insisted on staying on my route. He was actually belligerent about it.)

His personnel file? How had Rick found that? Oh, she didn't want to know.

She glanced at the other names. Rick had listed why he included them. Most of them had quit, retired, or been fired around the same date. Some had relatives here. Others had moved here. Still others had transferred here, but some of them, he noted, had been working on the days when he knew the Creep had been near the house.

*If you want to dig a little further,* he had written, *I have a jpg file with #1 Suspect's photo in it.*

In for a penny, in for a pound, as her mother used to say. Tasha clicked on the desktop, then found the jpg file sitting below the Internet browser. She double-clicked the file, and a photograph came up.

Like all institutional photographs, it had a washed-out look. The subject was a thin man with a receding hairline and weak chin. His nose was long and crooked as if it had been broken, and he had a faint scar under his lower lip.

"Been in a few fights, have you?" she whispered to the photo.

He wore the dark uniform of a deliveryman, and his eyes reflected the camera's flash redly. She wished she could see those eyes better. They would tell her a lot.

The doorknob jiggled, and the lock snapped back. She glanced at the photo one last time. Well, there'd be no lying to Rick now about whether or not she'd seen the files.

"No fair with the shoes," she said, grabbing them and coming into the main room. Then she stopped.

For standing there, with a wide grin on his exceedingly pale face, was Herbert Beebe.

# CHAPTER 34

*Y*OU KNOW," Rick said, "Tasha is going to think we're somewhere in that damn restaurant."

They were standing on the edge of Pioneer Plaza, near the Starbucks. Behind them, a group of pierced, tattooed, and dread-locked teenagers were playing hacky sack. Police officers on horses were patrolling the street. And down the brick stairs, a group of women gathered. Placards lay on the ground around them. They were obviously planning some kind of protest.

"Well, none of the other restaurants are that full," Lou said. "Pick one and we'll let Tasha know where we are."

"Deal." Rick was so hungry, he was tempted to go into Starbucks and buy anything sweet and gooey. Instead he pointed at a restaurant across the street. It was an upscale French restaurant that served all day. He'd been wanting to try it for weeks.

"All right," Lou said. "You realize that's probably not on the depart-ment's budget."

Rick grinned. "Jessamyn will pay for yours."

"She's such a gentleman," Lou said.

They walked to the sidewalk, passing a flower vendor as they went. Rick resisted the urge to browse. He wanted to buy flowers for Tasha, to show her just how important she'd become. But he didn't dare with Lou along.

Although Lou seemed to know what had happened. He'd alluded to it once or twice. Rick simply hadn't responded. He'd promised Tasha that he wouldn't.

He hoped the note wasn't too out of line. He was less worried about the information he'd given her—he knew she'd use that—than he was about the signature line. It had seemed right at 7:30 after no sleep. Now, in the bright sunlight of a Portland morning, it seemed like he was rushing things. He'd probably scared her away.

"You're quiet," Lou said.

"Tired," Rick said.

"Not much sleep, huh?"

Rick glanced at him, trying to hear if there was a leer in Lou's voice. "Yesterday was rough."

"Yeah, I suppose."

This time, Rick did hear a bit of chiding. It made him defensive. He wanted to explain how difficult the day had been, even though the evening had more than made up for it.

"So," Rick said, feeling a little mean-spirited. "How was the concert?"

"Loud," Lou said.

"I thought you left awfully late," Rick said. "Wasn't sure you were going to make it."

"It was at the Rose Garden," Lou said. "They didn't care what time you get there."

"I'm sure your wife cared," Rick said, as they crossed the street at the light.

Lou shrugged. "She's been a police officer's wife for years. She knows the drill."

The phrase caught him. Rick hadn't really contemplated what it meant to be in love with a police officer. The worry, the complications, the constant ever-present fear that your loved one might not come home.

"How long did it take her to adjust?"

"To my schedule?" Lou opened the restaurant door. "She's never adjusted."

Wonderful, Rick thought.

"But she does put up with it, which is more than I could have expected." Lou had a fond expression on his face. It made him look tender, something Rick would have thought Lou's features couldn't achieve.

Obviously the man really loved his wife. Inconvenience or no. They put up with each other and supported each other. And that was what counted.

Then Rick felt uneasy. He glanced around the restaurant and saw nothing unusual. There were a handful of patrons, mostly people in business suits, talking earnestly over dishes covered in sauces. He checked the wait staff. None of them looked like the photographs he'd been scanning the night before.

Maybe his mental timer had just gone off. Tasha should be out of her shower by now, and heading down to the hotel's restaurant.

"I think we'd better let Tasha know where we are," Rick said.

Lou tossed him a cell phone. Rick caught it in one hand.

"Press 'star' twice," Lou said. "I've got Tasha's cell on the speed dial. If she's already out of the room, this'll guarantee that we find her."

At that moment, the hostess approached them carrying two menus designed to look like parchment. "Breakfast?" she asked with a French accent that Rick could only hope was fake.

"Yes," Lou said as if she'd been withholding food from him.

She didn't seem to notice. "This way," she said, and led them into the main dining room. She led them to a black booth flanked on both sides by large vases filled with roses.

As Rick and Lou sat down, she handed them the menus.

"Let me tell you the specials," she said. As she recited, ingredient by ingredient, Rick's fist clenched around the cell phone.

His feeling of unease had grown, and he had no real idea why.

# CHAPTER 35

*J*ESSAMYN," BEEBE SAID with complete and utter joy.

Tasha didn't move. Rick had told her she looked nothing like Rita. Rita had curly red hair. Tasha's was blond —and wet. And when it was wet, it curled.

She resisted the urge to touch it. She made her lower lip tremble, just a little. She had to buy some time. Her handcuffs were in her purse, which was beside the sofa. Behind Beebe.

A thousand miles away.

"Who are you?" she asked, struggling to sound weak and terrified. She'd never felt weak in her entire life. Brooke used to say that was one of her problems.

"My name is Herbert Beebe, my dear." He was stronger than his photo made him look. He had a compact build, and muscular arms and back. Which only made sense, considering that he'd lifted heavy pack-ages most of his life. "I've come to rescue you."

He sounded so sincere, which made the last sentence sound completely ridiculous.

"Rescue... me?" She dropped her voice to a whisper, then looked toward the window, then the door, as if she were afraid Rick was going to overhear.

"I know what he's been doing to you, my darling. I've come to get you out. Let's hurry."

"But Rick..." She was trying not to glance at her purse. She supposed she could pull out her gun, but she didn't want to spook the man. She wanted to catch him by surprise.

"What about him?" Beebe asked.

"If he finds me, then—oh, God." She couldn't even make up what her imaginary Rick would do. If only she were the writer. But she wasn't. Her ability to make things up on the spot was flimsy at best.

"He won't find you, not if we hurry." Beebe glanced at the door, as if just mentioning Rick would make him appear.

"How—how did you know?"

Beebe smiled. "All the signs were there. Remember what I said to you in Chicago?"

She stared at him for a moment. Of course she didn't. That had been Rita. But she had to gamble. "That was you, wasn't it? Oh, I knew you'd come for me."

For a moment, she thought she went over the top. He was staring at her, a small frown on his face. "I told you to contact me. Why didn't you? The police said you'd called them."

She swallowed. Lies. She hated lies. "That wasn't me. That was Rick. I—I had to tell him."

"But you could have called."

She shook her head. "It wasn't bad then. I didn't realize what he can do." Then she paused, as if something had just come to her. As if the words "what he can do" triggered a horrible image in her mind. "You have to leave. If he catches you... ."

"I'll take care of him." Beebe pushed back his suit coat with his right hand. A semi-automatic hung from a holster at his hip. This man really had sunken into fantasy. If he fired that thing, he could release fifteen bullets before she even got to her gun.

"Is—is that thing loaded?" The stammer wasn't quite so hard to fake this time. She had expected violence from Beebe, but not a weapon that was designed for war.

"Oh, yeah." For a moment, his watery blue eyes glinted. Hard, dangerous, and crazy. What a lovely combination. Then the look vanished and the milquetoast Beebe reappeared. "Don't worry, beloved. I won't let anything harm you."

Beloved. Darling. The heroes in Jessamyn's novels—Rick's novels—used those endearments all the time. It was one of the few things that Tasha had never liked about the books.

They also had a lot of rescue fantasies in them.

She shivered slightly.

Beebe reached for her. "Let me get you out of here."

She didn't want him to touch her, but she didn't know if she should step away.

At the last minute, she figured out what to do. He believed Rick abused Jessamyn, and Tasha had seen her share of abused spouses when she was still a beat cop.

She cringed away from his touch.

"I won't hurt you," he said, sounding slightly offended.

"Rick, he—"

"He hurts you?" Beebe seemed to grow taller. "Maybe we should wait for him."

"N-No," Tasha said. She had to get to that purse. "I want to get out of here. You can get me out of here, right?"

"Of course I can, sweetie."

Did he have any idea how awful those words sounded? Probably not. He probably saw himself as tall, dark, and dashing. Probably no more so than right now, when he was rescuing the lady of his dreams.

"Then we have to leave now," Tasha said. "Rick will be back soon. He went to get breakfast."

"Who was the man with him?"

"Man?" It was Lou, but she didn't dare admit that. Unfortunately, nothing was coming to mind.

"He looked familiar. I know I've seen him recently—"

A phone rang. Her phone. Her cell phone.

Beebe looked around for the source of the sound.

"Th-That's my phone," Tasha said, wondering if she was overdoing the stammer. "Only Rick has the number."

The phone rang again. Beebe was frowning.

"If I don't answer it, he'll come and check on me."

Another ring.

"Where is it?" he asked.

"Let me get it. If I do anything out of the ordinary, he'll come here."

For the first time, Beebe looked a little panicked. So, for all his bravado, he was afraid of Rick. Good. That might help.

Beebe nodded.

Tasha launched herself across the room, narrowly missing him, and grabbed her purse. She thought of going directly for the handcuffs she kept in there, but that was too risky. Instead, she pulled out the cell phone and answered it.

"Tasha!" It was Rick. She let out a shaky little breath, hoping that the phone wasn't loud enough for Beebe to hear Rick's side of the conversation. "Lou and I—"

"I didn't get it right away because I was getting dressed." She was beginning to get this down, this pretending to be a victim thing. She could hear the terror in her own voice. Only it didn't sound like her voice.

"What?" Rick asked.

"I'm sorry. I know you want me to answer in two rings." Her left hand was still inside her purse, inching toward the handcuffs.

Beebe was watching her closely.

"Tasha, it's Rick."

"I know, sweetie," she said, giving Beebe a wild-eyed look. "But I couldn't get to the phone any faster. Don't yell at me, please."

"What the hell is this, Tash?"

"I don't want to go back to that room, Rick. Please. Don't make me."

Beebe's eyes widened. Either she was very good at her new acting job, or she was very bad.

Rick let out a small whistling breath. "I'll be right there, Tash."

"Don't do anything, please. I'll be fine." This time, it was her speaking. She didn't want Rick up here—not Rick the man who attacked flower delivery guys. She wanted Lou to come here as back-up. That was all she needed.

"He hasn't hurt you, has he?"

"Of course not."

"Good." And then Rick hung up.

She closed the phone slowly, and stuck it back in her purse. Her hands were shaking. Great. Now she had Rick to worry about. She only hoped he would be honest with Lou.

As she let go of the phone, she grabbed the handcuffs, prying one side open.

"Is he coming here?" Beebe asked.

"I don't think so," she said, knowing that an absolute reassurance would be bad. Beebe expected Rick to be nasty, so she had to play it that way.

"Then let's get out of here." Beebe reached out a hand to help her up.

She took his hand, let him pull her forward, then twisted his arm around his back. "I don't think we're going anywhere," she said.

# CHAPTER 36

*H*E'S THERE," Rick said as he hung up, tossing the phone back to Lou.

Lou caught the phone. "The perp?"

Rick nodded. "And he thinks Tasha is Jessamyn."

"Thank the Lord for small favors." Lou threw down a ten, and was struggling to get out of the booth.

Rick slid out quickly and ran out of the restaurant. After the restaurant's darkness, the sunlight nearly blinded him. He hurried down the street, not waiting for Lou. Lou would catch up. But Rick had to get there.

Tasha was alone with the Creep, and God knew what he would do to her. She was there because of Rick. And yes, he knew that she could take care of herself, but he also knew that things went wrong. And something like this could go very wrong.

He glanced over his shoulder. Lou was running behind him, phone pressed to his ear. Probably calling for back-up.

Rick careened into a middle-aged man, and nearly lost his balance. "Sorry," Rick said, continuing forward.

The man cursed him, but Rick didn't stop. His gaze was on the Old Multnomah Hotel's sign two blocks ahead. People were pulling their cars up front as if nothing was wrong. Valets were opening doors, carrying luggage, chatting.

Did they know Tasha was in trouble?

The distance seemed so much longer than any distance he'd ever run before. He'd have to go in, take the stairs, find hotel security—or maybe he'd leave that to Lou.

He would just get there.

Tasha needed him.

He hoped he would reach her in time.

# CHAPTER 37

TASHA SECURED THE handcuffs to her belt, then grabbed for Beebe's other hand, but he swung around, nearly knocking her off balance. She still had his wrist, and she concentrated on holding it as he whirled her around the room. His free hand was moving. She couldn't see it, and she knew that was a bad sign.

He hurled her into the coffee table, hitting her knee and sending pain shooting through her leg. She concentrated on bringing her hand up on his wrist until she found his thumb.

He shoved her toward the couch, and she slipped a foot beneath his leg, yanking it out from underneath him. He seemed to anticipate her, twisting his leg, and catching hers.

She brought her knee up, slamming it into his crotch. He yelped with pain. At that moment, she bent his thumb all the way back, and he screamed. Then she bent his wrist back as well, forcing him to kneel on the floor.

She yanked his free hand behind his back. Getting the cuffs would be the trick. She hated this part. She bent his thumb back as far as she could, forcing him forward until he was prone. Then she stuck a knee in his back as she wrestled his arms.

At that moment, the door opened. She didn't turn to look, trusting it was Rick. She loosened her grip on Beebe's thumb, caught both hands in hers, and reached for her handcuffs.

Then he reared back and flipped her off him. She tumbled sideways and hit her head on the coffee table. Pain shot through her and she struggled not to pass out.

## CHAPTER 38

OR A MOMENT, Rick froze in the doorway. Tasha had the Creep, and then had lost him because Rick had come in at the wrong point. Tasha was lying beside the coffee table, her eyes barely open.

The Creep had risen to his knees, and was fumbling at his side.

"You're not Jessamyn!" he screamed, and pulled a gun, leveling at Tasha's head.

Rick had had enough. He lunged at the Creep, tackling him. He landed near the table and chairs, jarring his arm. The gun went off, shooting what sounded like a hundred rounds, blowing a hole in the window. Shattered glass fell all around them.

Rick hoped it had missed Tasha. He could see her shadow moving. She was fumbling for something.

The Creep struggled against him. The little bastard was strong. Rick had grabbed his waist, not his arms, and that hampered all of his movements.

The Creep flipped him and slammed him against the floor. The breath left Rick's body, but he managed, somehow, to free a hand and grasp the Creep's gun arm.

"That's it." The voice belonged to Tasha.

The Creep froze. Tasha was pointing a gun at his head. Her green eyes blazed and she looked fierce.

"Where's Jessamyn?" the Creep wailed.

Tasha's gaze met Rick's, and then she smiled. A slow, impish smile. "Jessamyn?" she repeated. "Why, you're holding him."

"Je-Jessamyn?" the Creep asked, sounding stunned.

"Haven't you ever heard of pen names, you idiot?" Rick asked, tightening his grip on the Creep's gun arm. Tasha reached over and grabbed the Creep's gun out of his hand.

"Pen names?" The Creep looked confused. "But I met Jessamyn. In Chicago. She—"

"Her name was Rita," Rick snapped. He wasn't willing to let go of the Creep's arm yet. "She was my girlfriend, and you drove her off."

"No," the Creep said. "She was Jessamyn. I know she was Jessamyn. She *lived* in your house."

"Not when you met her."

The Creep blinked once, then frowned. His face was pudgy and poorly defined, but Rick recognized him anyway. That was the man he'd found in his computer search the night before.

"What the hell is this?"

Rick glanced behind him. Lou was at the door, with hotel security flanking his back. The rent-a-cops looked terrified.

"This," Rick said cheerfully, "is the Creep. Creep, this is Lou. He's a detective with the Portland police."

The Creep looked up at Lou. "I didn't do anything."

"Then why is Detective Morgan holding a gun to your head?"

The Creep's eyes got wider. "I—She—I—She's the blond? But her hair should be up."

"He thought I was his imaginary friend." Tasha hadn't moved from her position. She looked ready to shoot the Creep if he so much as breathed wrong.

Rick's hand was getting tired from clutching the Creep's gun arm. "Anyone have handcuffs?"

"I do," Lou said, "but you guys look so pretty there, posing, that I thought I'd enjoy the view for a moment."

"Lou," Tasha said through gritted teeth. "I could shoot twice. One of the bullets could easily hit Mr. Beebe here, but the other could go wild. No one would blame me if my partner took some friendly fire."

"Doesn't seem that friendly to me." Lou crossed the room and yanked Beebe's arm. "Breaking and entering, pissing all over someone's house, menacing, attempted murder, oh, man, have we got some things to talk about."

"I haven't given him any warnings," Tasha said.

"Don't worry. I'll take care of the formalities. We got some guys meeting us downstairs." Lou grinned. "Besides, it looks like you gotta dry your hair."

"You owe me breakfast!" Tasha said.

The Creep turned toward her, looking even smaller now. "If you're not Jessamyn, where is she?"

The plaintive sentence sent a shiver through Rick. He thought they'd already dealt with that.

Tasha seemed unaffected. "Jessamyn only exists on the cover of books."

Lou took the Creep's arms and dragged him out the door. The Creep looked up at him. "But I saw her. In Chicago. Please. You're a police officer. You have to look for her. He's hiding her somewhere...."

Tasha slammed the door closed, then leaned on it. Her hair was damp and curling. Her cheeks were flushed.

She looked beautiful.

Rick was still on the floor. He had a hunch standing up would be work. His head ached. "He didn't hurt you, did he?"

She holstered her gun. "Bruised a little. But I'm not sure he'll have the use of his right hand any time soon."

"He's going to go for insanity, isn't he?"

She shrugged. "He could be crazy as a loon, but as long as he knows right from wrong, he won't win an insanity plea. And no certifiably crazy person could have tracked us to this hotel."

"I used my own name to check in," Rick said.

"Still," she said. "It takes a bit of smarts to find you. And motivation."

"What happens now?" Rick asked.

"Statements all around. Delayed breakfast most likely. Then we have to charge him, and the legal dance begins."

"But he's out of my life?"

Her gaze was compassionate. "If we stop him, Rick."

He felt his stomach clench. "What does that mean?"

"As long as Jessamyn is secret, he's going to believe you're hiding her."

Rick eased himself off the floor. Damn. It was as painful as he thought it was going to be. He'd bruised a lot going down too. And that run took a bit out of him. He hadn't run like that since he moved from Chicago. "So? He'll be in jail."

"For a few days. But from the information you found, this is a first time offense. He'll probably make bail."

Rick let out a large sigh. It wasn't going to end. It would never end. "So I have to let the world know I'm Jessamyn?"

"They'll find out anyway. If I were Beebe's defense attorney, I'd play up the Jessamyn angle."

He turned away from Tasha, and went to the window just to collect himself. He knew even better than Tasha what was coming. The tabloids, the constant media reports, the silly television interviews he'd have to endure.

*Why'd you do it, Mr. Chance? Why did you want the entire country to think you were a woman?*

*A woman's pen name, Mr. Chance? Robert James Waller did it without one.*

He heard Tasha walk across the floor. She stopped just behind him. He could feel her warmth against his back, her breath against his neck, but she didn't touch him.

"You know," she said, "it'll be easier to go through all this if you have someone standing beside you."

"Yeah, well," he said, "life has never worked that way."

"I'd like to be there. I'd like to be the person at your side."

"Why?" he said bitterly. "So that the tabloids will have more fodder? Female Cop Falls for Lying Writer. Is It True Love or Just Research for the Next Book?"

"What if it's both?" she said.

He turned. She was so close to him that he had to strain not to touch her. "Tasha, they're not going to believe anything. It's going to be hell for a while."

She gave him that impish smile again. "I can handle hell."

He shook his head. "Why would you do that?"

"Because I love you, Rick."

"Are you serious?" His heart was beating hard. He felt giddy. He had the strange thought that the sensation he'd been describing in his books wasn't adequate enough to describe this feeling, this mixture of hope and terror that filled him.

Her smile faded and she suddenly looked uncertain. "I've never been more serious in my life."

"But we just met last Friday. Yesterday, you thought I assaulted a deliveryman."

"And today you did." She shrugged. "See, I can adapt."

"Tasha—"

"Rick, you believe in love at first sight. I know it from your books. Besides, we've gone through more in the past five days than most people do in years of dating."

He may have used that line in his books. He wasn't sure. "But your family—they already disapprove of me."

"That was before they knew you were rich."

The muscles in his shoulders tightened. Tasha must have noticed because her smile returned.

"Relax," she said. "I probably have more money in trust than you and Jessamyn earned in the past eight years."

"I wouldn't bet on it," he said. He longed to touch her. "Tash, what you're proposing—it would take a hell of a commitment. Your life would be trashed too."

She smiled at him. "For you, I'd do anything."

"Anything?" he asked.

"Well." She tilted her head as if she were considering that idea. "I don't think I could do a society wedding. Or the yacht club. Or any more pink taffeta dresses."

He slipped his hand in her hair. "I think we can make a commitment without that."

"We?" she asked.

He nodded. "If you commit to me, I commit to you. And I don't take commitment lightly, Tasha."

"Neither do I," she said.

They stared at each other for a moment, and then she caught his hand and pulled him close. They kissed. A deep, passionate warm kiss. A kiss that even put the one from the night before to shame.

He wrapped his arms around her. And before he completely lost himself to sensation, he had one thought:

With her at his side, he could survive anything.

# CHAPTER 39

*R*ICK SUDDENLY HAD a lot of personal business to complete. And before he did any of it, he had to talk to Jane, and he had to do it alone. Tasha wanted to be with him, but he wouldn't let her.

Instead of cooking Jane dinner on Friday, he did it the evening after they caught the Creep.

Rick invited his sister to his home after all, cooked her a fantastic roast chicken dinner, and watched her eat it, his stomach knotted in a ball. For the first part of the meal, she took in his home, especially the refrigerator, which seemed like a great toy to her. After a while, she set her fork down.

"Are you going to eat or did you invite me over to poison me?"

He picked up his own fork. He had never felt less like eating in his life. "I wanted to talk to you."

"If it's about Teri, don't bother," Jane said. "I never should have believed her."

"She was credible."

"Then," Jane said. "But she pulled a similar stunt a few years ago with one of your old friends. Did you know that?"

He shook his head. He hadn't kept up with his old friends.

"And I realized just how dumb I was."

"You weren't dumb, Jane. Everyone believed her."

"Mom and Dad didn't."

He pushed his plate away. "Yes, they did. They yelled at me."

"For getting involved with Teri."

"For not living up to my responsibilities."

Jane nodded. "They didn't believe her by the end, Rick. They wanted to tell you that."

He folded his hands in his lap. "Thanks for that. Even if it isn't true."

"Are you accusing me of making up stories?" she asked.

"No." He took a deep breath. In for a penny, in for a pound, as Tasha said. "I'm the one who does that."

Jane grinned. "Are you confessing?"

He froze. "To what?"

"To writing all those Jessamyn Chance books?"

He frowned. "What makes you think that?"

"Oh..." Jane shrugged. "Maybe it was the details of Mom and Dad's plane crash in that first book. Or the story of Teri in *Betrayal*. Or maybe it was the little things, like the way you described our family's house so perfectly in *Pretty One*. Or the way a young boy chipped his tooth in *Brainy*, just like you did when you were twelve. Or—"

"Why didn't you say anything?" He was stunned. He hadn't expected her to know.

"I wanted you to tell me, Rick."

"But I didn't tell anyone."

"What about Tasha?"

He waved a hand and sighed. "That's a whole new story."

"I want to hear it," Jane said, and shoved his plate back at him.

"She already knew?" Tasha said that night as she curled against him on his big bed. She had been pleased to learn that the bed was as comfortable as she had imagined it would be.

He nodded, drawing her close.

"And she didn't tell anyone?"

"Jane's cool."

"I'll say." Tasha wondered if her family was going to be as cool when they found out about Rick. Probably. He was rich, after all.

Ironically, as far as she was concerned, that was the least important part about him. His kindness, his warmth, and his intelligence—not to mention his fantastic body—they were all much more important than his bank balance.

In fact, she still hadn't confessed that she knew his bank balance. She'd been too busy finishing the case against Beebe, and arresting Damon Pfeiffer.

It had been a productive few days.

"What are you thinking?" he asked.

"I was remembering the first time I saw this bed," she said.

"Oh?"

"I was helping Lou search for the Creep. Do you know that I was paying more attention to the bed than I was to backing up Lou?"

"I'm not sure I wanted to know that," Rick said. He was generally fine with her job, but, she suspected, he would worry about her, like every cop's lover did.

"I usually pay attention," Tasha said. She had to reassure him.

"So what distracted you?" he asked.

"The thought of you. Sleeping here. Naked."

"Were you really thinking about me sleeping?" he asked, his voice low.

She smiled. Then she slipped her hands under the covers. "You know, you promised me a night in which we could do whatever we wanted."

He smiled back. "So I did."

"How come we put it off?"

"I don't know. Arrest warrants, statements, family obligations, repairs, wedding plans?"

She found what she had been searching for. He squirmed at her touch.

"And, um," he said, his voice breaking a little, "I seem to recall one or two sexual interludes in the last twenty-four hours."

"Interludes," she said, moving her hand. "Not an entire night. Awake. Doing all sorts of things that romance writers are supposed to specialize in."

"Putting together really witty sentences?" he asked.

"You know what I mean."

"Yes," he said softly. "I believe I do."

And then, as if to prove his point, he kissed her long and slow and passionately.

The way heroes always kissed.

In books.

I value honest feedback, and would love to hear your opinion in a review, if you're so inclined, on your favorite book retailer's site.

Be the first to know!

Please sign up for the Kristine Kathryn Rusch newsletter, and receive exclusive content, keep up with the latest news, releases and so much more—even the occasional giveaway.

So, what are you waiting for? To sign up, go to kristinekathrynrusch.com.

But wait! There's more. Sign up for the WMG Publishing newsletter, too, and get the latest news and releases from all of the WMG authors and lines, including Kristine Grayson, Kris Nelscott, Dean Wesley Smith, *Fiction River: An Original Anthology Magazine, Smith's Monthly,* and so much more.

To sign up go to wmgpublishing.com.

If you enjoyed *The Perfect Man,* you might like Kristine Kathryn Rusch's novel of romance, music, and mystery, *The Death of Davy Moss.* What follows is a preview chapter.

*This book is set in 1997. Since then, the music industry has changed so much that we can legitimately start this story with that lovely phrase:*
*Once Upon a Time...*

### Part One

...A new biography of legendary pop star **Davy Moss** appeared this week, this one by music critic and historian **Riley Platt**. Platt's thesis? Moss would have been one of the country's best musicians if he had survived the single-car collision that took his life fifteen years ago. Platt bases his theory on Moss's background as a childhood classical music prodigy and a few surviving compositions. Add this one to the collection of strange Moss cultish material that has arisen after his death...and cross it off your Christmas list.

— ROLLING STONE

EMILY LUKOVICH stopped in the foyer of the Sea Grotto Restaurant and took a deep breath. It calmed her a little. She had taken the job, she reminded herself, for good or bad. A consultant consulted. Even if the people she was advising didn't want to hear what she had to say.

She slid off her raincoat, adjusted the sleeves on her silk blouse, and touched her hair lightly. She had been in Oceanlake a week, and she still wasn't used to the informality of the town. No one dressed up here. Not even for business. She had shown up to her first appointment with the board of the Rolling Waves Casino in a Donna Karan suit and found herself so overdressed that it felt as if she had worn a bridal gown to a barn.

The hostess behind the desk smiled at her. Emily smiled back. At least this place was friendly. She needed friendly after her years in Vegas and Los Angeles. Even the casino was friendly.

She liked that.

"May I help you?" the hostess asked.

"I'm meeting someone," she said.

"Are you with the rehearsal dinner or the casino?"

"The casino," Emily said, glancing over her shoulder. Near the dance floor, a long table had been set up. A young couple sat at the head, with older people—obviously parents—in the seats beside them, and couples around the age of twenty filling the rest of the seats. No one had dressed up for that, either.

Emily would have. In fact, Emily had. She'd been a bridesmaid three times in the past year—never, as the cliché went, a bride. Not that she wanted to be. Once upon a time, she'd thought herself too avant-garde for marriage. Then she became too busy. And later, too hurt.

"This way please," the hostess said. She led Emily down three stairs, not pausing like Emily wanted to when she saw the view. The windows at the Sea Grotto overlooked the Pacific Ocean. It was steel gray and frothy, a winter ocean in twilight. Yet the stark beauty grabbed her, as it had every day since she had arrived. She almost wished she could give up everything and stay in this tiny Oregon town with its provincial casino and stunning scenery.

Almost.

She did like her job. It provided a way to stay in the music business without all the hassles of artist management. She had rebuilt her reputation and she got to hear all the up-and-coming bands, satisfying the hidden music geek inside her while keeping a hold on the business.

She had been hired by Rolling Waves as a consultant and promoter to get their concert series up and running. Rolling Waves, owned by a consolidated tribe of local Native Americans, had been profitable from the beginning. The casino board, tired of the local and regional acts it could draw, decided it wanted to compete on the Vegas level. It wanted big names to perform in its new concert hall, but didn't know how to get them.

Emily was supposed to set up the system, hire the first year's lineup, and then leave. She estimated she could do the job in six months. Normally she did it in three, but Rolling Waves was a difficult case. It was more remote than the other casinos she had dealt with, and the casino board wanted to learn how to do the promotion themselves.

The problem was—and had been since Emily arrived a few days after Christmas—that the board had no idea what "national level" meant. Tonight was a case in point. They had called her to the Sea Grotto to hear a local band and see if it was worth hiring for the casino bar.

She had expressly told them when she was hired that she did not work with local bands. She did not work regionally. She only worked nationally, hiring top acts for top venues. The key was to make Rolling Waves a top venue.

A local band would not do.

The hostess led Emily to a large booth. Only three of the board members were there: Tom Running Bear, Joe Escobal, and Paul Perdy. They were the important three. Tom Running Bear, a heavyset man with thick dark hair, was the casino's chief executive officer and the only board member who actually worked in the casino. Joe Escobal, the nominal head of the board, was a young man from one of the tribe's most important families. And Paul Perdy was a small elderly man who disappeared into the booth's back corner. Emily had learned immediately to pay attention to Paul. He was the real power in both the tribe and the casino, and with the flick of a hand could change a decision.

Bear slid over to make room for her. She hung her raincoat on the peg beside the booth and sat down. Her seat faced the dance floor and the rehearsal dinner table. She must have looked disgruntled because Joe Escobal smiled at her.

"We thought you should hear this band."

"I know." No band had set up yet. She was early. "You realize this isn't part of my contract."

"That's right," Bear said. "But we thought that if you liked them, it might save the casino some money—"

"We need to make a decision now, gentlemen," she said, her voice deliberately harsh. She had to take control of this group quickly or she had to resign and let them find someone else. She might be too high-powered for them. "Either you hire a consultant to help you bring in first-rate talent, or you hire a consultant to bring in the best of the local musicians. I don't work locally, and I don't manage musicians."

The words stung her as she spoke them. Managing musicians had been her first love. But she hadn't done it in years. Not since the Ricky Fink Band.

Bear put his hand on hers. "We know. And we're sorry if this is the wrong direction. But we don't just need musicians for the main hall. We need them for the bar and gaming areas as well."

She took a deep breath. So this was the area that their confusion stemmed from. She hadn't realized it.

"You've been doing a tremendous job hiring musicians for those slots," she said. "I'll bet you and I will have the same opinion of this band. I don't think you need help in that area. In fact, I don't think you need any help if you continue with the local acts in all the arenas, including the concert hall. You only need me to go national."

"People come here to game," Paul said softly, and when she looked at him, his brown eyes moved away from hers. Ah, so there was her opposition. It was becoming clear to her now.

"Yes, they do," she said, "but let me be honest with you, Paul. Rolling Waves is two-and-a-half hours from Portland by car. You cannot fly here. The tourists come for the beach. While they're here, they might go to the casino. Business is wonderful in the summer. It's the off-season that I can help you with."

She slid her hand from Bear's and leaned forward so that she could see Paul's face more clearly.

"Let's say, for the sake of argument, that we hold a Faith Hill/Tim McGraw concert here on Valentine's Day, and then do a sweetheart package, offering concert tickets, a discounted hotel room at the Grotto here, and a nice dinner in the casino restaurant. We advertise this all through the Pacific Northwest. We become a destination. The people who use the tickets, the hotel room, and the meal, will spend the rest of their weekend in the casino, pulling slots, playing bingo, or losing on the blackjack tables."

"On Valentine's?" Joe asked somewhat skeptically.

"You can't be romantic all the time," Emily said, and felt a heat rise in her cheeks as she spoke. As if she knew. She hadn't had a relationship in years. She had been too busy, and the consulting work she did hadn't allowed her to meet people in the new communities. Three months in Kansas City, followed by three months in Tennessee, followed by three months in Illinois did not allow her time to herself at all. The six months she had planned here in Oceanlake felt like a luxury.

"You think you can get Faith Hill?" Paul asked.

"Not this year," Emily said. "Maybe not even next. But if we work hard enough to make this the most exciting venue in the Northwest, I think we could get her three years from now—and pick our weekend."

Paul snorted slightly, but said nothing. Joe shot Emily an apologetic smile.

"We've had this argument before, Paul," he said. "Let's give Emily a chance."

"She's costing a lot of money for a chance."

"I really don't want a chance," she said. "You hired me. If you don't need my services, there are plenty of others who do."

Harsh. So harsh. She heard herself, and marveled. She had learned that harshness in the last few years. Maybe if she had learned it earlier, she wouldn't have lost her reputation. Maybe she could have found a new job, managing a new band. Maybe she wouldn't have lost everything when her relationship with Ricky Fink ended.

"We need you," Joe said, without looking at Paul. "Right now, Rolling Waves is a novelty, but that will wear off. Two other casinos are being built on the coast, and they'll be competition for the tourist crowd. We'll need to be a draw then. And we have to prepare now."

Bear nodded. "It was our mix-up. We didn't know what to do about our lounge acts."

"Keep them," she said. "You're very good at choosing them."

"Since you're already here," he said, "will you listen to the band?"

She smiled. "You sound like you have a stake in them."

"No stake," Joe said. "They called us. None of us has ever heard them."

"But we wouldn't mind a fourth opinion."

She leaned back in the booth. "I wouldn't mind staying if we don't talk about business. It's been a long week."

"That it has," Bear said.

He was the nicest man she'd ever worked with. She could tell that already. And she liked both him and his wife. They had made her supper on her first night in town. Maybe, after six months in Oceanlake, she would have a few nights like this—friendly nights that would help her relax.

She ordered a drink and settled back in the booth, letting the conversation flow around her. The people in the Sea Grotto at this time of year were mostly locals out for a special night. That rehearsal dinner looked like fun. There was one empty chair at the table. She wondered who it belonged to, and why that person hadn't come.

A movement near the door caught her eye. A tall man entered and shook the rain off his dark hair. He looked familiar, and she felt as if she had seen him before a long, long time ago. He had an angular face and electric blue eyes. Like the other locals, he wore a flannel shirt and faded jeans.

He was scanning the room, looking for someone. Probably a woman.

A lucky woman.

She smiled to herself and looked away, not wanting to be caught staring at a stranger. The men at the table were arguing about how good a local musician had to be, and she sat back to listen. Outside the window, the ocean glistened. It had whispered to her since she arrived that something was going to change.

Something had to change.

And she suspected that something was her.

# ABOUT THE AUTHOR

*New York Times* bestselling author Kristine Kathryn Rusch writes in almost every genre. Generally, she uses her real name (Rusch) for most of her writing. Under that name, she publishes bestselling science fiction and fantasy, award-winning mysteries, acclaimed mainstream fiction, controversial nonfiction, and the occasional romance. Her novels have made bestseller lists around the world and her short fiction has appeared in eighteen best of the year collections. She has won more than twenty-five awards for her fiction, including the Hugo, *Le Prix Imaginales*, the *Asimov's* Readers Choice award, and the *Ellery Queen Mystery Magazine* Readers Choice Award.

Publications from *The Chicago Tribune* to *Booklist* have included her Kris Nelscott mystery novels in their top-ten-best mystery novels of the year. The Nelscott books have received nominations for almost every award in the mystery field, including the best novel Edgar Award, and the Shamus Award.

She writes goofy romance novels as award-winner Kristine Grayson.

She also edits. Beginning with work at the innovative publishing company, Pulphouse, followed by her award-winning tenure at *The Magazine of Fantasy & Science Fiction*, she took fifteen years off before returning to editing with the original anthology series *Fiction River,* published by WMG Publishing. She acts as series editor with her husband, writer Dean Wesley Smith, and edits at least two anthologies in the series per year on her own.

To keep up with everything she does, go to kriswrites.com and sign up for her newsletter. To track her many pen names and series, see their individual websites (krisnelscott.com, kristinegrayson.com, krisdelake.com, retrievalartist.com, divingintothewreck.com). She lives and occasionally sleeps in Oregon.

*Keep informed:*
www.kriswrites.com